WOMEN OF THE
HARLEM RENAISSANCE
ANTHOLOGY SERIES

This anthology series gathers short stories, essays, one-act plays, and poems by the unsung Black women writers who helped shape an era.

The series includes two types of volumes:

Short-Take Anthologies
Concise, theme-based collections under 100 pages.

Expanded Anthologies
More comprehensive volumes that expand on the themes or authors introduced in the Short-Take volumes.

- Texts are carefully transcribed from the original publications.
- Short introductions provide reliable historical context.
- Overlap between volumes is minimal, allowing the books to function as a continuous collection.

HalesitePress.com

ESSENTIAL SHORT STORIES BY WOMEN OF THE HARLEM RENAISSANCE

VOLUMES 1 & 2

A WOMEN OF THE HARLEM RENAISSANCE 'EXPANDED' ANTHOLOGY

Introduction by
KAREN RAE LEVINE

HALESITE PRESS

CONTENTS

VOLUME 1

VOLUME 2

MORE STORIES

EDITORIAL NOTES

Research for this collection was conducted over multiple years and drew on archival periodicals, newspapers, and anthologies published during the period of the Harlem Renaissance. Each work was carefully transcribed from its original publication and checked against archival copies to ensure textual accuracy. Spelling, punctuation, and dialect have been preserved as they appear in the source texts, except for the silent correction of clear typographical errors introduced through historical printing or scanning.

Selections in this series are organized thematically or by author to create focused collections that remain approachable for students, educators, and general readers. Editorial intervention has been kept intentionally minimal. Introductions provide historical context but avoid interpretive analysis so that the writers' voices remain central.

The introductions that accompany each volume are intentionally brief but are based on extensive research. They provide historical context and focused biographical information about the writers and the circumstances in which the works were produced. These introductions draw on both established scholarship and newly available sources, including archival materials and period publications, and reexamine earlier biographical studies. Their purpose is to illuminate the historical and cultural context of the works rather than to offer new literary interpretation. When literary analysis is included, it is presented through quotations from scholars whose work has shaped the study of Harlem Renaissance literature.

SOURCE NOTES

A complete research bibliography and supporting indices used in preparing this volume are maintained by the editor as part of an ongoing research archive and are not reproduced in full in this edition.

The editor also maintains a complete index of more than 200 short stories, one-act plays, essays, and poems that received a prize or honorable mention in the annual literary contests conducted by *The Crisis* and *Opportunity*. These contests were administered independently in 1925, 1926, and 1927, and the index is based on the published contest results.

LITERARY CONTESTS

In this series of anthologies, each story, essay, play, or poem recognized in these contests is identified by a subtitle indicating its place or honorable mention, category, or special award, contest year, and the periodical that held the contest.

Also acknowledged is the winner of the 1923 contest for "Best Short Story by a Negro Student," hosted by *The Crisis* and sponsored by Virginia's Delta Omega Chapter of the Alpha Kappa Alpha Sorority. Judged by Jessie Redmon Fauset, W.E.B. Du Bois, and Arthur Spingarn, "To a Wild Rose" by Ottie B. Graham was the unanimous winner.

The Crisis

The 1925 and 1926 *Crisis* contests included Short Stories, Essays, Plays, and Poetry. In 1927 these categories were combined into a single award for "Literary Art and Expression," recognizing individuals for bodies of work.

Special Awards

- The Chesnutt Honoraria recognized the three best contributions published in *The Crisis* during 1927. In April 1928 the award was reinstated as a monthly prize for the best contribution, picture, or article.

Opportunity

Opportunity literary categories included Short Stories, Essays, Plays, Personal Experience Sketches, and Poetry.

Special Awards

- The Alexander Pushkin Poetry Prize (1926–1927) recognized the "most ambitious and most mature work of the Negro poet."
- The Buckner Award (1926–1927) honored works from any category demonstrating "conspicuous promise."
- The Van Vechten Award recognized the best story, play, essay, or poem published in *Opportunity* during 1927.

PREFACE

As I was exploring short stories by women in the early twentieth century, I came across a beautiful, insightful story by a Black woman I'd never heard of. Then another. And another. Each one was vibrant, original, and emotionally complex. As I looked further, I found the mountain beneath the iceberg—a wealth of remarkable short works largely unknown to mainstream readers and often difficult to access.

First, I had to reexamine not only my own education but the education system itself. In nearly all US public high schools today, the study of Harlem Renaissance literature is optional and left to the discretion of individual teachers and districts. But even that much is fairly recent. Before 2017, New York State's English standards didn't mention the Harlem Renaissance at all.

I'm fairly certain I wasn't introduced to any Black writers in my high school years on Long Island in the 1970s, and literature was only a small part of my undergraduate education in Engineering. But when I looked back at the literature component of my MFA in Creative Writing— earned at a progressive New York City university in 2006—I was struck by the absence of Black voices.

It was mostly by chance, and with great humility, that I came to understand the breadth of the exclusion of Black literature from the American canon—and the need for that to change.

As I researched and read the works of Black writers of the Harlem Renaissance, I found a deeper layer of exclusion. Zora Neale Hurston is widely recognized in that circle, and more women writers are slowly beginning to gain attention, but most of the literature of the era taught and celebrated today is overwhelmingly written by men.

This imbalance raised more questions I wanted to explore. A look at African American anthologies published in the 1920s confirmed the disparity—only 12% of the works included were written by women.[1] Still, I had my doubts, and that uncertainty led me down a path of research more intense—and ultimately more rewarding—than I'd anticipated.

I conducted an extensive study of the national African American literary contests held between 1925 and 1927 by the prominent periodicals, *The Crisis* and *Opportunity*. I was surprised to discover that 40% of the over 200 awarded short stories, one-act plays, essays, and poems combined were written by women. Women also authored half of the short stories published in these periodicals.[2] It became more and more clear to me that women were not on the fringes of a literary movement—they were actively shaping it.

I also examined the short stories by women that were selected for inclusion in post-era anthologies compiled by African American literary historians and editors. My initial survey of 18 relevant texts revealed more than 70 unique stories by more than 30 different writers.[3] To expand the scope to include poems, plays, and essays, I turned to contemporary discourse and collections by scholars Cheryl Wall, Lorraine Elena Roses, Maureen Honey, and others.

---

1. *The Book of American Negro Poetry* (1922), *Negro Poets and Their Poems* (1923), *An Anthology of Verse by American Negroes* (1924), *The New Negro* (1925), *Caroling Dusk* (1927), and *Ebony and Topaz* (1927).

2. Musser, Judith. "African American Women's Short Stories in the Harlem Renaissance: Bridging a Tradition." In *MELUS*, Summer 1998, p. 44.

3. These were academic anthologies that highlighted only Black writers, were published after 1990, and included at least one short story by a woman written between 1912 and 1930.

I used the results of both studies as a foundation for building a meaningful collection of short works. I identified those selected for historical anthologies or recognized in the literary contests of the era as those most admired at the time. Works frequently reprinted in contemporary anthologies I marked as the most studied since. Through targeted searches of original periodicals and literary journals, I uncovered dozens of additional stories, poems, essays, and plays—some of which had never been reprinted.

But I wanted to do more than recover these works. I wanted to make them accessible. So I set out to create something different: short, approachable collections designed for students, educators, and everyday readers. That meant organizing my now-extensive collection into themed volumes that would resonate with modern audiences.

As a white writer and editor, I come to this work with deep respect and a strong sense of responsibility. I'm aware of the risks of speaking over, interpreting, or curating in ways that reinforce the very exclusions this series hopes to correct. That awareness shaped my approach at every stage. My role has been to gather, not explain. I've kept introductions brief and informative rather than interpretive.

It's impossible to completely remove the editor's experience from the selection process of any anthology. Every decision, from choosing a theme to selecting individual pieces, is shaped by what the editor knows, values, and finds compelling. That said, I've tried to keep my influence intentional, transparent, and as limited as possible. The process of curating each volume was guided by two factors: (a) my combined knowledge of the writing most admired during the Harlem Renaissance and the works most studied in the years since, and (b) a commitment to including all of the work specified by a theme, not just a selective sampling. For example, the poetry collection devoted to Jessie Redmon Fauset includes every poem she published between 1912 and 1929, including translations, children's verse, and illustrations.

In some cases, I took thoughtful liberties by shaping collections around patterns that emerged from the material itself, such as a volume of essays by writers exploring their experiences as women of color in the 1920s, or a set of short stories by six different writers, each offering a distinct take on the theme of "passing." For every collection, the criteria for inclusion are clearly explained in the introductions so readers can understand how and why the pieces were selected. This project is not about my literary scholarship. It's about helping to make space for these writers to be read, heard, and appreciated on their own terms.

This series of anthologies was created to amplify, not explain; to gather, not revise; and to invite readers into a rich, often-overlooked archive of brilliant and essential writing. My hope is that each collection serves as both an introduction and an invitation to read more deeply, ask more questions, and continue the work of recognition and restoration.

INTRODUCTION

The acknowledgment and appreciation of fiction by women of the Harlem Renaissance is growing. Their short stories offer distinctive premises and perspectives that, taken together, provide a vital counterbalance to the historically male-dominated narratives of the era. This volume gathers the most compelling stories by remarkable women, from those that have gained wider recognition to those who remain lesser known but are equally deserving.

Women wrote nearly half of the short stories published in the era's leading African American periodicals, *The Crisis* and *Opportunity*, and more than half of those published in Black literary journals.[1] Men and women were also closely matched in the national literary contests held by those periodicals between 1925 and 1927. Of the 69 identified winners in the Short Story and Personal Experience Sketch categories combined, 45% (31) were authored by women.[2] The contest results are especially

---

1. Based on remarks by Judith Musser (see Preface) and data extracted from "An Index of Literary Materials in 'The Crisis,' 1910-1935" by Jean Fagan Yellin, *CLA Journal*, vol. 15, no. 2, 1971. The literary journals noted are *Fire!!, The Saturday Evening Quill, Black Opals, Harlem,* and *Carolina Magazine.*

2. The information was gathered from an extensive study by the editor of the history, politics, and outcomes of *The Crisis* and *Opportunity* literary contests. The statistics are based on a compilation of award announcements published in those periodicals. For the

significant because the honorees, selected from hundreds of anonymous submissions, reflect the opinions of esteemed literary figures such as Alain Locke, James Weldon Johnson, H. G. Wells, and Sinclair Lewis. (The Preface includes an overview of the contests.)

Before and during the Harlem Renaissance, the white-dominated publishing industry was largely closed to African Americans and often openly racist. The literary contests were part of a deliberate effort by Black leaders, including the editors of *The Crisis* and *Opportunity*, W.E.B. Du Bois and Charles S. Johnson, to challenge that exclusion and elevate authentic African American voices in the national literary arena. Their success transformed the landscape of American literature. Between 1905 and 1920, no more than five African Americans had published significant books.[3] Between 1920 and 1935, the bookshelves filled with more than 50 volumes of fiction, nonfiction, drama, and poetry by Harlem Renaissance writers.

Women, however, were not among the group of writers who had been actively championed. In spite of this, Jessie Redmon Fauset, Nella Larsen, and Zora Neale Hurston earned early success in mainstream publishing. But their literary careers were destined to fade into obscurity. The voices of women were drowned out by the compounded forces of racism in the national sphere, gender bias within the African American community, and restrictive societal expectations imposed by both.

"This pattern of short-lived success followed by years of anonymity," writes scholar Cheryl A. Wall, "suggests how difficult it was for a black woman in the early twentieth century to sustain a career as a writer. For many women, the competing demands of marriage and career, along with the requirement that their art advance the cause of racial equality, created an untenable situation."[4]

In the initial decades of post-era studies, this lack of continued visibility

---

purposes of this anthology, the categories of Short Stories and Personal Experience Sketches are both treated as short stories.

3. Lewis, David Levering. When Harlem was in Vogue. United Kingdom, Oxford University Press, 1989, p. 89.

4. Wall, Cheryl A.. "Women of the Harlem Renaissance." *The Cambridge Companion to African American Women's Literature*. Cambridge University Press, 2009.

fostered a perception, more easily reinforced by the prevailing male bias, that because women's voices weren't prevalent, they weren't as important. "Many scholars characterized African-American literature," writes scholar Lorraine Elena Roses, "even during the Harlem Renaissance, as primarily a male event and mentioned women's participation only in passing."[5]

In the wake of the 1960s Civil Rights Movement, a new wave of interest in Black cultural history took shape. Alice Walker's rediscovery of Zora Neale Hurston in the 1970s marked a turning point in the recovery of women writers of the Harlem Renaissance. Black feminist scholarship was expanding, and by the 1990s, a welcome surge of academic publications and anthologies affirmed the lasting value of the era's nearly forgotten women authors.

"[S]cholars have tended to ignore women who wrote short stories during the Harlem Renaissance," writes Professor Judith Musser, "and thus have misrepresented the era. By refocusing on these stories, we come to a broader perspective on the values this era represented. In addition, these women's short stories also provide a link in the long and rich tradition of African American women's writing."[6]

Despite hopes for greater inclusivity, the turn of the twenty-first century brought little meaningful change to the representation of short stories by women in anthologies of African American literature. In the fiction section of *The Portable Harlem Renaissance Reader* (2020), only a quarter of the stories and excerpts are written by women.[7] In *The Norton Anthology of African American Literature* (4th Edition, 2025), there isn't enough fiction in the Harlem Renaissance section for a meaningful comparison, but only 20% of more than 100 selections are by women.[8]

Countering this shortfall, however, is a growing body of biographies, historical fiction, digital archives, articles, and reprints of novels, plays,

---

5. Roses, Lorraine Elena. *Harlem's Glory: Black Women Writing, 1900-1950. Harvard University Press*, 1996, p. 2.
6. Musser, Judith. "African American Women's Short Stories in the Harlem Renaissance: Bridging a Tradition." In *MELUS*, Summer 1998, p. 28.
7. Seven out of 30 short stories and novel excerpts.
8. 22 out of 107 short stories, essays, excerpts, and poems.

and poetry collections, devoted to restoring the voices and legacies of the women of the era.

This volume is designed to complement the continuing efforts to narrow the gap in recognition and representation. It's an invitation to explore a broader field of short stories and an introduction to the women who wrote them.

The method of selecting the stories for the collection is unique. It reflects a fusion of the opinions of the contest judges in the 1920s and the perspectives of modern scholars who, decades later, reexamined the literary merit of that same community of writers. It represents an intersection of experts, past and present, grounded in their shared belief that short stories by both men and women hold equal literary value.

The short stories by women that received recognition in the contests are identified as some—but not all—of the "most admired" at the time. (Several prominent fiction writers, including Jessie Redmon Fauset, Nella Larsen, and Angelina Weld Grimké, did not participate.) Many of these stories were never published or preserved and have been lost to time. Fortunately, 14 of the 29 are available for reprint. "To a Wild Rose" by Ottie B. Graham, the winner of the "Best Short Story by a Negro Student" in 1923, has been added to the list of "most admired."

A survey of short stories reprinted in nine anthologies that either focus on women or account for them in equal measure revealed 62 unique works originally published between 1912 and 1930.[9] Ranking the stories by frequency of appearance across volumes offers a reasonable indication of the stories that have been "most studied" by informed scholars.

Six prize-winning stories not included in these anthologies were added to the list.

The writers who appear most frequently are Zora Neale Hurston, Jessie Redmon Fauset, Nella Larsen, Marita O. Bonner, and Dorothy West. The three most anthologized stories are "Sanctuary" by Nella Larsen, "Mary

---

9. There's no definitive timeline for the era. These parameters were set for ease and consistency.

Elizabeth" by Jessie Redmon Fauset, and "Wedding Day" by Gwendolyn Bennett.

In the spirit of simultaneously introducing readers to an under-explored genre and showcasing a wide range of overlooked authors, when multiple stories by the same writer were on the combined list of "most admired" and "most studied," only a single story was selected to represent that author. The result is a concise and meaningful collection of 26 stories by 26 different writers that serves as both an overview and a starting point for deeper exploration.

This book is part of a series of anthologies offered in two formats: 'Short-Take' collections (under 100 pages) and more comprehensive 'Expanded' editions. This 'Expanded' anthology is a combination of two 'Short-Take' volumes of *Essential Short Stories*, with the addition of nine more compelling tales.

The captivating narratives in this sweeping collection offer insights and perspectives unique to the women who experienced the Harlem Renaissance. Through their presence, perseverance, and talent, these traditionally overlooked writers played a crucial role in the advancement of Black women's literature. Each story is both a treasure and a pleasure to read.

The Writers and Their Stories

• **Gwendolyn Bennett** was a multitalented artist and writer who wrote a recurring column in *The Crisis* and co-founded and edited the acclaimed literary journal *Fire!!* In her short story, "Wedding Day," a Black man moves to Paris to escape the intense and humiliating racism in the U.S. While courting another expatriate, he learns that the dehumanizing American mindset has followed him there.

• **Marita O. Bonner** was a prolific writer of short stories, essays, and plays. With a lyrical, imaginative, and sometimes experimental writing style, she addressed themes of racism, gender bias, and economic hardship. She presents "Drab Rambles" in two parts, both of which reveal the brutal intersection of racism and urban poverty. In the first part, a woman has to accept the sexual advances of her boss or face the dire consequences of unemployment. In the second, a sick man is crushed by a racist and dismissive healthcare system.

• **Nellie Rathbone Bright** was an active Philadelphia educator and poet who co-founded the literary journal, *Opals*, and co-authored a history book for children that stressed diversity. "Black" is her account of a solo trip on a steamship and the discrimination she faced as a woman of color, from the struggle to purchase tickets to disembarking from the steerage section she had been unexpectedly forced to occupy.

• **Eunice Hunton Carter**, a celebrated activist, attorney, and international leader, was the first Black woman appointed as New York State Assistant District Attorney. In "The Corner," a woman reflects on the nighttime opulence and daytime poverty she observes through the window of a comfortable Harlem apartment.

• The only biographical information for **Ethel R. Clark** is that she was living in Attleboro, Massachusetts when the honorable mention for "In Houses of Glass" was announced. The focus of her story is Honey, a schoolgirl forced to make a dramatic and telling adjustment to an African American family after the abrupt death of her white-passing mother.

• **Anita Scott Coleman**, a writer, teacher, and mother of five who lived much of her life in New Mexico, added a Southwestern perspective to the Harlem-based movement. Dozens of her stories and poems were published in local newspapers and national magazines. "Three Dogs and a Rabbit," one of her five award-winning narratives, tells the tale of a widow accused of hiding a Black fugitive. She responds to her accusers by relating her life story, ending with the revelation of her misjudged identity.

• **Mae Cowdery** was a young bohemian poet who sometimes pushed the limits of poetic convention by including elements of eroticism and same-sex love. "Lai-li" is Cowdery's haunting tale of a weary sea captain returning to an island in search of his lost love.

• **Caroline Bond Day**, one of the first African Americans to graduate from Radcliffe, was an anthropologist, educator, and author of *A Study of Some Negro-White Families in the United States* (1932). Her Personal

Experience Sketch recounts how she is treated differently when wearing a pink hat that inadvertently leads others to assume she's white.

• **Alice Dunbar-Nelson** began her involvement as an activist and writer before the artistic boom that defined the Harlem Renaissance, publishing two volumes of short stories in 1895 and 1899. In "Hope Deferred," a newly married man who recently graduated as a civil engineer is excited about starting the next chapter of his life. He finds, however, that employment is less about his qualifications than the color of his skin.

• **Jessie Redmon Fauset**, a versatile and prolific writer, was the influential literary editor of *The Crisis* magazine. In "Mary Elizabeth," an expressive housekeeper gives a pampered African American woman an underhanded lesson in the personal suffering that reverberated in the aftermath of slavery.

• **Marie Louise French**'s story "There Never Fell a Night so Dark" didn't win first place in a 1925 literary contest, but in the opinion of one of the renowned judges, Charles W. Chesnutt, it was "the best of the lot." Unfortunately, the life of the author remains a mystery.

• **Edythe Mae Gordon** was a poet and fiction writer. She and her husband organized a Boston writer's salon that produced an annual literary journal, *The Saturday Evening Quill*. "Subversion," a story of illness and heartbreak, appeared in the journal's first issue and was subsequently listed in the *O. Henry Memorial Award Prize Stories of 1928* as one of the year's distinguished "short short stories."

• **Ottie B. Graham** was a fiction writer, playwright, and performing artist who won first place in a 1923 fiction contest sponsored by an African American sorority. "To a Wild Rose" follows a spirited woman through slavery and freedom. The tale-within-a-tale addresses themes of love and identity.

• **Angelina Weld Grimké**, the daughter of a former slave and the great-niece of white abolitionists, was a respected poet, playwright, and fiction writer. In "Goldie," she delivers an unflinching portrayal of lynching and the profound devastation it leaves in its wake.

• **Zora Neale Hurston**, independent and gregarious, burst into Harlem's literary scene in 1925, becoming a popular writer of short stories, essays, plays, and novels. She was also a diligent and respected anthropologist. The title character in her award-winning short story "Spunk" kills the husband of his married lover. Spunk manages to escape justice—but not the haunting of the man he murdered. Two other stories by Hurston recognized in literary contests are "Muttsy" and "Black Death."

• **Nella Larsen,** best known for her novels *Passing* and *Quicksand*, was the first African American woman to receive a Guggenheim Fellowship. "Sanctuary" has enjoyed critical acclaim for many years. It's the suspenseful story of Jim, hunted by sheriffs for killing a man. He begs his friend's mother to hide him. The mother's choice and the identity of the victim are compelling.

• **May Miller** was a prolific, award-winning playwright. "Door-Stops," Miller's only published short story, is daring for its time. It's the tale of Irma, whose misplaced love leads to temptation and a life of prostitution.

• **Brenda Ray Moryck,** a diligent educator, journalist, and activist, dedicated her life and writing to social issues. Her story, "Days," relates the struggles of an African American couple who combat stereotypes in an ethnically mixed neighborhood.

• **Maude Irwin Owens** was an accomplished writer and visual artist. The title character in "Bathesda of Sinners Run" is the descendant of women with healing powers thought to be linked to Christian fervor. A surprising confrontation with an angry group of townswomen forces Bathesda to reexamine her connection to nature, God, and healing.

• **Leila Amos Pendleton** was an educator and activist who wrote an African American history textbook used in the Washington, D.C. public schools. In "The Foolish and the Wise," a housemaid, wiser than she realizes, observes discrepancies in her employer's culturally biased portrayal of Socrates.

• **Florida Ruffin Ridley** was one of the first Black public school teachers in Boston and edited *The Woman's Era*, the first national newspaper published by and for African American women. In "Two Gentlemen of

Boston," two close school friends—one white, one Black—are driven apart after a fight sparked by a racist remark by one about the other.

• Although **Adeline F. Ries's** life story is unknown, she left a lasting legacy in a single short story. The title character in "Mammy," angry and grieving, proves to be far from the stereotype of a submissive woman content in her life as an enslaved caregiver.

• **Eloise Bibb Thompson** was an educator, activist, playwright, poet, and journalist. Her roots in Louisiana informed her short stories. In "Masks," an African American mask-maker in New Orleans is consumed with a desire for white-passing descendants. His crisis of identity upends the lives of his family for generations.

• **Dorothy West** moved to Harlem when she was a teenager and had a long career as a writer and editor. She penned her second novel at 87. Her short story "The Typewriter" shared second place in a literary contest with Zora Neale Hurston's "Muttsy." It centers on a poor, urban Black man who imagines an alternate life as he dictates fictitious letters to a daughter practicing her typing skills.

• A Philadelphia native, **Idabelle Yeiser** was a writer, poet, and educator dedicated to developing and promoting culturally unbiased academic programs. In her award-winning personal experience sketch, "Letters," Yeiser describes her travels in Algeria and Tunisia. At the time, this was an uncommon excursion for African American women.

VOLUME 1

SANCTUARY

NELLA LARSEN

On the Southern coast, between Merton and Shawboro, there is a strip of desolation some half a mile wide and nearly ten miles long between the sea and old fields of ruined plantations. Skirting the edge of this narrow jungle is a partly grown-over road which still shows traces of furrows made by the wheels of wagons that have long since rotted away or been cut into firewood. This road is little used, now that the state has built its new highway a bit to the west and wagons are less numerous than automobiles.

In the forsaken road a man was walking swiftly. But in spite of his hurry, at every step he set down his feet with infinite care for the night was windless and the heavy silence intensified each sound; even the breaking of a twig could be plainly heard. And the man had need of caution as well as haste.

Before a lonely cottage that shrank timidly back from the road the man hesitated a moment, then struck out across the patch of green in front of it. Stepping behind a clump of bushes close to the house, he looked in through the lighted window at Annie Poole, standing at her kitchen table mixing the supper biscuits.

He was a big, black man with pale brown eyes in which there was an odd mixture of fear and amazement. The light showed streaks of gray soil on his heavy, sweating face and great hands, and on his torn clothes. In his woolly hair clung bits of dried leaves and dead grass.

He made a gesture as if to tap on the window, but turned away to the door instead. Without knocking he opened it and went in.

II

The woman's brown gaze was immediately on him, though she did not move. She said, "You ain't in no hurry, is you, Jim Hammer?" It wasn't, however, entirely a question.

"Ah's in trubble, Mis' Poole," the man explained, his voice shaking, his fingers twitching.

"W'at you done done now?"

"Shot a man, Mis' Poole."

"Trufe?" The woman seemed calm. But the word was spat out.

"Yas'm. Shot 'im." In the man's tone was something of wonder, as if he himself could not quite believe that he had really done this thing which he affirmed.

"Daid?"

"Dunno, Mis' Poole. Dunno."

"White man o' niggah?"

"Cain't say, Mis' Poole. White man, Ah reckons."

Annie Poole looked at him with cold contempt. She was a tiny, withered woman—fifty perhaps—with a wrinkled face the color of old copper, framed by a crinkly mass of white hair. But about her small figure was some quality of hardness that belied her appearance of frailty. At last she spoke, boring her sharp little eyes into those of the anxious creature before her.

"An' w'at am you lookin' foh me to do 'bout et?"

"Jes' lemme stop till dey's gone by. Hide me till dey passes. Reckon dey ain't fur off now." His begging voice changed to a frightened whimper. "Foh de Lawd's sake, Mis' Poole, lemme stop."

And why, the woman inquired caustically, should she run the dangerous risk of hiding him?

"Obadiah, he'd lemme stop ef he was to home." the man whined.

Annie Poole sighed. "Yas," she admitted, slowly, reluctantly, "Ah spec' he would. Obadiah, he's too good to youall no 'count trash." Her slight shoulders lifted in a hopeless shrug. "Yas, Ah reckon he'd do et. Emspecial' seein how he allus set such a heap o' store by you. Cain't see w'at foh, mahse'f. Ah shuah don' see nuffin' in you but a heap o' dirt."

But a look of irony, of cunning, of complicity passed over her face. She went on, "Still, 'siderin' all an' all, how Obadiah's right fon' o' you, an' how white folks is white folks, Ah'm a-gwine hide you dis one time."

Crossing the kitchen, she opened a door leading into a small bedroom, saying, "Git yo'se'f in dat dere feather baid an' Ah'm a-gwine put de clo's on de top. Don' reckon dey'll fin' you ef dey does look foh you in mah house. An Ah don' spec' dey'll go foh to do dat. Not lessen you been keerless an' let 'em smell you out gittin' hyah." She turned on him a withering look.

"But you allus been triflin'. Cain't do nuffin propah. An' Ah'm a-tellin' you ef dey warn't white folks an' you a po' niggah, Ah shuah wouldn't be lettin' you mess up mah feather baid dis ebenin', 'cose Ah jes' plain don' want you hyah. Ah done kep' mahse'f outen trubble all mah life. So's Obadiah."

"Ah's powahful 'bliged to you, Mis' Poole. You shuah am one good 'oman. De Lawd'll mos' suttinly—"

Annie Poole cut him off." Dis ain't no time foh all dat kin' o' fiddle-de-roll. Ah does mah duty as Ah sees et 'thout no thanks from you. Ef de Lawd had gib you a white face 'stead o' dat dere black one, Ah shuah would turn you out. Now hush yo' mouf an' git yo'se'f in. An' don' git movin' and scrunchin' undah dose covahs and git yo'se'f kotched in mah house."

Without further comment the man did as he was told. After he had laid his soiled body and grimy garments between her snowy sheets, Annie Poole carefully rearranged the covering and placed piles of freshly laundered linen on top. Then she gave a pat here and there, eyed the result, and finding it satisfactory, went back to her cooking.

III

Jim Hammer settled down to the racking business of waiting until the approaching danger should have passed him by. Soon savory odors seeped in to him and he realized that he was hungry. He wished that Annie Poole would bring him something to eat. Just one biscuit. But she wouldn't, he knew. Not she. She was a hard one, Obadiah's mother.

By and by he fell into a sleep from which he was dragged back by the rumbling sound of wheels in the road outside. For a second fear clutched so tightly at him that he almost leaped from the suffocating shelter of the bed in order to make some active attempt to escape the horror that his capture meant. There was a spasm at his heart, a pain so sharp, so slashing that he had to suppress an impulse to cry out. He felt himself falling. Down, down, down. ... Everything grew dim and very distant in his memory. ... Vanished. ... Came rushing back.

Outside there was silence. He strained his ears. Nothing. No footsteps. No voices. They had gone on then. Gone without even stopping to ask Annie Poole if she had seen him pass that way. A sigh of relief slipped from him. His thick lips curled in an ugly, cunning smile. It had been smart of him to think of coming to Obadiah's mother's to hide. She was an old demon, but he was safe in her house.

He lay a short while longer listening intently, and, hearing nothing, started to get up. But immediately he stopped, his yellow eyes glowing like pale flames. He had heard the unmistakable sound of men coming toward the house. Swiftly he slid back into the heavy, hot stuffiness of the bed and lay listening fearfully.

The terrifying sounds drew nearer. Slowly. Heavily. Just for a moment he thought they were not coming in— they took so long. But there was a light knock and the noise of a door being opened. His whole body went taut. His feet felt frozen, his hands clammy, his tongue like a weighted, dying thing. His pounding heart made it hard for his straining ears to hear what they were saying out there.

"Ebenin', Mistah Lowndes." Annie Poole's voice sounded as it always did, sharp and dry.

There was no answer. Or had he missed it? With slow care he shifted his position, bringing his head nearer the edge of the bed. Still he heard nothing. What were they waiting for? Why didn't they ask about him?

Annie Poole, it seemed, was of the same mind. "Ah don' reckon youall done traipsed 'way out hyah jes' foh yo' healf," she hinted.

"There's bad news for you, Annie, I'm 'fraid." The sheriff's voice was low and queer.

Jim Hammer visualized him standing out there—a tall, stooped man, his white tobacco-stained mustache drooping limply at the ends, his nose hooked and sharp, his eyes blue and cold. Bill Lowndes was a hard one too. And white.

"W'atall bad news, Mistah Lowndes?" The woman put the question quietly, directly.

"Obadiah—" the sheriff began—hesitated—began again. "Obadiah—ah —er he's outside, Annie. I'm 'fraid—"

"Shucks! You done missed. Obadiah, he ain't done nuffin', Mistah Lowndes. Obadiah!" she called stridently, "Obadiah! git hyah an' splain yo'se'f."

But Obadiah didn't answer, didn't come in. Other men came in. Came in with steps that dragged and halted. No one spoke. Not even Annie Poole. Something was laid carefully upon the floor.

"Obadiah, chile," his mother said softly, "Obadiah, chile." Then, with sudden alarm, "He ain't daid, is he? Mistah Lowndes! Obadiah, he ain't daid?"

Jim Hammer didn't catch the answer to that pleading question. A new fear was stealing over him.

"There was a to-do, Annie," Bill Lowndes explained gently, "at the garage back o' the factory. Fellow tryin' to steal tires. Obadiah heerd a noise an' run out with two or three others. Scared the rascal all right. Fired off his gun an' run. We allow et to be Jim Hammer. Picked up his cap back there. Never was no 'count. Thievin' an' sly. But we'll git 'im, Annie. We'll git 'im."

The man huddled in the feather bed prayed silently. "Oh, Lawd! Ah didn't go to do et. Not Obadiah, Lawd. You knows dat. You knows et." And into his frenzied brain came the thought that it would be better for him to get up and go out to them before Annie Poole gave him away. For he was lost now. With all his great strength he tried to get himself out of the bed. But he couldn't.

"Oh Lawd!" he moaned, "Oh Lawd!" His thoughts were bitter and they ran through his mind like panic. He knew that it had come to pass as it said somewhere in the Bible about the wicked. The Lord had stretched out his hand and smitten him. He was paralyzed. He couldn't move hand or foot. He moaned again. It was all there was left for him to do. For in the terror of this new calamity that had come upon him he had forgotten the waiting danger which was so near out there in the kitchen.

His hunters, however, didn't hear him. Bill Lowndes was saying, "We been a-lookin' for Jim out along the old road. Figured he'd make tracks for Shawboro. You ain't noticed anybody pass this evenin', Annie?"

The reply came promptly, unwaveringly. "No, Ah ain't sees nobody pass. Not yet."

IV

Jim Hammer caught his breath.

"Well," the sherriff concluded, "we'll be gittin' along. Obadiah was a mighty fine boy. Ef they was all like him—. I'm sorry, Annie. Anything I c'n do let me know."

"Thank you, Mistah Lowndes."

With the sound of the door closing on the departing men, power to move came back to the man in the bedroom. He pushed his dirt-caked feet out from the covers and rose up, but crouched down again. He wasn't cold now, but hot all over and burning. Almost he wished that Bill Lowndes and his men had taken him with them.

Annie Pool had come into the room.

It seemed a long time before Obadiah's mother spoke. When she did there were no tears, no reproaches; but there was a raging fury in her voice as she lashed out, "Git outen mah feather baid, Jim Hammer, an' outen mah house, an' don' nevah stop thankin' yo' Jesus he done gib you dat black face."

MARY ELIZABETH

JESSIE REDMON FAUSET

Mary Elizabeth was late that morning. As a direct result, Roger left for work without telling me good-bye, and I spent most of the day fighting the headache which always comes if I cry.

For I cannot get a breakfast. I can manage a dinner,—one just puts the roast in the oven and takes it out again. And I really excel in getting lunch. There is a good delicatessen near us, and with dainty service and flowers, I get along very nicely. But breakfast! In the first place, it's a meal I neither like nor need. And I never, if I live a thousand years, shall learn to like coffee. I suppose that is why I cannot make it.

"Roger," I faltered, when the awful truth burst upon me and I began to realize that Mary Elizabeth wasn't coming, "Roger, couldn't you get breakfast downtown this morning? You know last time you weren't so satisfied with my coffee."

Roger was hostile. I think he had just cut himself, shaving. Anyway, he was horrid.

"No, I can't get my breakfast downtown!" He actually snapped at me. "Really, Sally, I don't believe there's another woman in the world who would send her husband out on a morning like this on an empty stomach. I don't see how you can be so unfeeling."

Well, it wasn't "a morning like this," for it was just the beginning of November. And I had only proposed his doing what I knew he would have to do eventually.

I didn't say anything more, but started on that breakfast. I don't know why I thought I had to have hot cakes! The breakfast really was awful! The cakes were tough and gummy and got cold one second, exactly, after I took them off the stove. And the coffee boiled, or stewed, or scorched, or did whatever the particular thing is that coffee shouldn't do. Roger sawed at one cake, took one mouthful of the dreadful brew, and pushed away his cup.

"It seems to me you might learn to make a decent cup of coffee," he said icily. Then he picked up his hat and flung out of the house.

I think it is stupid of me, too, not to learn how to make coffee. But, really, I'm no worse than Roger is about lots of things. Take "Five Hundred." Roger knows I love cards, and with the Cheltons right around the corner from us and as fond of it as I am, we could spend many a pleasant evening. But Roger will not learn. Only the night before, after I had gone through a whole hand with him, with hearts as trumps, I dealt the cards around again to imaginary opponents and we started playing. Clubs were trumps, and spades led. Roger, having no spades, played triumphantly a Jack of Hearts and proceeded to take the trick.

"But Roger," I protested, "you threw off."

"Well," he said, deeply injured, "didn't you say hearts were trumps when you were playing before?"

And when I tried to explain, he threw down the cards and wanted to know what difference it made; he'd rather play casino, anyway! I didn't go out and slam the door.

But I couldn't help from crying this particular morning. I not only value Roger's good opinion, but I hate to be considered stupid.

Mary Elizabeth came in about eleven o'clock. She is a small, weazened woman, very dark, somewhat wrinkled, and a model of self-possession. I wish I could make you see her, or that I could reproduce her accent, not that it is especially colored,—Roger's and mine are much more so—but her pronunciation, her way of drawing out her vowels, is so distinctively Mary Elizabethan!

I was ashamed of my red eyes and tried to cover up my embarrassment with sternness. "Mary Elizabeth," said I, "you are late!" Just as though she didn't know it.

"Yas'm, Mis' Pierson," she said, composedly, taking off her coat. She didn't remove her hat,—she never does until she has been in the house some two or three hours. I can't imagine why. It is a small, black, dusty affair, trimmed with black ribbon, some dingy white roses and a sheaf of wheat. I give Mary Elizabeth a dress and hat now and then, but, although I recognize the dress from time to time, I never see any change in the hat. I don't know what she does with my ex-millinery.

"Yas'm," she said again, and looked comprehensively at the untouched breakfast dishes and the awful viands, which were still where Roger had left them.

"Looks as though you'd had to git breakfast yoreself," she observed brightly. And went out in the kitchen and ate all those cakes and drank that unspeakable coffee! Really she did, and she didn't warm them up either.

I watched her miserably, unable to decide whether Roger was too finicky or Mary Elizabeth a natural-born diplomat.

"Mr. Gales led me an awful chase last night," she explained. "When I got home yistiddy evenin', my cousin whut keeps house fer me (!) tole me Mr. Gales went out in the mornin' en hadn't come back."

"Mr. Gales," let me explain, is Mary Elizabeth's second husband, an octogenarian, and the most original person, I am convinced, in existence.

"Yas'm," she went on, eating a final cold hot-cake, "en I went to look fer 'im, en had the whole perlice station out all night huntin' 'im. Look like they wusn't never goin' to find 'im. But I ses, 'Jes' let me look fer enough en long enough en I'll find 'im,' I ses, en I did. Way out Georgy Avenue, with the hat on ole Mis' give 'im. Sent it to 'im all the way fum Chicaga. He's had it fifteen years,—high silk beaver. I knowed he wusn't goin' too fer with that hat on.

"I went up to 'im, settin' by a fence all muddy, holdin' his hat on with both hands. En I ses, 'Look here, man, you come erlong home with me, en let me put you to bed.' En he come jest as meek! No-o-me, I knowed he wusn't goin' fer with ole Mis' hat on."

"Who was old 'Mis,' Mary Elizabeth?" I asked her.

"Lady I used to work fer in Noo York," she informed me. "Me en Rosy, the cook, lived with her fer years. Ole Mis' was turrible fond of me, though her en Rosy used to querrel all the time. Jes' seemed like they couldn't git erlong. 'Member once Rosy run after her one Sunday with a knife, en I kep 'em apart. Reckon Rosy musta bin right put out with ole Mis' that day. By en by her en Rosy move to Chicaga, en when I married Mr. Gales, she sent 'im that hat. That old white woman shore did like me. It's so late, reckon I'd better put off sweepin' tel termorrer, ma'am."

I acquiesced, following her about from room to room. This was partly to get away from my own doleful thoughts—Roger really had hurt my feelings—but just as much to hear her talk. At first I used not to believe all she said, but after I investigated once and found her truthful in one amazing statement, I capitulated.

She had been telling me some remarkable tale of her first husband and I was listening with the stupefied attention, to which she always reduces me. Remember she was speaking of her first husband.

"En I ses to 'im. I ses, 'Mr Gale—' "

"Wait a moment, Mary Elizabeth," I interrupted, meanly delighted to have caught her for once. "You mean your first husband, don't you?"

"Yas'm," she replied. "En I ses to 'im, 'Mr. Gale! I ses—' "

"But, Mary Elizabeth," I persisted, "that's your second husband, isn't it,—Mr. Gale?"

She gave me her long-drawn "No-o-me! My first husband was Mr. Gale and my second is Mr. *Gales*. He spells his name with a Z, I reckon. I ain't never see it writ. Ez I wus sayin', I ses to Mr. Gale—"

And it was true! Since then I have never doubted Mary Elizabeth.

She was loquacious that afternoon. She told me about her sister, "where's got a home in the country and where's got eight children." I used to read Lucy Pratt's stories about little Ephraim or Ezekiel, I forget his name, who always said "where's" instead of "who's," but I never believed it really till I heard Mary Elizabeth use it. For some reason or other she never mentions her sister without mentioning the home, too. "My sister where's got a home in the country" is her unvarying phrase.

"Mary Elizabeth," I asked her once, "does your sister live in the country, or does she simply own a house there?"

"Yas'm," she told me.

She is fond of her sister. "If Mr. Gales wus to die," she told me complacently, "I'd go to live with her."

"If he should die," I asked her idly, "would you marry again?"

"Oh, no-o-me!" She was emphatic. "Though I don't know why I shouldn't, I'd come by it hones'. My father wus married four times."

That shocked me out of my headache. "Four times, Mary Elizabeth, and you had all those step-mothers!" My mind refused to take it in.

"Oh, no-o-me! I always lived with mamma. She was his first wife."

I hadn't thought of people in the state in which I had instinctively placed Mary Elizabeth's father and mother as indulging in divorce, but as Roger says slangily, "I wouldn't know."

Mary Elizabeth took off the dingy hat. "You see, papa and mamma—" the ineffable pathos of hearing this woman of sixty-four, with a husband of eighty, use the old childish terms!

"Papa and mamma wus slaves, you know, Mis' Pierson, and so of course they wusn't exackly married. White folks wouldn't let 'em. But they wus awf'ly in love with each other. Heard mamma tell erbout it lots of times, and how papa wus the han'somest man! Reckon she wus long erbout sixteen or seventeen then. So they jumped over a broomstick, en they wus jes as happy! But not long after I come erlong, they sold papa down South, and mamma never see him no mo' fer years and years. Thought he was dead. So she married again."

"And he came back to her, Mary Elizabeth?" I was overwhelmed with the woefulness of it.

"Yas'm. After twenty-six years. Me and my sister where's got a home in the country—she's really my half-sister, see Mis' Pierson,—her en mamma en my step-father en me wus all down in Bumpus, Virginia, workin' fer some white folks, and we used to live in a little cabin, had a front stoop to it. En one day an ole cullud man come by, had a lot o' whiskers. I'd saw him lots of times there in Bumpus, lookin' and peerin' into every cullud woman's face. En jes' then my sister she call out, 'Come here, you Ma'y Elizabeth,' en that old man stopped, en he looked at me en he looked at me, en he ses to me, 'Chile, is yo' name Ma'y Elizabeth?'

"You know, Mis' Pierson, I thought he was jes' bein' fresh, en I ain't paid no 'tention to 'im. I ain't sed nuthin' ontel he spoke to me three or four times, en then I ses to 'im, 'Go 'way fum here, man, you ain't got no call to be fresh with me. I'm a decent woman. You'd oughta be ashamed of yoreself, an ole man like you.' "

Mary Elizabeth stopped and looked hard at the back of her poor wrinkled hands.

"En he says to me, 'Daughter,' he ses, jes' like that, 'daughter,' he ses, 'hones' I ain't bein' fresh. Is yo' name shore enough Ma'y Elizabeth?'

"En I tole him, 'Yas'r.'

" 'Chile,' he ses, 'whar is yo' daddy?'

" 'Ain't got no daddy,' I tole him peart-like. 'They done tuk 'im away fum me twenty-six years ago. I wusn't but a mite of a baby. Sol' 'im down the river. My mother often talks about it.' And, oh, Mis' Pierson, you shoulda see the glory come into his face!

" 'Yore mother!' he ses kinda out of breath, 'yore mother! Ma'y Elizabeth, whar is your mother?' "

'Back thar on the stoop,' I tole 'im. 'Why, did you know my daddy?'

"But he didn't pay no 'tention to me, jes' turned and walked up the stoop whar mamma was settin'! She wus feelin' sorta porely that day. En you oughta see me steppin' erlong after 'im.

"He walked right up to her and giv' her one look. 'Oh, Maggie,' he shout out, 'oh, Maggie! Ain't you know me? Maggie, ain't you know me?'

"Mamma look at 'im and riz up outa her cheer. 'Who're you?' she ses kinda trimbly, callin' me Maggie thata way? Who're you?'

"He went up real close to her, then, 'Maggie,' he ses, jes like that, kinda sad 'n tender, 'Maggie!' And hel' out his arms.

"She walked right into them. 'Oh,' she ses, 'it's Cassius! It's Cassius! It's my husban' come back to me! It's Cassius!' They wus like two mad people.

"My sister Minnie and me, we jes' stood and gawped at 'em. There they wus, holding on to each other like two pitiful childrun, en he tuk her hands and kissed 'em.

" 'Maggie,' he ses, you'll come away with me, won't you? You gona take me back, Maggie? We'll go away, you en Ma'y Elizabeth en me. Won't we, Maggie?'

"Reckon my mother clean fergot my step-father. 'Yes, Cassius,' she ses, 'we'll go away.' And then she sees Minnie, en it all comes back to her. 'Oh, Cassius,' she ses, 'I cain't go with you, I'm married again, en this time fer real. This here gal's mine and three boys, too, and another chile comin' in November!' "

"But she went with him, Mary Elizabeth," I pleaded. "Surely she went with him after all those years. He really was her husband."

I don't know whether Mary Elizabeth meant to be sarcastic or not. "Oh, no-o-me, mamma couldn't a done that. She wus

a good woman. Her ole master, whut done sol' my father down river, brung her up too religious fer that, en anyways, papa was married again, too. Had his fourth wife there in Bumpus with 'im."

The unspeakable tragedy of it!

I left her and went up to my room, and hunted out my dark-blue serge dress which I had meant to wear again that winter. But I had to give Mary Elizabeth something, so I took the dress down to her.

She was delighted with it. I could tell she was, because she used her rare and untranslatable expletive.

"Haytian!" she said. "My sister where's got a home in the country, got a dress looks somethin' like this, but it ain't as good. No-o-me. She got hers to wear at a friend's weddin',—gal she was riz up with. Thet gal married well, too, lemme tell you; her husband's a Sunday School sup'rintender."

I told her she needn't wait for Mr. Pierson, I would put dinner on the table. So off she went in the gathering dusk, trudging bravely back to her Mr. Gales and his high silk hat.

I watched her from the window till she was out of sight. It had been such a long time since I had thought of slavery. I was born in Pennsylvania, and neither my parents nor grandparents had been slaves; otherwise I might have had the same tale to tell as Mary Elizabeth, or worse yet, Roger and I might have lived in those black days and loved and lost each other and futilely, damnably, met again like Cassius and Maggie.

Whereas it was now, and I had Roger and Roger had me.

How I loved him as I sat there in the hazy dusk. I thought of his dear, bronze perfection, his habit of swearing softly in excitement, his blessed stupidity. Just the same I didn't meet him at the door as usual, but pretended to be busy. He came rushing to me with the *Saturday Evening Post*, which is more to me than rubies. I thanked him warmly, but aloofly, if you can get that combination.

We ate dinner almost in silence for my part. But he praised everything,— the cooking, the table, my appearance.

After dinner we went up to the little sitting-room. He hoped I wasn't tired,—couldn't he fix the pillows for me? So!

I opened the magazine and the first thing I saw was a picture of a woman gazing in stony despair at the figure of a man disappearing around the bend of the road. It was too much. Suppose that were Roger and I! I'm afraid I sniffled. He was at my side in a moment.

"Dear loveliest! Don't cry. It was all my fault. You aren't any worse about coffee than I am about cards! And anyway, I needn't have slammed the door! Forgive me, Sally. I always told you I was hard to get along with. I've had a horrible day,—don't stay cross with me, dearest."

I held him to me and sobbed outright on his shoulder. "It isn't you, Roger," I told him, "I'm crying about Mary Elizabeth."

I regret to say he let me go then, so great was his dismay. Roger will never be half the diplomat that Mary Elizabeth is.

"Holy smokes!" he groaned. "She isn't going to leave us for good, is she?"

So then I told him about Maggie and Cassius. "And oh, Roger," I ended futilely, "to think that they had to separate after all those years, when he had come back, old and with whiskers!" I didn't mean to be so banal, but I was crying too hard to be coherent.

Roger had got up and was walking the floor, but he stopped then aghast.

"Whiskers!" he moaned. "My hat! Isn't that just like a woman?" He had to clear his throat once or twice before he could go on, and I think he wiped his eyes.

"Wasn't it the—" I really can't say what Roger said here,—"wasn't it the darndest hard luck that when he did find her again, she should be married? She might have waited."

I stared at him astounded. "But, Roger," I reminded him, "he had married three other times, he didn't wait."

"Oh—!" said Roger, unquotably, "married three fiddlesticks! He only did that to try to forget her."

Then he came over and knelt beside me again. "Darling, I do think it is a sensible thing for a poor woman to learn how to cook, but I don't care as long as you love me and we are together. Dear loveliest, if I had been Cassius,—he caught my hands so tight that he hurt them,—and I had married fifty times and had come back and found you married to someone else, I'd have killed you, killed you."

Well, he wasn't logical, but he was certainly convincing.

So thus, and not otherwise, Mary Elizabeth healed the breach.

WEDDING DAY

GWENDOLYN BENNETT

His name was Paul Watson and as he shambled down rue Pigalle he might have been any other Negro of enormous height and size. But as I have said, his name was Paul Watson. Passing him on the street, you might not have known or cared who he was, but any one of the residents about the great Montmartre district of Paris could have told you who he was as well as many interesting bits of his personal history.

He had come to Paris in the days before colored jazz bands were the style. Back home he had been a prize fighter. In the days when Joe Gans was in his glory Paul was following the ring, too. He didn't have that fine way about him that Gans had and for that reason luck seemed to go against him. When he was in the ring he was like a mad bull, especially if his opponent was a white man. In those days there wasn't any sympathy or nicety about the ring and so pretty soon all the ringmasters got down on Paul and he found it pretty hard to get a bout with anyone. Then it was that he worked his way across the Atlantic Ocean on a big liner—in the days before colored jazz bands were the style in Paris.

Things flowed along smoothly for the first few years with Paul's working here and there in the unfrequented places of Paris. On the side he used to give boxing lessons to aspiring youths or gymnastic young women. At that time he was working so steadily that he had little chance to find out what was going on around Paris. Pretty soon, however, he grew to be known among the trainers and managers began to fix up bouts for him. After one or two successful bouts a little fame began to come into being for him. So it was that after one of the prize-fights, a colored fellow came to his dressing room to congratulate him on his success as well as invite him to go to Montmartre to meet "the boys."

Paul had a way about him and seemed to get on with the colored fellows who lived in Montmartre and when the first Negro jazz band played in a tiny Parisian cafe Paul was among them playing the banjo. Those first years were without event so far as Paul was concerned. The members of that first band often say now that they wonder how it was that nothing happened during those first seven years, for it was generally known how great was Paul's hatred for American white people. I suppose the tranquility in the light of what happened afterwards was due to the fact that the cafe in which they worked was one in which mostly French people drank and danced and then too, that was before there were so many Americans visiting Paris. However, everyone had heard Paul speak of his intense hatred of American white folks. It only took two Benedictines to make him start talking about what he would do to the first "Yank" that called him "nigger." But the seven years came to an end and Paul Watson went to work in a larger cafe with a larger band, patronized almost solely by Americans.

I've heard almost every Negro in Montmartre tell about the night that a drunken Kentuckian came into the cafe where Paul was playing and said:

"Look heah, Bruther, what you all doin' ovah heah?"

"None ya bizness. And looka here, I ain't your brother, see?"

"Jack, do you heah that nigger talkin' lak that tah me?"

As he said this, he turned to speak to his companion. I have often wished that I had been there to have seen the thing happen myself. Every tale I have heard about it was different and yet there was something of truth in each of them. Perhaps the nearest one can come to the truth is by saying that Paul beat up about four full-sized white men that night besides doing a great deal of damage to the furniture about the cafe. I couldn't tell you just what did happen. Some of the fellows say that Paul seized the nearest table and mowed down men right and left, others say he took a bottle, then again the story runs that a chair was the instrument of his fury. At any rate, that started Paul Watson on his siege against the American white person who brings his native prejudices into the life of Paris.

It is a verity that Paul was the "black terror." The last syllable of the word, nigger, never passed the lips of a white man without the quick reflex action of Paul's arm and fist to the speaker's jaw. He paid for more glassware and cafe furnishings in the course of the next few years than is easily imaginable. And yet, there was something likable about Paul. Perhaps that's the reason that he stood in so well with the policemen of the neighborhood. Always some divine power seemed to intervene in his behalf and he was excused after the payment of a small fine with advice about his future conduct. Finally, there came the night when in a frenzy he shot the two American sailors.

They had not died from the wounds he had given them hence his sentence had not been one of death but rather a long term of imprisonment. It was a pitiable sight to see Paul sitting in the corner of his cell with his great body hunched almost double. He seldom talked and when he did his words were interspersed with oaths about the lowness of "crackers." Then the World War came.

It seems strange that anything so horrible as that wholesale slaughter could bring about any good and yet there was something of a smoothing quality about even its baseness. There has never been such equality before or since such as that which the World War brought. Rich men fought by the side of paupers; poets swapped yarns with dry-goods salesmen, while Jews and Christians ate corned beef out of the same tin. Along with the general leveling influence came France's pardon of her prisoners in order that they might enter the army. Paul Watson became free and a French soldier. Because he was strong and had innate daring in his heart he was placed in the aerial squad and cited many times for bravery. The close of the war gave him his place in French society as a hero. With only a memory of the war and an ugly scar on his left cheek he took up his old life.

His firm resolutions about American white people still remained intact and many chance encounters that followed the war are told from lip to lip proving that the war and his previous imprisonment had changed him little. He was the same Paul Watson to Montmartre as he shambled up rue Pigalle.

Rue Pigalle in the early evening has a sombre Beauty—gray as are most Paris streets and other-worldish. To those who know the district it is the Harlem of Paris and rue Pigalle is its dusky Seventh Avenue. Most of the colored musicians that furnish Parisians and their visitors with entertainment live somewhere in the neighborhood of Rue Pigalle. Some time during every day each of these musicians makes a point of passing through rue Pigalle. Little wonder that almost any day will find Paul Watson going his shuffling way up the same street.

He reached the corner of rue de la Bruyere and with sure instinct his feet stopped. Without half thinking he turned into "the Pit." Its full name is The Flea Pit. If you should ask one of the musicians why it was so called, he would answer you to the effect that it was called "the pit" because all the "fleas" hang out there. If you did not get the full import of this explanation, he would go further and say that there were always "spades" in the pit and they were as thick as fleas. Unless you could understand this latter attempt at clarity you could not fully grasp what the Flea Pit means to the Negro musicians in Montmartre. It is a tiny cafe of the genus that is called bistro in France. Here the fiddle players, saxophone blowers, drumbeaters and ivory ticklers gather at four in the afternoon for a porto or a game of billiards. Here the cabaret entertainers and supper musicians meet at one o'clock at night or thereafter for a whiskey and soda, or more billiards. Occasional sandwiches and a "quiet game" also play their parts in the popularity of the place. After a season or two it becomes a settled fact just what time you may catch so-and-so at the famous "Pit."

The musicians were very fond of Paul and took particular delight in teasing him. He was one of the chosen few that all of the musicians conceded as being "regular." It was the pet joke of the habitues of the cafe that Paul never bothered with girls. They always said that he could beat up ten men but was scared to death of one woman. "Say fellow, when ya goin' a get hooked up?"

"Can't say, Bo. Ain't so much on skirts."

"Man alive, ya don't know what you're missin'—somebody little and cute telling ya sweet things in your ear. Paris is full of women folks."

"I ain't much on 'em all the same. Then too, they're all white."

"What's it to ya? This ain't America."

"Can't help that. Get this—I'm collud, see? I ain't got nothing for no white meat to do. If a woman eva called me nigger I'd have to kill her, that's all!"

"You for it, son. I can't give you a thing on this Mr. Jefferson Lawd way of lookin' at women.

"Oh, tain't that. I guess they're all right for those that wants 'em. Not me!"

"Oh you ain't so forty. You'll fall like all the other spades I've ever seen. Your kind falls hardest."

And so Paul went his way—alone. He smoked and drank with the fellows and sat for hours in the Montmartre cafes and never knew the companionship of a woman. Then one night after his work he was walking along the street in his queer shuffling way when a woman stepped up to his side.

"Voulez vous."

"Naw, gowan away from here."

"Oh, you speak English, don't you?"

"You an 'merican woman?"

"Used to be 'fore I went on the stage and got stranded over here."

"Well, get away from here. I don't like your kind!"

"Aw, Buddy, don't say that. I ain't prejudiced like some fool women."

"You don't know who I am, do you? I'm Paul Watson and I hate American white folks, see?"

He pushed her aside and went on walking alone. He hadn't gone far when she caught up to him and said with sobs in her voice:—

"Oh, Lordy, please don't hate me 'cause I was born white and an American. I ain't got a sou to my name and all the men pass me by cause I ain't spruced up. Now you come along and won't look at me cause I'm white."

Paul strode along with her clinging to his arm. He tried to shake her off several times but there was no use. She clung all the more desperately to him. He looked down at her frail body shaken with sobs, and something caught at his heart. Before he knew what he was doing he had said:—

"Naw, I ain't that mean. I'll get you some grub. Quit your cryin'. Don't like seein' women folks cry."

It was the talk of Montmartre. Paul Watson takes a woman to Gavarnni's every night for dinner. He comes to the Flea Pit less frequently, thus giving the other musicians plenty of opportunity to discuss him.

"How times do change. Paul, the woman-hater, has a Jane now."

"You ain't said nothing, fella. That ain't all. She's white and an 'merican, too."

"That's the way with these spades. They beat up all the white men they can lay their hands on but as soon as a gang of golden hair with blue eyes rubs up close to them they forget all they ever said about hatin' white folks."

"Guess he thinks that skirt's gone on him. Dumb fool!"

"Don' be no chineeman. That old gag don' fit for Paul. He cain't understand it no more'n we can. Says he jess can't help himself, everytime she looks up into his eyes and asks him does he love her. They sure are happy together. Paul's goin' to marry her, too. At first she kept saying that she didn't want to get married cause she wasn't the marrying kind and all that talk. Paul jus' laid down the law to her and told her he never would live with no woman without being married to her. Then she began to tell him all about her past life. He told her he didn't care nothing about what she used to be jus' so long as they loved each other now. Guess they'll make it."

"Yeah, Paul told me the same tale last night. He's sure gone on her all right."

"They're gettin' tied up next Sunday. So glad it's not me. Don't trust these American dames. Me for the Frenchies."

"She ain't so worse for looks, Bud. Now that he's been furnishing the green for the rags."

"Yeah, but I don't see no reason for the wedding bells. She was right—she ain't the marrying kind."

... and so Montmartre talked. In every cafe where the Negro musicians congregated Paul Watson was the topic for conversation. He had suddenly fallen from his place as bronze God to almost less than the dust.

The morning sun made queer patterns on Paul's sleeping face. He grimaced several times in his slumber, then finally half-opened his eyes. After a succession of dream-laden blinks he gave a great yawn, and rubbing his eyes, looked at the open window through which the sun shone brightly. His first conscious thought was that this was the bride's day and that bright sunshine prophesied happiness for the bride throughout her married life. His first impulse was to settle back into the covers and think drowsily about Mary and the queer twists life brings about, as is the wont of most bridge-grooms on their last morning of bachelorhood. He put this impulse aside in favor of dressing quickly and rushing downstairs to telephone to Mary to say "happy wedding day" to her.

One huge foot slipped into a worn bedroom slipper and then the other dragged painfully out of the warm bed were the courageous beginnings of his bridal toilette. With a look of triumph he put on his new grey suit that he had ordered from an English tailor. He carefully pulled a taffeta tie into place beneath his chin, noting as he looked at his face in the mirror that the scar he had received in the army was very ugly—funny, marrying an ugly man like him.

French telephones are such human faults. After trying for about fifteen minutes to get Central 32.01 he decided that he might as well walk around to Mary's hotel to give his greeting as to stand there in the lobby of his own, wasting his time. He debated this in his mind a great deal. They were to be married at four o'clock. It was eleven now and it did seem a shame not to let her have a minute or two by herself. As he went walking down the street towards her hotel he laughed to think of how one always cogitates over doing something and finally does the thing he wanted to in the beginning anyway.

———

Mud on his nice gray suit that the English tailor had made for him. Damn—gray suit—what did he have a gray suit on for, anyway. Folks with black faces shouldn't wear gray suits. Gawd, but it was funny that time when he beat up that cracker at the Periquet. Fool couldn't shut his mouth he was so surprised. Crackers—damn 'em—he was one nigger that wasn't 'fraid of 'em. Wouldn't he have a hell of a time if he went back to America where black was black. Wasn't white nowhere, black wasn't. What was that thought he was trying to get ahold of—bumping around in his head—something he started to think about but couldn't remember it somehow.

The shrill whistle that is typical of the French subway pierced its way into his thoughts. Subway—why was he in the subway—he didn't want to go any place. He heard doors slamming and saw the blue uniforms of the conductors swinging on to the cars as the trains began to pull out of the station. With one or two strides he reached the last coach as it began to move up the platform. A bit out of breath he stood inside the train and looking down at what he had in his hand he saw that it was a tiny pink ticket. A first class ticket in a second class coach. The idea set him to laughing. Everyone in the car turned and eyed him, but that did not bother him. Wonder what stop he'd get off—funny how these French said descend when they meant get off—funny he couldn't pick up French—been here so long. First class ticket in a second class coach!— that was one on him. Wedding day today, and that damn letter from Mary. How'd she say it now, "just couldn't go through with it," white women just don't marry colored men, and she was a street woman, too. Why couldn't she have told him flat that she was just getting back on her feet at his expense. Funny that first class ticket he bought, wish he could see Mary—him a-going there to wish her "happy wedding day," too. Wonder what that French woman was looking at him so hard for? Guess it was the mud.

HOPE DEFERRED

ALICE DUNBAR-NELSON

The direct rays of the August sun smote on the pavements of the city and made the soda-water signs in front of the drug stores alluringly suggestive of relief. Women in scant garments, displaying a maximum of form and a minimum of taste, crept along the pavements, their mussy light frocks suggesting a futile disposition on the part of the wearers to keep cool. Traditional looking fat men mopped their faces, and dived frantically into screened doors to emerge redder and more perspiring. The presence of small boys, scantily clad and of dusky hue and languid steps marked the city, if not distinctively southern, at least one on the borderland between the North and the South.

Edwards joined the perspiring mob on the hot streets and mopped his face with the rest. His shoes were dusty, his collar wilted. As he caught a glimpse of himself in a mirror of a shop window, he smiled grimly. "Hardly a man to present himself before one of the Lords of Creation to ask a favor," he muttered to himself.

Edwards was young; so young that be had not outgrown his ideals. Rather than allow that to happen, he had chosen one to share them with him, and the man who can find a woman willing to face poverty for her husband's ideals has a treasure far above rubies, and more precious than one with a thorough understanding of domestic science. But ideals do not always supply the immediate wants of the body, and it was the need of the wholly material that drove Edwards wilted, warm and discouraged into the August sunshine.

The man in the office to which the elevator boy directed him looked up impatiently from his desk. The windows of the room were open on a court-yard where green tree tops waved in a humid breeze; an electric fan whirred, and sent forth flashes of coolness; cool looking leather chairs invited the dusty traveler to sink into their depths.

Edwards was not invited to rest, however. Cold gray eyes in an impassive pallid face fixed him with a sneering stare, and a thin icy voice cut in on his half spoken words with a curt dismissal in its tone.

"Sorry, Mr.—Er—, but I shan't be able to grant your request."

His "Good Morning" in response to Edwards' reply as he turned out of the room was of the curtest, and left the impression of decided relief at an unpleasant duty discharged.

"Now where?" He had exhausted every avenue, and this last closed the door of hope with a finality that left no doubt in his mind. He dragged himself down the little side street, which led home, instinctively, as a child draws near to its mother in its trouble.

Margaret met him at the door, and their faces lighted up with the glow that always irradiated them in each other's presence. She drew him into the green shade of the little room, and her eyes asked, though her lips did not frame the question.

"No hope," he made reply to her unspoken words.

She sat down suddenly as one grown weak.

"If I could only just stick it out, little girl," he said, "but we need food, clothes, and only money buys them, you know."

"Perhaps it would have been better if we hadn't married—" she suggested timidly. That thought had been uppermost in her mind for some days lately.

"Because you are tired of poverty?" he queried, the smile on his lips belying his words.

She rose and put her arms about his neck. "You know better than that; but because if you did not have me, you could live on less, and thus have a better chance to hold out until they see your worth."

"I'm afraid they never will." He tried to keep his tones even, but in spite of himself a tremor shook his words. "The man I saw to-day is my last hope; he is the chief clerk, and what he says controls the opinions of others. If I could have gotten past his decision, I might have influenced the senior member of the firm, but he is a man who leaves details to his subordinates, and Mr. Hanan was suspicious of me from the first. He isn't sure," he continued with a little laugh, which he tried to make sound spontaneous, "whether I am a stupendous fraud, or an escaped lunatic."

"We can wait; your chance will come," she soothed him with a rare smile.

"But in the meanwhile—" he finished for her and paused himself.

A sheaf of unpaid bills in the afternoon mail, with the curt and wholly unnecessary "Please Remit" in boldly impertinent characters across the bottom of every one drove Edwards out into the wilting sun. He knew the main street from end to end; he could tell how many trolley poles were on its corners; he felt that he almost knew the stones in the buildings, and that the pavements were worn with the constant passing of his feet, so often in the past four months had he walked, at first buoyantly, then hopefully, at last wearily up and down its length.

The usual idle crowd jostled around the baseball bulletins. Edwards joined them mechanically. "I can be a side-walk fan, even if I am impecunious." He smiled to himself as he said the words, and then listened idly to a voice at his side, "We are getting metropolitan, see that!"

The "That" was an item above the baseball score. Edwards looked and the letters burned themselves like white fire into his consciousness.

STRIKE SPREADS TO OUR CITY.
WAITERS AT ADAMS' WALK OUT
AFTER BREAKFAST THIS MORNING.

"Good!" he said aloud. The man at his side smiled appreciatively at him; the home team had scored another run, but unheeding that Edwards walked down the street with a lighter step than he had known for days.

The proprietor of Adams' restaurant belied, both his name and his vocation. He could have been rubicund, corpulent, American; instead he was wiry, lank, foreign in appearance. His teeth projected over a full lower lip, his eyes set far back in his head and were concealed by wrinkles that seemed to have been acquired by years of squinting into men's motives.

"Of course I want waiters," he replied to Edwards' question, "any fool knows that." He paused, drew in his lower lip within the safe confines of his long teeth, squinted his eye intently on Edwards. "But do I want colored waiters? Now, do I?"

"It seems to me there's no choice for you in the matter," said Edwards good-humoredly.

The reply seemed to amuse the restaurant keeper immensely; he slapped the younger man on the back with a familiarity that made him wince both physically and spiritually.

"I guess I'll take you for head waiter." He was inclined to be jocular, even in the face of the disaster which the morning's strike had brought him. "Peel off and go to work. Say, stop!" as Edwards looked around to take his bearings, "What's your name?"

"Louis Edwards."

"Uh huh, had any experience?"

"Yes, some years ago, when I was in school."

"Uh huh, then waiting ain't your general work."

"No."

"Uh huh, what do you do for a living?"

"I'm a civil engineer."

One eye-brow of the saturnine Adams shot up, and he withdrew his lower lip entirely under his teeth.

"Well, say man, if you're an engineer, what you want to be strike-breaking here in a waiter's coat for, eh?"

Edwards' face darkened, and he shrugged his shoulders. "They don't need me, I guess," he replied briefly. It was an effort, and the restaurant keeper saw it, but his wonder overcame his sympathy.

"Don't need you with all that going on at the Monarch works? Why, man, I'd a thought every engineer this side o' hell would be needed out there."

"So did I; that's why I came here, but—"

"Say, kid, I'm sorry for you, I surely am; you go on to work."

"And so," narrated Edwards to Margaret, after midnight, when he had gotten in from his first day's work, "I became at once head waiter, first assistant, all the other waiters, chief boss, steward, and high-muck-a-muck, with all the emoluments and perquisites thereof."

Margaret was silent; with her ready sympathy she knew that no words of hers were needed then, they would only add to the burdens he had to bear. Nothing could be more bitter than this apparent blasting of his lifelong hopes, this seeming lowering of his standard. She said nothing, but the pressure of her slim brown hand in his meant more than words to them both.

"It's hard to keep the vision true," he groaned.

If it was hard that night, it grew doubly so within the next few weeks. Not lightly were the deposed waiters to take their own self-dismissal and supplanting. Daily they menaced the restaurant with their surly attentions, ugly and ominous. Adams shot out his lower lip from the confines of his long teeth and swore in a various language that he'd run his own place if he had to get every nigger in Africa to help him. The three or four men whom he was able to induce to stay with him in the face of missiles of every nature, threatened every day to give up the battle. Edwards was the force that held them together. He used every argument from the purely material one of holding on to the job now that they had it, through the negative one of loyalty to the man in his hour of need, to the altruistic one of keeping the place open for colored men for all time. There were none of them of such value as his own personality, and the fact that he stuck through all the turmoil. He wiped the mud from his face, picked up the putrid vegetables that often strewed the floor, barricaded the doors at night, replaced orders that were destroyed by well-aimed stones, and stood by Adams' side when the fight threatened to grow serious.

Adams was appreciative. "Say, kid, I don't know what I'd a done without you, now that's honest. Take it from me, when you need a friend anywhere on earth, and you can send me a wireless, I'm right there with the goods in answer to your S. O. S."

This was on the afternoon when the patrol, lined up in front of the restaurant, gathered in a few of the most disturbing ones, none of whom, by the way, had ever been employed in the place. "Sympathy" had pervaded the town.

The humid August days melted into the sultry ones of September. The self-dismissed waiters had quieted down, and save for an occasional missile, annoyed Adams and his corps of dark-skinned helpers no longer. Edwards had resigned himself to his temporary discomforts. He felt, with the optimism of the idealist, that it was only for a little while; the fact that he had sought work at his profession for nearly a year had not yet discouraged him. He would explain carefully to Margaret when the day's work was over, that it was only for a little while; he would earn enough at this to enable them to get away, and then in some other place he would be able to stand up with the proud consciousness that all his training had not been in vain.

He was revolving all these plans in his mind one Saturday night. It was at the hour when business was dull, and he leaned against the window and sought entertainment from the crowd on the street. Saturday night, with all the blare and glare and garishness dear to the heart of the middle-class provincial of the smaller cities, was holding court on the city streets. The hot September sun had left humidity and closeness in its wake, and the evening mists had scarce had time to cast coolness over the town. Shop windows glared wares through colored lights, and phonographs shrilled popular tunes from open store doors to attract unwary passersby. Half-grown boys and girls, happy in the license of Saturday night on the crowded streets, jostled one another and pushed in long lines, shouted familiar epithets at other pedestrians with all the abandon of the ill-breeding common to the class. One crowd, in particular, attracted Edwards' attention. The girls were brave in semi-decollete waists, scant short skirts and exaggerated heads, built up in fanciful designs; the boys with flamboyant red neckties, striking hat-bands, and white trousers. They made a snake line, boys and girls, hands on each others' shoulders, and rushed shouting through the press of shoppers, scattering the inattentive right and left. Edwards' lip curled, "Now, if those were colored boys and girls—"

His reflections were never finished, for a patron moved towards his table, and the critic of human life became once more the deferential waiter.

He did not move a muscle of his face as he placed the glass of water on the table, handed the menu card, and stood at attention waiting for the order, although he had recognized at first glance the half-sneering face of his old hope—Hanan, of the great concern which had no need of him. To Hanan, the man who brought his order was but one of the horde of menials who satisfied his daily wants and soothed his vanity when the cares of the day had ceased pressing on his shoulders. He had not even looked at the man's face, and for this Edwards was grateful.

A new note had crept into the noise on the streets; there was in it now, not so much mirth and ribaldry as menace and anger. Edwards looked outside in slight alarm; he had grown used to that note in the clamor of the streets, particularly on Saturday nights; it meant that the whole restaurant must be prepared to quell a disturbance. The snake line had changed; there were only flamboyant hat-bands in it now, the decolleté shirt waists and scant skirts had taken refuge on another corner. Something in the shouting attracted Hanan's attention, and he looked up wonderingly.

"What are they saying?" he inquired. Edwards did not answer; he was so familiar with the old cry that he thought it unnecessary.

"Yah! Yah! Old Adams hires niggers! Hires niggers!"

"Why, that is so," Hanan looked up at Edwards' dark face for the first time. "This is quite an innovation for Adams' place. How did it happen?"

"We are strike-breakers," replied the waiter quietly, then he grew hot, for a gleam of recognition came into Hanan's eyes.

"Oh, yes, I see. Aren't you the young man who asked me for employment as an engineer at the Monarch works?"

Edwards bowed, he could not answer; hurt pride surged up within him and made his eyes hot and his hands clammy.

"Well, er—I'm glad you've found a place to work; very sensible of you, I'm sure. I should think, too, that it is work for which you would be more fitted than engineering."

Edwards started to reply, but the hot words were checked on his lips. The shouting had reached a shrillness which boded immediate results, and with the precision of a missile from a warship's gun, a stone hurtled through the glass of the long window. It struck Edwards' hand, glanced through the dishes on the tray which he was in the act of setting on the table, and tipped half its contents over Hanan's knee. He sprang to his feet angrily, striving to brush the debris of his dinner from his immaculate clothing, and turned angrily upon Edwards.

"That is criminally careless of you!" he flared, his eyes blazing in his pallid face. "You could have prevented that; you're not even a good waiter, much less an engineer."

And then something snapped in the darker man's head. The long strain of the fruitless summer; the struggle of keeping together the men who worked under him in the restaurant; the heat, and the task of enduring what was to him the humiliation of serving, and this last injustice, all culminated in a blinding flash in his brain. Reason, intelligence, all was obscured, save a man hatred, and a desire to wreak his wrongs on the man, who, for the time being, represented the author of them. He sprang at the white man's throat and bore him to the floor. They wrestled and fought together, struggling, biting, snarling, like brutes in the dèbris of food and the clutter of overturned chairs and tables.

The telephone rang insistently. Adams wiped his hands on a towel, and carefully moved a paint brush out of the way, as he picked up the receiver.

"Hello!" he called. "Yes, this is Adams, the restaurant keeper. Who? Uh huh. Wants to know if I'll go his bail? Say, that nigger's got softening of the brain . Course not, let him serve his time, making all that row in my place; never had no row here before. No, I don't never want to see him again."

He hung up the receiver with a bang, and went back to his painting. He had almost finished his sign, and he smiled as he ended it with a flourish:

WAITERS WANTED. NONE BUT
WHITE MEN NEED APPLY

Out in the county work-house, Edwards sat on his cot, his head buried in his hands. He wondered what Margaret was doing all this long hot Sunday, if the tears were blinding her sight as they did his; then he started to his feet, as the warden called his name. Margaret stood before him, her arms outstretched, her mouth quivering with tenderness and sympathy, her whole form yearning towards him with a passion of maternal love.

"Margaret! You here, in this place?"

"Aren't you here?" she smiled bravely, and drew his head towards the refuge of her bosom. "Did you think I wouldn't come to see you?"

"To think I should have brought you to this," he moaned.

She stilled his reproaches and heard the story from his lips. Then she murmured with bloodless mouth, "How long will it be?"

"A long time, dearest—and you?"

"I can go home, and work," she answered briefly, "and wait for you, be it ten months or ten years—and then—?"

"And then—" they stared into each other's eyes like frightened children. Suddenly his form straightened up, and the vision of his ideal irradiated his face with hope and happiness.

"And then, Beloved," he cried, "then we will start all over again. Somewhere, I am needed; somewhere in this world there are wanted dark-skinned men like me to dig and blast and build bridges and make straight the roads of the world, and I am going to find that place— with you.

She smiled back trustfully at him. "Only keep true to your ideal, dearest," she whispered, "and you will find the place. Your window faces the south, Louis. Look up and out of it all the while you are here, for it is there, in our own southland, that you will find the realization of your dream."

SPUNK

SECOND PRIZE, SHORT STORY, 1925 OPPORTUNITY CONTEST

ZORA NEALE HURSTON

A giant of a brown skinned man sauntered up the one street of the Village and out into the palmetto thickets with a small pretty woman clinging lovingly to his arm.

"Looka theah, folkses!" cried Elijah Mosley, slapping his leg gleefully. "Theah they go, big as life an' brassy as tacks."

All the loungers in the store tried to walk to the door with an air of nonchalance but with small success.

"Now pee-eople!" Walter Thomas gasped, "Will you look at 'em!"

"But that's one thing Ah likes about Spunk Banks—he ain't skeered of nothin' on God's green footstool—*nothin'!* He rides that log down at saw-mill Jus' like he struts 'round wid another man's wife—jus' don't give a kitty. When Tes' Miller got cut to giblets on that circle-saw, Spunk steps right up and starts ridin'. The rest of us was skeered to go near it."

A round shouldered figure in overalls much too large, came nervously in the door and the talking ceased. The men looked at each other and winked.

"Gimme some soda-water. Sass'prilla Ah reckon," the new-comer ordered, and stood far down the counter near the open pickled pig-feet tub to drink it.

Elijah nudged Walter and turned with mock gravity to the new-comer.

"Say Joe, how's everything up yo' way? How's yo' wife?"

Joe started and all but dropped the bottle he held in his hands. He swallowed several times painfully and his lips trembled.

"Aw 'Lige, you oughtn't to do nothin' like that," Walter grumbled. Elijah ignored him.

"She jus' passed heah a few minutes ago goin' thata way," with a wave of his hand in the direction of the woods.

Now Joe knew his wife had passed that way. He knew that the men lounging in the general store had seen her, moreover, he knew that the men knew *he* knew. He stood there silent for a lone moment staring blankly, with his Adam's apple twitching nervously up and down his throat. One could actually *see* the pain he was suffering, his eyes, his face, his hands and even the dejected slump of his shoulders. He set the bottle down upon the counter. He didn't bang it, just eased it out of his hand silently and fiddled with his suspender buckle.

"Well, Ah'm goin' after her today. Ah'm goin' an' fetch her back. Spunk's done gone too fur."

He reached deep down into his trouser pocket and drew out a hollow ground razor, large and shiny, and passed his moistened thumb back and forth over the edge.

"Talkin' like a man, Joe. Course that's yo fambly affairs, but Ah like to see grit in anybody."

Joe Kanty laid down a nickel and stumbled out into the street.

Dusk crept in from the woods. Ike Clarke lit the swinging oil lamp that was almost immediately surrounded by candle-flies. The men laughed boisterously behind Joe's back as they watched him shamble woodward.

"You oughtn't to said whut you did to him, 'Lige,—look how it worked him up," Walter chided.

"And Ah hope it did work him up. Tain't even decent for a man to take and take like he do."

"Spunk will sho' kill him."

"Aw, Ah doan't know. You never kin tell. He might turn him up an' spank him fur settin' in the way, but Spunk wouldn't shoot no unarmed man. Dat razor he carried outa heah ain't gonna run Spunk down an' cut him, an' Joe ain't got the nerve to go up to Spunk with it knowing he totes that Army 45. He makes that break outa heah to bluff us. He's gonna hide that razor behind the first likely palmetto root an' sneak back home to bed. Don't tell me nothin' 'bout that rabbit-foot colored man. Didn't he meet Spunk an' Lena face to face one las' week an' mumble sumthin' to Spunk 'bout lettin' his wife alone?"

"What did Spunk say?" Walter broke in— "Ah like him fine but tain't right the way he carries on wid Lena Kanty, jus' cause Joe's timid 'bout fightin'."

"You wrong theah, Walter. 'Tain't cause Joe's timid at all, it's cause Spunk wants Lena. If Joe was a passle of wile cats Spunk would tackle the job just the same. He'd go after *anything* he wanted the same way. As Ah wuz sayin' a minute ago, he tole Joe right to his face that Lena was his. 'Call her,' he say to Joe. 'Call her and see if she'll come. A woman knows her boss an' she answers when he calls.' 'Lena, ain't I yo' husband?' Joe sorter whines out. Lena looked at him real disgusted but she don't answer and she don't move outa her tracks. Then Spunk reaches out an' takes hold of her arm an' says: 'Lena, youse mine. From now on Ah works for you an' fights for you an' Ah never wants you to look to nobody for a crumb of bread, a stitch of close or a shingle to go over yo' head, but *me* long as Ah live. Ah'll git the lumber foh owah house tomorrow. Go home an' git yo' things together!' "

" 'Thass mah house' Lena speaks up. 'Papa gimme that.' "

" 'Well,' says Spunk, 'doan give up whut's yours, but when youse inside don't forgit youse mine, an' let no other man git outa his place wid you!' "

"Lena looked up u him with her eyes so full of love that they wuz runnin' over an' Spunk seen it an' Joe seen it too, and his lip started to tremblin' and his Adam's apple was galloping up and down his neck like a race horse. Ah bet he's wore out half a dozen Adam's apples since Spunk's been on the job with Lena. That's all he'll do. He'll be back heah after while swallowin' an' workin' his lips like he wants to say somethin' an' can't."

"But didn't he do nothin' to stop 'em?"

"Nope, not a frazzlin' thing—jus' stood there. Spunk took Lena's arm and walked oft jus' like nothin' ain't happened and he stood there gazin' after them till they was outa sight. Now you know a woman don't want no man like that. I'm jus' waitin' to see whut he's goin' to say when he gits back."

II

But Joe Kanty never came back, never. The men in the store heard the sharp report of a pistol somewhere distant in the palmetto thicket and soon Spunk came walking leisurely, with his big black Stetson set at the same rakish angle and Lena clinging to his arm, came walking right into the general store. Lena wept in a frightened manner.

"Well," Spunk announced calmly, "Joe come out there wid a meatax an' made me kill him."

He sent Lena home and led the men back to Joe—Joe crumple and limp with his right hand still clutching his razor.

"See mah back? Mah cloes cut clear through. He sneaked up an' tried to kill me from the back, but Ah got him, an' got him good, first shot," Spunk said.

The men glared at Elijah, accusingly.

"Take him up an' plant him in 'Stoney lonesome'," Spunk said in a careless voice. "Ah didn't wanna shoot him but he made me do it. He's a dirty coward, jumpin' on a man from behind."

Spunk turned on his heel and sauntered away to where he knew his love wept in fear for him and no man stopped him. At the general store later on, they all talked of locking him up until the sheriff should come from Orlando, but no one did anything but talk.

A clear cass of self-defense, the trial was a short one, and Spunk walked out of the court house to freedom again. He could work again, ride the dangerous log-carriage that fed the singing, snarling biting, circle-saw; he could stroll the soft dark lanes with his guitar. He was free to roam the woods again; he was free to return to Lena. He did all of these things.

III

"Whut you reckon, Walt?" Elijah asked one night later. "Spunk's gittin' ready to marry Lena!"

"Naw! Why Joe ain't had time to git cold yit. Nohow Ah didn't figger Spunk was the marryin' kind."

"Well, he is," rejoined Elijah. "He done moved most of Lena's things—and her along wid 'em—over to the Bradley house. He's buying it. Jus' like Ah told yo' all right in heah the night Joe wuz kilt. Spunk's crazy 'bout Lena. He don't want folks to keep on talkin' 'bout her—thass reason he's rushin' so. Funny thing 'bout that bob-cat, wan't it?"

"Whut bob-cat, 'Lige? Ah ain't heered 'bout none."

"Ain't cher? Well, night befo' las was the fust night Spunk an' Lena moved together an' jus' as they was goin' to bed, a big black bob-cat, black all over, you hear me, *black*, walked round and round that house and howled like forty, an' when Spunk got his gun an' went to the winder to shoot it, he says it stood right still an' looked him in the eye, an' howled right at him. The thing got Spunk so nervoused up he couldn't shoot. But Spunk says twan't no bob-cat nohow. He says it was Joe done sneaked back from Hell!"

"Humph!" sniffed Walter, "he oughter be nervous after what he done. Ah reckon Joe come back to dare him to marry Lena, or to come out an' fight. Ah bet he'll be back time and agin, too. Know what Ah think? Joe wuz a braver man than Spunk."

There was a general shout of derision from the group.

"Thass a fact," went on Walter. "Lookit whut he done; took a razor an' went out to fight a man he knowed toted a gun an' wuz a crack shot, too; 'nother thing Joe wuz skeered of Spunk, skeered plumb stiff! But he went jes' the same. It took him a long time to get his nerve up. 'Tain't nothin for Spunk to fight when he ain't skeered of nothin'. Now, Joe's done come back to have it out wid the man that's got all he ever had. Y'll know Joe ain't never had nothin' nor wanted nothin' besides Lena. It musta been a h'ant cause ain' nobody never seen no black bob-cat."

"'Nother thing," cut in one of the men, "Spunk waz cussin' a blue streak today cause he 'lowed dat saw wuz wobblin'—almos' got 'im once. The machinist come, looked it over an' said it wuz alright. Spunk musta been leanin' t'wards it some. Den he claimed somebody pushed 'im but 'twant nobody close to 'im. Ah wuz glad when knockin' off time come. I'm skeered of dat man when he gits hot. He'd beat you full of button holes as quick as he's look atcher."

IV

The men gathered the next evening in a different mood, no laughter. No badinage this time.

"Look 'Lige, you goin' to set up wid Spunk?"

"Naw, Ah reckon not, Walter. Tell yuh the truth, Ah'm a lil bit skittish. Spunk died too wicket—died cussin' he did. You know he thought he wuz done outa life."

"Good Lawd, who'd he think done it?"

"Joe."

"Joe Kanty? How come?"

"Walter, Ah b'leeve Ah will walk up thata way an' set. Lena would like it Ah reckon."

"But whut did he say, 'Lige?"

Elijah did not answer until they had left the lighted store and were strolling down the dark street.

"Ah wuz loadin' a wagon wid scantlin' right near the saw when Spunk fell on the carriage but 'fore Ah could git to him the saw got him in the body—awful sight. Me an' Skint Miller got him off but it was too late.

Anybody could see that. The fust thing he said wuz: 'He pushed me, 'Lige—the dirty hound pushed me in the back!'—He was spittin' blood at ev'ry breath. We laid him on the sawdust pile with his face to the East so's he could die easy. He helt mah han' till the last, Walter, and said: 'It was Joe, 'Lige—the dirty sneak shoved me ... he didn't dare come to mah face ... but Ah'll git the son-of-a-wood louse soon's Ah get there an' make hell too hot for him. ... Ah felt him shove me. ... !' Thass how he died.

"If spirits kin fight, there's a powerful russle goin' on somewhere ovah Jordan cause Ah b'leeve Joe's ready for Spunk an' ain't skeered anymore —yas, Ah b'leeve Joe pushed 'im mahself."

They had arrived at the house. Lena's lamentations were deep and loud. She had filled the room with magnolia blossoms that gave off a heavy sweet odor. The keepers of the wake tipped about whispering in frightened tones. Everyone in the Village was there, even old Jeff Kanty, Joe's father, who a few hours before would have been afraid to come within ten feet of him, stood leering triumphantly down upon the fallen giant as if his fingers had been the teeth of steel that laid him low.

The cooling board consisted of three sixteen-inch boards on saw horses, a dingy sheet was his shroud.

The women ate heartily of the funeral baked meats and wondered who would be Lena's next. The men whispered coarse conjectures between guzzles of whiskey.

THE TYPEWRITER

SECOND PRIZE (TIE), SHORT STORY, 1926 OPPORTUNITY CONTEST

DOROTHY WEST

It occurred to him, as he eased past the bulging knees of an Irish wash lady and forced an apologetic passage down the aisle of the crowded car, that more than anything in all the world he wanted not to go home. He began to wish passionately that he had never been born, that he had never been married, that he had never been the means of life's coming into the world. He knew quite suddenly that he hated his flat and his family and his friends. And most of all the incessant thing that would "clatter clatter" until every nerve screamed aloud, and the words of the evening paper danced crazily before him, and the insane desire to crush and kill set his fingers twitching.

He shuffled down the street, an abject little man of fifty-odd years, in an ageless overcoat that flapped in the wind. He was cold, and he hated the North, and particularly Boston, and saw suddenly a barefoot pickaninny sitting on a fence in the hot, Southern sun with a piece of steaming corn bread and a piece of fried salt pork in either grimy hand.

He was tired, and he wanted his supper, but he didn't want the beans, and frankfurters, and light bread that Net would undoubtedly have. That Net had had every Monday night since that regrettable moment fifteen years before when he had told her—innocently—that such a supper tasted "right nice. Kinda change from what we always has."

He mounted the four brick steps leading to his door and pulled at the bell; but there was no answering ring. It was broken again, and in a mental flash he saw himself with a multitude of tools and a box of matches shivering in the vestibule after supper. He began to pound lustily on the door and wondered vaguely if his hand would bleed if he smashed the glass. He hated the sight of blood. It sickened him.

Some one was running down the stairs. Daisy probably. Millie would be at that infernal thing, pounding, pounding. ... He entered. The chill of the house swept him. His child was wrapped in a coat. She whispered solemnly, "Poppa, Miz Hicks an' Miz Berry's orful mad. They gointa move if they can't get more heat. The furnace's bin out all day. Mama couldn't fix it." He said hurriedly, "I'll go right down. I'll go right down." He hoped Mrs. Hicks wouldn't pull open her door and glare at him. She was large and domineering, and her husband was a bully. If her husband ever struck him it would kill him. He hated life, but be didn't want to die. He was afraid of God, and in his wildest flights of fancy couldn't imagine himself an angel. He went softly down the stairs.

He began to shake the furnace fiercely. And he shook into it every wrong, mumbling softly under his breath. He began to think back over his uneventful years, and it came to him as rather a shock that he had never sworn in all his life. He wondered uneasily if he dared say "damn." It was taken for granted that a man swore when he tended a stubborn furnace. And his strongest interjection was "Great balls of fire!"

The cellar began to warm, and he took off his inadequate overcoat that was streaked with dirt. Well, Net would have to clean that. He'd be damned—! It frightened him and thrilled him. He wanted suddenly to rush upstairs and tell Mrs. Hicks if she didn't like the way he was running things, she could get out. But he heaped another shovelful of coal on the fire and sighed. He would never be able to get away from himself and the routine of years.

He thought of that eager Negro lad of seventeen who had come North to seek his fortune. He had walked jauntily down Boylston Street, and even his own kind had laughed at the incongruity of him. But he had thrown up his head and promised himself: "You'll have an office here some day. With plate-glass windows and a real mahogany desk." But, though he didn't know it then, he was not the progressive type. And he became successively, in the years, bell boy, porter, waiter, cook, and finally janitor in a down town office building. He had married Net when he was thirty-three and a waiter. He had married her partly because—though he might not have admitted it—there was no one to eat the expensive delicacies the generous cook gave him every night to bring home. And partly because he dared hope there might be a son to fulfil his dreams. But Millie had come, and after her twin girls who had died within two weeks, then Daisy, and it was tacitly understood that Net was done with child-bearing.

Life, though flowing monotonously, had flowed peacefully enough until that sucker of sanity became a sitting-room fixture. Intuitively at the very first he had felt its undesirability. He had suggested hesitatingly that they couldn't afford it. Three dollars the eighth of every month. Three dollars: food and fuel. Times were hard, and the twenty dollars apiece the respective husbands of Miz Hicks and Miz Berry irregularly paid was only five dollars more than the thirty-five a month he paid his own Hebraic landlord. And the Lord knew his salary was little enough. At which point Net spoke her piece, her voice rising shrill. "God knows I never complain 'bout nothin'. Ain't no other woman got less than me. I bin wearin' this same dress here five years, an' I'll wear it another five. But I don't want nothin'. I ain't never wanted nothin'. An' when I does as', it's only for my children. You're a poor sort of father if you can't give that child jes' three dollars a month to rent that typewriter. Ain't 'nother girl in school ain't got one. An' mos' of 'ems bought an' paid for. You know yourself how Millie is. She wouldn't as' me for it till she had to. An' I ain't going to disappoint her. She's goin' to get that typewriter Saturday, mark my words."

On a Monday then it had been installed. And in the months that followed, night after night he listened to the murderous "tack, tack, tack" that was like a vampire slowly drinking his blood. If only he could escape. Bar a door against the sound of it. But tied hand and foot by the economic fact that "Lord knows we can't afford to have fires burnin' an' lights lit all over the flat. You'all gotta set in one room. An' when y'get tired settin' y'c'n go to bed. Gas bill was somep'n scandalous last month."

He heaped a final shovelful of coal on the fire and watched the first blue flames. Then, his overcoat under his arm, he mounted the cellar stairs. Mrs. Hicks was standing in her kitchen door, arms akimbo. "It's warmin'," she volunteered.

"Yeh," he was conscious of his grime-streaked face and hands, "it's warmin'. I'm sorry 'bout all day."

She folded her arms across her ample bosom. "Tending a furnace ain't a woman's work. I don't blame your wife none 'tall."

Unsuspecting he was grateful. "Yeh, it's pretty hard for a woman. I always look after it 'fore I goes to work, but some days it jes' ac's up."

"Y'oughta have a janitor, that's what y'ought," she flung at him. "The same cullud man that tends them apartments would be willin'. Mr. Taylor has him. It takes a man to run a furnace, and when the man's away all day—"

"I know," he interrupted, embarrassed and hurt, "I know. Tha's right, Miz Hicks tha's right. But I ain't in a position to make no improvements. Times is hard."

She surveyed him critically. "Your wife called down 'bout three times while you was in the cellar. I reckon she wants you for supper."

"Thanks," he mumbled and escaped up the back stairs.

He hung up his overcoat in the closet, telling himself, a little lamely, that it wouldn't take him more'n a minute to clean it up himself after supper. After all Net was tired and prob'bly worried what with Miz Hicks and all. And he hated men who made slaves of their women folk. Good old Net. He tidied up in the bathroom, washing his face and hands carefully and cleanly so as to leave no—or very little—stain on the roller towel. It was hard enough for Net, God knew.

He entered the kitchen. The last spirals of steam were rising from his supper. One thing about Net she served a full plate. He smiled appreciatively at her unresponsive back, bent over the kitchen sink. There was no one could bake beans just like Net's. And no one who could find a market with frankfurters quite so fat.

He sank down at his place. "Evenin', hon."

He saw her back stiffen. "If your supper's cold, 'tain't my fault. I called and called."

He said hastily, "It's fine, Net, fine. Piping."

She was the usual tired housewife. "Y'oughta et your supper 'fore you fooled with that furnace. I ain't bothered 'bout them niggers. I got all my dishes washed 'cept yours. An' I hate to mess up my kitchen after I once get it straightened up."

He was humble. "I'll give that old furnace an extra lookin' after in the mornin'. It'll las' all day to-morrow, hon."

"An' on top of that," she continued, unheeding him and giving a final wrench to her dish towel, "that confounded bell don't ring. An'—"

"I'll fix it after supper," he interposed hastily.

She hung up her dish towel and came to stand before him looming large and yellow. "An' that old Miz Berry, she claim she was expectin' comp'ny. An' she knows they must 'a' come an' gone while she was in her kitchen an' couldn't be at her winder to watch for 'em. Old liar," she brushed back a lock of naturally straight hair. "She wasn't expectin' nobody."

"Well, you know how some folks are—"

"Fools! Half the world," was her vehement answer. "I'm goin' in the front room an' set down a spell. I bin on my feet all day. Leave them dishes on the table. God knows I'm tired, but I'll come back an' wash 'em." But they both knew, of course, that he, very clumsily, would.

At precisely quarter past nine when he, strained at last to the breaking point, uttering an inhuman, strangled cry, flung down his paper, clutched at his throat and sprang to his feet, Millie's surprised young voice, shocking him to normalcy, heralded the first of that series of great moments that every humble little middle-class man eventually experiences.

"What's the matter, poppa? You sick? I wanted you to help me."

He drew out his handkerchief and wiped his hot hands. "I declare I must 'a' fallen asleep an' had a nightmare. No, I ain't sick. What you want, hon?"

"Dictate me a letter, poppa. I c'n do sixty words a minute.—You know, like a business letter. You know, like those men in your building dictate to their stenographers. Don't you hear 'em sometimes?

"Oh, sure, I know, hon. Poppa'll help you. Sure. I hear that Mr. Browning —Sure."

Net rose. "Guess I'll put this child to bed. Come on now, Daisy, without no fuss.—Then I'll run up to pa's. He ain't bin well all week."

When the door closed behind them, he crossed to his daughter, conjured the image of Mr. Browning in the process of dictating, so arranged himself, and coughed importantly.

"Well, Millie—"

"Oh, poppa, is that what you'd call your stenographer?" she teased. "And anyway pretend I'm really one—and you're really my boss, and this letter's real important."

A light crept into his dull eyes. Vigor through his thin blood. In a brief moment the weight of years fell from him like a cloak. Tired, bent, little old man that he was, he smiled, straightened, tapped impressively against his teeth with a toil-stained finger, and became that enviable emblem of American life: a business man.

"You be Miz Hicks, huh, honey? Course we can't both use the same name. I'll be J. Lucius Jones. J. Lucius. All them real big doin' men use their middle names. Jus' kinda looks big doin', doncha think, hon? Looks like money, huh? J. Lucius." He uttered a sound that was like the proud cluck of a strutting hen. "J. Lucius." It rolled like oil from his tongue.

His daughter twisted impatiently. "Now, poppa—I mean Mr. Jones, sir— please begin. I am ready for dictation, sir."

He was in that office on Boylston Street, looking with visioning eyes through its plate-glass windows, tapping with impatient fingers on its real mahogany desk.

"Ah—Beaker Brothers, Park Square Building, Boston, Mass. Ah— Gentlemen: In reply to yours of the seventh instant would state—"

Every night thereafter in the, weeks that followed, with Daisy packed off to bed, and Net "gone up to pa's" or nodding inobtrusively in her corner, there was the chameleon change of a Court Street janitor to J. Lucius Jones, dealer in stocks and bonds. He would stand, posturing, importantly flicking imaginary dust from his coat lapel, or, his hands locked behind his back, he would stride up and down, earnestly and seriously debating the advisability of buying copper with the market in such a fluctuating state. Once a week, too, he stopped in at Jerry's, and after a preliminary purchase of cheap cigars, bought the latest trade papers, mumbling an embarrassed explanation: "I got a little money. Think I'll invest it in reliable stock."

The letters Millie typed and subsequently discarded, he rummaged for later, and under cover of writing to his brother in the South, laboriously, with a great many fancy flourishes, signed each neatly typed sheet with the exalted J. Lucius Jones.

Later, when he mustered the courage, he suggested tentatively to Millie that it might be fun—just fun, of course!—to answer his letters. One night—he laughed a good deal louder and longer than necessary—he'd be J. Lucius Jones, and the next night—here he swallowed hard and looked a little frightened—Rockefeller or Vanderbilt or Morgan—just for fun, y'undestand! To which Millie gave consent. It mattered little to her one way or the other. It was practise, and that was what she needed. Very soon now she'd be in the hundred class. Then maybe she could get a job!

He was growing very careful of his English. Occasionally—and it must be admitted, ashamedly—he made surreptitious ventures into the dictionary. He had to, of course. J. Lucius Jones would never say "Y'got to" when he meant "It is expedient." And, old brain though he was, he learned quickly and easily, juggling words with amazing facility.

Eventually be bought stamps and envelopes—long, important-looking envelopes—and stammered apologetically to Millie, "Honey, poppa thought it'd help you if you learned to type envelopes, too. Reckon you'll have to do that too, when y'get a job. Poor old man," he swallowed painfully, "came round selling these envelopes. You know how 'tis. So I had to buy 'em." Which was satisfactory to Millie. If she saw through her father, she gave no sign. After all, it was practise, and Mr. Hennessey had promised the smartest girl in the class a position in the very near future. And she, of course, was smart as a steel trap. Even Mr. Hennessey had said that—though not in just those words.

He had got in the habit of carrying those self-addressed envelopes in his inner pocket where they bulged impressively. And occasionally he would take them out—on the car usually—and smile upon them. This one might be from J. P. Morgan. This one from Henry Ford. And a million-dollar deal involved in each. That narrow, little spinster, who, upon his sitting down, had drawn herself away from his contact, was shunning J. Lucius Jones!

Once, led by some sudden, strange impulse, as an outgoing car rumbled up out of the subway, he got out a letter, darted a quick, shamed glance about him, dropped it in an adjacent box, and swung aboard the car, feeling, dazedly, as if he had committed a crime. And the next night he sat in the sitting-room quite on edge until Net said suddenly, "Look here, a real important letter come to-day for you, pa. Here 'tis. What you s'pose it says," and he reached out a hand that trembled. He made brief explanation. "Advertisement, hon. Thassal."

They came quite frequently after that, and despite the fact that he knew them by heart, he read them slowly and carefully, rustling the sheet, and making inaudible, intelligent comments. He was, in these moments, pathetically earnest.

Monday, as he went about his janitor's duties, he composed in his mind the final letter from J. P. Morgan that would consummate a big business deal. For days now letters had passed between them. J. P. had been at first quite frankly uninterested. He had written tersely and briefly. Which was meat to J. Lucius. The compositions of his brain were really the work of an artist. He wrote glowingly of the advantage of a pact between them. Daringly he argued in terms of billions. And at last J. P. had written his next letter would be decisive. Which next letter, this Monday, as he trailed about the office building, was writing itself on his brain.

That night Millie opened the door for him. Her plain face, was transformed. "Poppa—poppa, I got a job! Twelve dollars week to start with! Isn't that *swell!*"

He was genuinely pleased. "Honey, I'm glad. Right glad," and went up the stairs, unsuspecting.

He ate his upper hastily, went down into the cellar to see about his fire, returned and carefully tidied up, informing his reflection in the bathroom mirror," Well, J. Lucius, you c'n expect that final letter any day now."

He entered the sitting-room. The phonograph was playing. Daisy was singing lustily. Strange. Net was talking animatedly, to—Millie, but with needle and thread over a neat, little frock. His wild glance darted to the table. The pretty, little centerpiece, the bowl and wax flowers all neatly arranged: the typewriter gone from its accustomed place. It seemed an hour before he could speak. He felt himself trembling. Went hot and cold.

"Millie—your typewriter's—gone!"

She made a deft little in and out movement with her needle. "It's the eighth, you know. When the man came to-day for the money, I sent it back. I won't need it no more—now!—The money's on the mantle-piece, poppa."

"Yeh," he muttered. "All right."

He sank down in his chair, fumbled for the paper, found it.

DRAB RAMBLES

FIRST PRIZE, LITERARY ART AND
EXPRESSION, 1927 CRISIS CONTEST

MARITA O. BONNER

I am hurt. There is blood on me. You do not care. You do not know me. You do not know me. You do not care. There is blood on me. Sometimes it gets on you. You do not care I am hurt. Sometimes it gets on your hands—on your soul even. You do not care. You do not know me.

You do not care to know me, you say, because we are different. We are different you say.

You are white, you say. And I am black.

You are white and I am black and so we are different, you say. If I am whiter than you, you say I am black.

You do not know me.

I am all men tinged in brown. I am all men with a touch of black. I am you and I am myself.

You do not know me. You do not care, you say.

I am an inflow of God, tossing about in the bodies of all men: all men tinged and touched with black.

I am not pure Africa of five thousand years ago. I am you—all men tinged and touched. Not old Africa into somnolence by a jungle that blots out all traces of its antiquity.

I am all men. I am tinged and touched. I am colored. All men tinged and touched; colored in a brown body.

Close all men in a small space, tinge and touch the Space with one blood —you get a check-mated Hell.

A check-mated Hell, seething in a brown body, I am.

I am colored. A check-mated Hell seething in a brown body. You do not know me.

You do not care—you say.

But still, I am you—and all men.

I am colored. A check-mated Hell seething in a brown body.

Sometimes I wander up and down and look. Look at the tinged-in-black, the touched-in-brown. I wander and see how it is with them and wonder how long—how long Hell can seethe before it boils over.

How long can Hell be check-mated?

Or if check-mated can solidify, if this is all it is?

If this is all it is.

THE FIRST PORTRAIT

He was sitting in the corridor of the Out-Patients Department. He was sitting in a far corner well out of the way. When the doors opened at nine o'clock, he had been the first one in. His heart was beating fast. His heart beat faster than it should. No heart should beat so fast that you choke at the throat when you try to breathe. You should not feel it knocking— knocking—knocking—now against your ribs, now against something deep within you. Knocking against something deep, so deep that you cannot fall asleep without feeling a cutting, pressing weight laid against your throat, over your chest. A cutting, pressing weight that makes you struggle to spring from the midst of your sleep. Spring up.

It had beat like that now for months. At first he had tried to work it off. Swung the pick in his daily ditch digging—Faster—harder. But that had not helped it at all. It had beaten harder and faster for the swinging. He had tried castor-oil to run it off of his system. Someone told him he ate too much meat and smoked too much. So he had given up his beloved ham and beef and chicken and tried to swing the pick on lighter things.

It would be better soon.

His breath had began to get short then. He had to stop oftener to rest between swings. The foreman, Mike Leary, had cursed at first and then moved him back to the last line of diggers. It hurt him to think he was not so strong as he had been.—But it would be better soon.

He would not tell his wife how badly his heart knocked. It would be better soon. He could not afford to lay off from work. He had to dig. Nobody is able to lay off work when there is a woman and children to feed and cover.

The castor oil had not helped. The meat had been given up, even his little pleasure in smoking. Still the heart beat too fast. Still the heart beat so he felt it up in the chords on each side of his neck below his ears.— But it would be better soon.

It would be better. He had asked to be let off half a day so he could be at the hospital at ten o'clock. Mike had growled his usual curses when he asked to get off.

"What the hell is wrong wit' you? All you need is a good dose of whiskey!"

He had gone off. When the doors of the Out-Patient's Department opened, he was there. It took him a long time to get up the stairs. The knocking was in his throat so. Beads of perspiration stood grey on his black-brown forehead. He closed his eyes a moment and leaned his head back. A sound of crying made him open them. On the seat beside a woman held a baby in her arms. The baby was screaming itself red in the face, wriggling and twisting to get out of its mother's arms on the side where the man sat. The mother shifted the child from one side to the other and told him with her eyes, "You ought not to be here!"

He had tried to smile over the knocking at the baby. Now he rolled his hat over in his hands and looked down.

When he looked up, he turned his eyes away from the baby and its mother. The knocking pounded. Why should a little thing like that make his heart pound. He must be badly off to breathe so fast over nothing. The thought made his heart skip and pound the harder.

But he would be better soon. Other patients began to file in. Soon the nurse at the desk began to read names aloud. He had put his card in first but she did not call him first. As she called each name, a patient stood up and went through some swinging doors.

Green lights—men in white coats—nurses in white caps and dresses filled the room it would seem, from the glimpses caught through the door. It seemed quiet and still, too, as if everyone were listening to hear something.

Once the door swung open wildly and an Italian came dashing madly through—a doctor close behind him. The man threw himself on a bench: "Oh God! Oh God! I ain't that sick, I ain't so sick I gotta die! No! You don't really know. I ain't so sick!"

The doctor leaned over him and said something quietly. The nurse brought something cloudy in a glass. The man drank it. By and by he was led out—hiccuping but quieter.

Back in his corner, his heart beat smotheringly. Suppose that had been he? Sick enough to die! Was the dago crazy, trying to run away? Run as he would, the sickness would be always with him. For himself, he would be better soon.

"Peter Jackson! Peter Jackson. Peter Jackson. Five, Sawyer Avenue!" The nurse had to say it twice before he heard through his thoughts.

Thump. The beat of his heart knocked him to his feet. He had to stand still before he could move.

"Here! This way." The nurse said it so loudly—so harshly—that the entire room turned around to look at him.

She need not he so hateful. He only felt a little dizzy. Slowly he felt along the floor with his feet. Around the corner of the bench. Across the space beside the desk. The nurse pushed open the door and pressed it back. "Dr. Sibley?" she called.

The door swung shut behind him. Along each side of the room were desks. Behind each, sat a doctor. When the nurse called "Dr. Sibley," no one answered, so Jackson stood at the door. His heart rubbed his ribs unnecessarily.

"Say! Over here!"

The words and the voice made his heart race again.—But he would be better now. He turned toward the direction of the voice, met a cool pair of blue eyes boring through tortoise-rimmed glasses. He sat down.

The doctor took a sheet of paper. "What's your name?"

His heart had been going so that when he said "Peter Jackson," he could make no sound the first time.

"What's your name, I said."

"Peter Jackson."

"How old are you?"

"Fifty-four."

"Occupation? Where do you work?"

"Day laborer for the city."

"Can you afford to pay a doctor?"

Surprise took the rest of his breath away for a second. The question had to be repeated.

"I guess so. I never been sick."

"Well, if you can afford to pay a doctor, you ought not to come here. This clinic is for foreigners and people who cannot pay a doctor. Your people have some of your own doctors in this city."

The doctor wrote for such a long time on the paper then that he thought he was through with him and he started to get up.

"Sit down." The words caught him before he was on his feet. "I haven't told you to go anywhere."

"I thought—," Jackson hung on his words uncertain.

"You needn't! Don't think! Open your shirt." And the doctor fitted a pair of tubes in his ears and shut out his thoughts.

He fitted the tubes in his ears and laid a sieve-like piece of rubber against his patient's chest. Laid it up. Laid it down. Finally he said: "What have you been doing to this heart of yours? All to pieces. All gone."

Gone. His heart was all gone. He tried to say something but the doctor snatched the tube away and turned around to the desk and wrote again.

Again he turned around: "Push up your sleeve," he said this time.

The sleeve went up. A piece of rubber went around his arm above the elbow. Something began to squeeze—knot—drag on his arm.

"Pressure almost two hundred," the doctor shot at him this time. "You can't stand this much longer."

He turned around. He wrote again. He wrote and pushed the paper away. "Well," said the doctor, "you will have to stop working and lie down. You must keep your feet on a level with your body."

Jackson wanted to yell with laughter. Lie down. If he had had breath enough, he would have blown all the papers off the desk, he would have laughed so. He looked into the blue eyes. "I can't stop work," he said.

The doctor shrugged: "Then," he said, and said no more.

Then! Then what?

Neither one of them spoke.

Then what?

Jackson wet his lips: "You mean—you mean I got to stop work to get well?"

"I mean you have to stop if you want to stay here."

"You mean even if I stop you may not cure me?"

The blue eyes did go down toward the desk then. The answer was a question.

"You don't think I can make a new heart, do you? You only get one heart. You are born with that. You ought not to live so hard."

Live hard? Did this man think he had been a sport? Live hard. Liquor, wild sleepless nights—sleep-drugged, rag-worn, half-shoddy days? That instead of what it had been. Ditches and picks. Births and funerals. Stretching a dollar the length of ten. A job, no job; three children and a wife to feed; bread thirteen cents a loaf. For pleasure, church—where he was too tired to go—sometimes. Tobacco that he had to consider twice before he bought.

"I ain't lived hard! I ain't lived hard!" he said suddenly. "I have worked harder than I should, that's all."

"Why didn't you get another job?" the doctor snapped. "Didn't need to dig ditches all your life."

Jackson drew himself up; "I had to dig ditches because I am an ignorant black man. If I was an ignorant white man, I could get easier jobs. I could even have worked in this hospital."

Color flooded the doctor's face. Whistles blew and shrieked suddenly outside.

Twelve o'clock. Mike would be looking for him.

He started for the door. Carefully. He must not waste his strength. Rent, food, clothes. He could not afford to lay off.

He had almost reached the door when a hand shook him suddenly. It was the doctor close behind him. He held out a white sheet of paper: "Your prescription," he explained, and seemed to hesitate. "Digitalis. It will help some. I am sorry."

Sorry for what? Jackson found the side-walk and lit his pipe to steady himself. He had almost reached the ditches when he remembered the paper. He could not find it. He went on.

THE SECOND PORTRAIT

By twelve o'clock, noon, the washroom of Kale's Fine Family Laundry held enough steam to take the shell off of a turtle's back. Fill tubs with steaming water at six o'clock, set thirty colored women to rubbing and shouting and singing at the tubs and by twelve o'clock noon the room is over full of steam. The steam is thick—warm—and it settles on your flesh like a damp fur rug. Every pore sits agape in your body; agape—dripping.

Kale's Fine Family Laundry did a good business. Mr. Kale believed in this running on oiled cogs. Cogs that slip easily—oiled from the lowest to the highest.

Now the cogs lowest in his smooth machinery were these thirty tubs and the thirty women at the tubs. I put the tubs first, because they were always there. The women came and went. Sometimes they merely went. Most all of them were dark brown and were that soft bulgy fat that no amount of hard work can rub off of some colored women. All day long they rubbed and scrubbed and sang or shouted and cursed or were silent according to their thirty natures.

Madie Frye never sang or shouted or cursed aloud. Madie was silent. She sang and shouted and cursed within. She sang the first day she came there to work. Sang songs of thanksgiving within her. She had needed that job. She had not worked for ten months until she came there. She had washed dishes in a boarding house before that. That was when she first came from Georgia. She had liked things then. Liked the job, liked the church she joined, liked Tom Nolan, the man for whom she washed dishes.

One day his wife asked Madie if she had a husband. She told her no. She was paid off. Madie, the second, was born soon after. Madie named her unquestioningly Madie Frye. It never occurred to her to name her Nolan, which would have been proper.

Madie bore her pain in silence, bore her baby in a charity ward, thanked God for the kindness of a North and thanked God that she was not back in Culvert when Madie was born, for she would have been turned out of church.

Madie stopped singing aloud then. She tried to get jobs—dishwashing—cleaning—washing clothes—but you cannot keep a job washing someone's clothes or cleaning their house and nurse a baby and keep it from yelling the lady of the house into yelling tantrums.

Madie, second, lost for her mother exactly two dozen jobs between her advent and her tenth month in her mother's arms.

Madie had not had time to feel sorry for herself at first. She was too busy wondering how long she could hold each job. Could she keep Madie quiet until she paid her room rent? Could she keep Mrs. Jones from knowing that Madie was down under the cellar stairs in a basket every day while she was upstairs cleaning, until she got a pair of shoes?

By the time she went to work in Kale's Hand Laundry, she had found the baby a too great handicap to take to work. She began to leave Madie with her next door neighbor, Mrs. Sundell, who went to church three times every Sunday and once in the week. She must be good enough to keep Madie while her mother worked. She was. She kept Madie for two dollars a week and Madie kept quiet for her and slept all night long when she reached home with her mother. Her mother marveled and asked Mrs. Sundell how she did it.

"Every time she cries, I give her paregoric. Good for her stomach."

· · ·

So the baby grew calmer and calmer each day. Calmer and quieter. Her mother worked and steamed silently down in Kale's tub-room. Worked, shouting songs of thanksgiving within her for steady money and peaceful nights.

June set in, and with it, scorching days. Days that made the thick steam full of lye and washing-powder eat the lining out of your lungs. There was a set of rules tacked up inside the big door that led into the checking-room that plainly said: "This door is never to be opened between the hours of six in the morning and twelve noon. Nor between the hours of one and six p.m."

That was to keep the steam from the checkers. They were all white and could read and write so they were checkers.

One day Madie put too much lye in some boiling water. It choked her. When she drew her next breath, she was holding her head in the clean cool air of the checking-room. She drew in a deep breath and coughed. A man spun across the floor and a white hand shot to the door. "Why the hell don't you obey rules?" He slammed the door and Madie stumbled back down the stairs.

A girl at the end tub looked around. "Was that Mr. Payne?" she asked.

Madie was still dazed; "Mr. Payne?" she asked.

"Yah. The man what closed the door."

"I don't know who he was."

The other laughed and drew closer to her. "Better know who he is," she said.

Madie blinked up at her. "Why?"

The girl cocked an eye: "Good to know him. You can stay off sometimes —if he likes you." That was all that day.

Another day Madie was going home. Her blank brown face was freshly powdered and she went quietly across the checking-room. The room was empty it seemed at first. All the girls were gone. When Madie was half across the room she saw a man sitting in the corner behind a desk. He looked at her as soon as she looked at him. It was the man who had yanked the door out of her hand, she thought. Fear took hold of her. She began to rush.

Someone called. It was the man at the desk. "Hey, what's your rush?" The voice was not loud and bloody this time. It was soft—soft—soft—like a cat's foot. Madie stood still afraid to go forward—afraid to turn around.

"What, are you afraid of me?" Soft like a cat's foot. "Come here."

—Good to know him—

Madie made the space to the outer door in one stride. The door opened in. She pushed against it.

"Aw, what's the matter with you?" Foot-steps brought the voice nearer. A white hand fitted over the doorknob as she slid hers quickly away.

Madie could not breathe. Neither could she lift her eyes. The door opened slowly. She had to move backwards to give it space. Another white hand brushed the softness of her body.

She stumbled out into the alley. Cold sweat stood out on her.

Madie second had cost her jobs and jobs. She came by Madie keeping that first job.

Madie was black brown. The baby was yellow. Was she now going to go job hunting or have· a sister or brother to keep with Madie second?

Cold perspiration sent her shivering in the alley.

And Madie cursed aloud.

———

Not in my day or your tomorrow—perhaps—but somewhere in God's day of meting—somewhere in God's day of measuring full measures overflowing—the blood will flow back to you—and you will care.

THREE DOGS AND A RABBIT

THIRD PRIZE, SHORT STORY,
1925 CRISIS CONTEST

ANITA SCOTT COLEMAN

"This, that I'm about to relate," said Timothy Phipps, "isn't much of a story, though, you might upon hearing it weave it into a ripping good yarn. I'm not much of a talker or writer. Now maybe when I'm in my cups or in the last stages of a delirious fever—I might attempt to—write." He tilted bis head, with its fringe of rough grey hair, a bit backwards and sidewise and laughed. His laughter seeming to echo—write, write, write.

Tinkling with fine spirits and good humor, he ceased laughing to inquire roguishly: "What, say, are the ingredients of a story? A plot? Ah, yes, a plot. Ho! ho! ho! The only plot in this rigmarole, my dear fellow, is running, hard to catch, a sure enough running plot. Characters. To be sure we must have characters: A pretty girl, a brave hero, a villain and love. A setting. Of course there must be a setting, an atmosphere, a coloring. We'll say moonlight and a rippling brook and a night bird singing nocturnal hymns in a forest and love. Love pirouetting in the silvery moonlight, love splashing and singing in a rippling brook. Love trilling and fluting in a bird's song—Love and a pretty girl—Love and a brave hero—Love and a villain made penitent and contrite; because of love. Bye the bye, there is no living person who could not fancy the beginning, imagine the entanglements, conceive the climax, unfold the developments, reveal the solution and picture the final, having such

64

material at hand. But," laughed Timothy, "none such—none such in what I'm a-telling."

Shedding his joviality for a more serious mien, he queried—

"Have you ever thought how very few really lovely women one meets in a life time? Our pretty young debutantes are far too sophisticated; while our age-mellowed matrons affect *naiveté*, and our bustling house-wives are too preoccupied with directing the destinies of nations to be attractive in the least.

"Men? Bother the men. We are but animals at best. Alert and crafty, lazy and jovial; just as chance decrees, and monotonously alike in our dependence upon woman. All of us are made or marred by our contacts with women. Whenever chance draws her draperies aside to allow a lovely woman to cross our path, it leaves an ineffaceable mark upon our contenance and traces indelible patterns of refinement upon our character.

"Unfortunately, I am of a critical turn of mind together with a pernicious inclination to believe with the ancient Greeks that an ugly body houses an ugly soul and that loveliness dwells only in beautiful temples.

"Certainly, certainly this inclination has led me into more than one blind alley. Ah, if I could only wield the pen as skillfully as I can this—" He flourished a carving knife, for we were at table and he was occupied at the moment in carving the *pièce de résistance*. "I would tell the world how untrue my premise is. And what a cruel fallacy outer loveliness ofttimes proves itself to be.

"Despite this, my contrary nature clings like a leech to the belief that beautiful temples are invariably beautiful within.

"And it chanced, I say chanced, since there is the probability that someone not half so lovely might have done the same deed, and had such been the case my belief would have suffered a terrible set-back. It chanced that the loveliest woman I ever saw was the most beautiful.

"I saw her first under amazing circumstances. Circumstances so extraordinary they seem unreal to this day, but I won't linger upon them, because they make another story. My second sight of her was in a crowded court-room and it was then while she sat very primly upon the culprit's bench that I had my first opportunity really to see her.

"She was a little woman. Feel as you like towards all other types, but a little woman has her appeal. Especially, a little old woman with silvery hair, and an unnamable air about her, that is like fingers forever playing upon the chords of sweetest memories. All this, and a prettiness beside, a trifle faded of course, but dainty and fragile and lovely—rare, you might say as a bit of old, old lace. And kindliness overlaying this, to lend a charm to her beauty that jewel or raiment could not render. Her silvery hair crinkled almost to the point of that natural curliness which Negro blood imparts. The kind of curl that no artificial aid so far invented can duplicate. Her eyes were extremely heavy-lidded, which is, as you know, a purely Negro attribute, and her mouth had a fullness, a ripeness, exceedingly—*African.*

"That she was anything other than a White American was improbable, improbable indeed. She, the widow of old Colonel Ritton, deceased, of Westview. As dauntless and intrepid a figure as ever lived to make history for his country. His career as an Indian fighter, pioneer and brave, open opposer of the lawlessness which held sway over the far West in the late sixties is a thing that is pointed to with pride and made much of, by Americans. Three notable sons, high standing in their respective vocations, paid her the homage due the mother of such stalwart, upright men as themselves. Two daughters, fêted continuously because of their beauty, were married into families, whose family-tree flourished like the proverbial mustard-seed, unblighted before the world.

"There had to be some reason why a lady of her standing was forced to appear in court. The truth is, it was not because of the greatness of her offense; but because of the unusualness of her misconduct which had raised such a hue and cry; until drastic method had to be resorted to.

"The charge against her was one of several counts, the plaintiffs being three very stout gentlemen, florid-faced, heavy-jowled, wide-paunched to a man. Each of them diffused a pomposity; which while being imposing managed somehow to be amusing. Their very manner bespoke their grim determination to punish the defendant. Their portly bodies fairly bristled with the strength of this intention. The muscles in their heavy faces worked as though the currents of their thoughts were supplied by volts of wonderment, shocking and bewildering. They charged, first: That the defendant willfully hampered them in the fulfillment of their authorized duty. Second: That the defendant had knowingly aided a criminal to evade the hands of the law, by sheltering the said criminal in or about her premises. Third: That the defendant had spoken untruthfully with intent to deceive by denying all knowledge of said criminal's whereabouts. Fourth: That the concealment of said criminal constituted a tort; the criminal being of so dangerous a character, his being at liberty was a menace to the commonwealth."

Timothy Phipps paused, as he busied himself, serving generous slices of baked ham to his guests. In the act of laying a copious helping upon his own plate, he commenced again, to unreel his yarn.

"There is no joy in life so satisfying, so joyous, as that of having our belief strengthened—to watch iridescent bubbles—our castles in the air—settle, unbroken upon firm old earth. To hear our doubts go singing through the chimneys of oblivion. Ah, that's joy indeed. And it is what I experienced that never-to-be forgotten day in the dinkiest little courtroom in the world.

"A rainy spell was holding sway and a penetrating drizzle oozed from the sky as though the clouds were one big jelly-bag hung to drip, drip, drip. I was sogged with depression, what with the weather and the fact that I was marooned in a very hostile section of my native land, it was little wonder that my nerves were jumpy and a soddenness saturated my spirits, even though I knew that the fugitive was free and making a rough guess at it, was to remain so. But an emotion, more impelling than curiosity forced me to linger to witness the outcome of old Mrs. Ritton's legal skirmish.

"From a maze of judicial meanderings, these facts were made known.

"The old Ritton house was a big rambling structure built at some period so long ago, the time was forgotten. It was not a place of quick escapes, for no such thing as fleeing fugitives had been thought of, in its planning. Unexpected steps up and steps down made hasty flight hazardous. Unlooked for corners and unaccountable turns called for leisurely progress and long halls with closed doors at their furtherest end, opening into other chambers, were hindrances no stranger could shun. All told, the house as it stood was a potent witness against the defendant, each of its numerous narrow-paned windows screeched the fact that none but the initiated could play at hide-and-seek within its walls.

"Many pros and cons were bandied about as to why the run-away Negro had entered Ritton's house. That he had done an unwonted thing went without saying—since hunted things flee to the outposts of Nature, shunning human habitation as one does a pestilence: to the long, long road girt by a clear horizon, where dipping sky meets lifting earth, on, on to the boundless space, away to the forest where wild things hover, or a dash to the mountains to seek out sheltering cave and cavern.

"At first, it was thought that entering the Ritton house was a 'dodge' but subsequent happenings had proven the supposition false. It was quite clear that he had gone in for protection and had found it.

"The claimants carefully explained to the court, how they had chased the Negro down Anthony, up Clements and into Marvin, the street which ran north and south beneath the Ritton-house windows. They were but a few lengths behind the fugitive—not close enough, you understand, to lay hold upon him; nor so near that they could swear that someone signaled from an open window in the Ritton house. How-be-it, they saw the Negro swerve from the street, dart through the Rittons' gate, dash down the walk, and enter the Ritton house. Less than five minutes afterwards they, themselves, pursued the Negro step by step into the building; to find upon entering it a room so spacious that the several pieces of fine old furniture arranged within it did not dispel an effect of emptiness, while the brilliant light of early afternoon showered upon everything, sparklingly, as if to say, 'No place to hide in here' and over beside an open window old lady Ritton sat very calmly, knitting. And upon being questioned she had strenuously denied that a black man had preceded them into her chamber.

"Finally the point was reached, when the defendant took the stand. And the Lord knows, so much depended, that is, as far as I was concerned, upon what she would or would not say—well, what she said, makes my story.

" 'Gentlemen, the thing you desire me to tell you, I cannot. Though, I think if I could make you understand a little of my feelings, you will cease—all of you being gentlemen—endeavoring to force me to divulge my secret.

" 'You, all of you, have been born so unfettered that you have responded to your every impulse; perhaps it will be hard to realize the gamut of my restraint, when I swear to you, gentlemen, that in all my life, I have experienced no great passion and responded to the urge of only two impulses—two—but two—and these, gentlemen, have become for me a sacred trust.

" 'It was years ago when I felt the first impulse and answered it. It has no apparent connection to the present occurrence. Yet, possibly, for no other reason than an old lady's imagining, the memory of that first occasion has leaped across the years to interlace itself with this.

" 'Wait, gentlemen. I will tell you all about it. This turbulence has awakened old dreams and old longings and opened the doors of yester-years in the midst of an old lady's musing; but it is worth all the worry. Yes, 'tis worth it.

" 'It is strange what mighty chains are forged by impulses and none of us know the strength that is required to break them. My first impulse wrought me much of happiness—very much happiness, gentlemen. Bear with an old lady's rambling—your Honor, and I shall relate just how it happened.

" 'I was ten years old, when my master—

" 'Pardon'? Yes? Yes, Sirs—My master.

" 'I was ten years old, when my master gave up his small holdings in the South and came West with his family, his wife,—my mistress—a daughter and two sons and myself. We traveled what was then the tortuous trail that began east of the Mississippi and ended in the rolling plains beside the Rio Grande. Our trip lasted a fortnight longer than we expected or had planned for. Once along the way, we were robbed. Again, we were forced to break camp and flee because a warring band of Indians was drawing near. Afterwards, we found to our dismay, that a box of provisions had been forgotten or had been lost. Misfortune kept very close to us throughout our journey, our food was all but gone. There was wild game for the killing, but ammunition was too precious to be squandered in such manner. Master had already given the command that we were to hold in our stomachs and draw in our belts until we reached some point where we could restock our fast dwindling supplies.

" 'One day, an hour before sun-down, we struck camp in a very lovely spot—a sloping hill-side covered with dwarf cedars and scrub oaks, a hill-side that undulated and sloped until it merged into a sandy-golden bottomed ravine. We pitched our camp in a sheltered nook in this ravine. The golden sand still warm from the day's sunshine made a luxurious resting place for our weary bodies. Below us, a spring trickled up through the earth and spread like lengths of sheerest silk over the bed of sand.

" 'In a little while our camp-fire was sending up curling smoke-wreaths, smoke-blue into the balmy air and a pot of boiling coffee—our very last —added its fragrance to the spice of cedars and the pungency of oaks. Sundown came on, and a great beauty settled over everything. Nature was flaunting that side of herself which she reveals to the wanderer in solitary places: the shy kisses she bestows upon the Mountain's brow and, passion-warmed, glows in flagrant colors of the sunset; the tender embrace with which she wraps the plains and the glistening peace shines again in sparkling stars. Beauty that is serene and beauty that brings peace and calm and happiness and is never found in towns or crowded cities.

" 'Our three hounds—faithful brutes that had trailed beside us all the weary miles—sat on their haunches and lifted their heads to send up long and doleful cries into the stillness.

" ' "Here—here—" cried Master. "Quit that!—Come, come, we'll take a walk and maybe scare up something to fill the pot tomorrow." He ended by whistling to the prancing dogs and they were off. Up the hillside they went, the dogs, noses to earth, skulking at Master's heels or plunging into the under-brush on a make-believe scent.

" 'I sat in the warm sand, a lonely slavechild, watching Master and the dogs until they reached the hill-top. Almost on the instant, the dogs scared up a rabbit. What a din they made yelping, yip, yap, yap and

Master halooing and urging them to the race. The frightened rabbit ran like the wind, a living atom with the speed of a flying arrow. Straight as a shooting star, it sped: until turning suddenly it began bounding back along the way it had come. The ruse worked. The dogs sped past, hot on his trail of the dodging rabbit, many paces forward before they were able to stop short and pick up the scent once more. And the rabbit ran, oh, how he ran tumbling, darting, swirling down the hillside, terror-mad, fright-blind, on he came, the dogs on his trail once more, bounding length over length behind him. One last frantic dash, one desperate leap and the rabbit plunged into my lap. I covered the tiny trembling creature with my hands, just in time, before the great hounds sprang towards me. With great effort I kept them off and managed to conceal my captive in the large old-fashioned pocket of my wide skirt.

" 'Master, disgruntled at his dogs and quite ireful—it is no little thing for a hungry man to see a tempting morsel escape him—came up to question me. "That rabbit—that rabbit—which way did it go?"

" 'When I replied "Don't know," he became quite angry and beat me. Gentlemen, the scars of that long ago flogging I shall carry to my grave. Our food was nearly gone and it was I, the slave-girl, who knew the lack most sorely. But I did not give the rabbit over to my master.

"She paused a little while and in all my life I never before knew such quiet; you could actually feel the silence.

" 'It is strange, strange how far reaching the consequences of an impulse may be. Howard, my master's son, witnessed everything. He had always teased me. His favorite pastime had been to annoy the slave-girl with his pranks, but be changed from that day. That day, when he saw his father beat me. And it was he, Gentlemen, who taught me to forget the scars of serfdom and taught me the joys of freedom. In all truth, Sirs, I am the widow of Colonel Howard Monroe Ritton of Westview.'

"There is no use trying to tell you about that," declared Timothy. "It's an experience as indescribable as it is unforgettable. That little old white-haired woman standing alone in the midst of all those hostile people, tearing apart with such simple words the whole fabric of her life. I think it was her loveliness that held them spell-bound; the power of her beauty, that kept them straining their ears to catch every word she said.

As if suddenly awakened to her surroundings, she cleared her throat nervously, and hurriedly concluded her story.

" 'The necessity of my being here, Gentlemen, is the outcome of my second impulse, an impulse, Gentlemen, nothing more. Each afternoon I sit in my west chamber beside my sunny windows, there is a whole beautiful row of them, as one can see by passing along the street ... I like the sunshine which pours through them of an afternoon, and I like to knit. And I like to watch the passersby. And, I think, Gentlemen, whenever I sit there I can recall more easily the things that are passed, the old friends, the old places, the old loves and the old hurts, which, somehow, have no longer the power to bring pain.

" 'So I was peering—my eyes are not so good—into the street and I saw a cloud of dust, all of a sudden. I thrust my head a little ways through the window, then, I saw a man running; on looking closer, I saw that he was black.

" 'Then a queer thing happened, Gentlemen; the first time in years on years, I remembered the days of my bondage. And curiously, yes, curiously, I recalled. Wait. No, I did not recall it. I swear to you, Gentlemen, a picture formed before me; a hilly slope overgrown with trees of scrub oak and dwarf cedars—a golden sand-bottomed ravine and twilight falling upon miles on miles of wind-swept prairie, and peace, sweet and warm and kind, brushing my soul and turning my thoughts towards God. And I heard it, the strident yelps of three strong dogs. I saw it—a tiny furry rabbit running for its life. I tell you—it was real, Gentlemen. And while I looked, it faded—changed—glowed into another picture—the one that was being enacted out in the street. It glimmered back to fancy and flashed again to fact, so swiftly, I could not distinguish which. Then, Sirs, they merged and both were one ... The black man who was running so wildly was only a little terror-mad rabbit. The three stout gentlemen there, (she pointed, quite like a child toward the fat policemen, while a ripple of laughter floated across the room), and the crowd which followed after, very strangely, Gentlemen, every person in it had the visage of my master. I think, I cried out at that, Sirs. Yes. Certainly. I cried—at that.

" 'Then the black man was in my presence, inside my sunny west-chamber, and I was forced to act—act quickly—.

" 'The picture had to be finished, Gentlemen. The rabbit, no, the man—had to be protected. Thank you, Sirs. That is all.'

"Yes," said Timothy Phipps, pensively. "I was the running black gentleman in the story—" He tilted his head a bit backwards and sideways and laughed. His laughter echoing—joy—joy—joy!

VOLUME 2

TO A WILD ROSE

BEST SHORT STORY BY A NEGRO
STUDENT, THE CRISIS, 1923

OTTIE B. GRAHAM

"Ol' man, ol' man, why you looking at me so?" Tha's what you sayin', son. Tha's what you sayin'. Then you start a-singin' that song agin, an' I reckon I'm starin' agin. I'm just a-wonderin', son. I'm just a-wonderin'. How is it you can sing them words to a tune an' still be wantin' for material for a tale? "Georgia Rose." An' you jus' sing the words an' they don't say nothin' to you? Well listen to me, young un, an' write what you hear if you want to. Don't laugh none at all if I hum while I tell it, 'cause maybe I'll forget all about you; but write what you hear if you want to.

Thar's just me in my family, an' I never did know the rest. On one o' them slave plantations 'way down in the South I was a boy. Wan't no slave very long, but know all about it jus' a same. 'Cause I was proud, they all pestered me with names. The white uns called me red nigger boy an' the black uns called me red pore white. I never 'membered no mother—just the mammies 'round the place, so I fought when I had to and kep' my head high without tryin' to explain what I didn't understan'.

Thar was a little girl 'round the house, a ladies' maid. Never was thar angel more heavenly. Flo they called her, an' they said she was a young demon. An' they called her witch, an' said she was too proud. Said she was lak her mother. They said her mother come down from Oroonoka an' Oroonoka was the prince captured out o' Africa. England took the prince in the early days o' slavery, but I reckon we got some o' his kin. That mean we got some o' his pride, young un, that mean we got some o' his pride. Beautiful as was that creature, Flo, she could 'ford bein' proud. She was lak a tree—lak a tall, young tree, an' her skin was lak bronze, an' her hair lak coal. If you look in her eyes they was dreamin', an' if you look another time they was spaklin' lak black diamonds. Just made it occur to you how wonderful it is when somethin' can be so wild an' still so fine lak. "My blood is royal! My blood is African!" Tha's how she used to say. Tha's how her mother taught her. Oroonoka! African pride! Wild blood and fine.

Thar was a fight one day, one day when things was goin' peaceful. They sent down from the big house a great tray of bones from the chicken dinner. Bones for me! Bones for an extra treat! An' the men an' the women an' the girls an' the boys all come round in a ring to get the treat. The Butler stood in the center, grinnin' an' makin' pretty speeches about the dinner an' the guests up at the big house. An' I cried to myself, "Fool —black fool! Fool—black fool!" An' I started wigglin' through the legs in the crowd till I got up to the center. Then I stood up tall as I could and I hissed at the man, an' the words wouldn't stay down my throat, an' I hollered right out, "Fool—black fool!" An' 'fore he could do anything atall, I kicked over his tray of gravy an' bones. Bones for me! Bones for an extra treat!

The old fellah caught me an' started awackin', but I was young an' tough an' strong, an' I give him the beatin' of his life. Pretty soon come Flo to me. "Come here, Red-boy," she say, an' she soun' like the mistress talkin', only her voice had more music an' was softer. "Come here, Red-boy," she say, "we have to run away. *I* would not carry the tray out to the quarters, an' *you* kicked It over. We're big enough for floggin' now, an' they been talkin' about it at the big house. They scared to whip me, 'cause they know I'll kill the one that orders it done first chance I get. But they mean to do somethin', an' they mean to get you good, first thing."

We made little bundles and stole off at supper time when everybody was busy, an' we hid way down in the woods. 'Bout midnight they came almost on us. We knew they would come a-huntin'. The hounds gave 'em 'way with all their barkin', and the horses gave 'em 'way steppin' on shrubbery. The river was near an' we just stepped in; an' when we see we couldn't move much farther 'less they spot us, we walked waist deep to the falls. Thar we sat hidin' on the rocks, Flo an' me, with tho little falls a-tumblin' all over us, an' the search party walkin' up an' down the bank, cussin' an' swearin' that Flo was a witch. Thar we sat under the falls lak two water babies, me a-shiverin', an' that girl a-laughin'. Yes, such laughin'! Right then the song rose in my heart tha's been thar ever since. It's a song I could never sing, but tha's been thar all a same. Son, you never seen nothin' lak that. A wild thing lak a flower—lak a spirit—sittin' in the night on a rock, laughin' through the falls, with a laugh that trickled lak the water. Laughin' through the falls at the hunters.

After while they went away an' the night was still. We got back to the bank to dry, but how we gonna dry when we couldn't make a fire? Then my heart start a-singin' that song again as the light o' the moon come down in splashes on Flo. She begin to dance. Yes son, dance. An' son, you never seen nothin' lak that. A wild thing lak a flower the wind was a-chasin'—lak a spirit a-chasin' the wind. Dancin' in the woods in the light o' the moon.

"Come Red-boy, you gotta get dry." And we join hands an' whirled round together till we almost drop. Then we eat the food in our little wet bundles—wet bread an' wet meat an' fruit. An' we followed the river all night long, till we come to a little wharf about day break. A Negro overseer hid us away on a small boat. We sailed for two days, an' he kep' us fed in hidin'. When that boat stopped we got on a ferry, an' he give us to a man an' a woman. Free Negroes, he told us, an' left us right quick.

I ain't tellin' you, young un, where it all happen, cause that ain't so particular for your material. We didn't have to hide on the ferry-boat, an' everybody looked at us hard. The lady took Flo an' the man took me, an' we all sat on deck lak human bein's. When we left the ferry we rode in a carriage, an' finally we stopped travellin' for good. Paradise never could a' been sweeter than our new home was for me. They said it was in Pennsylvania. A pretty white house with wild flowers everywhere. An' they went out an' brought back Flo to set 'em off. An' when I'd see her movin' round among 'em, an' I'd ask her if she wasn't happy, she'd throw back that throat o' bronze, an' smile lak all o' Glory. "I knew I'd be free, Red-boy. Tha's what my mother said I'd have to be. My blood is African!

My blood is royal!" Then the song come a-singin' itself again in my heart, an' I hush up tight. Wild thing waterin' wild things—wild thing in a garden.

Thar come many things with the years; the passin' o' slavery an' the growin' up o' Flo. Thar wasn't nothin' else much that made any difference. I went to the city to work, but I went to visit Flo an' the people most every fortnight. One time I told her about my love; told her I wanted her to be my wife. An' she threw back her curly head, but she didn't smile her bright smile. She closed her black eyes lak as though she was in pain, an' lak as though the pain come from pity. An' I hurried up an' said I knew I should a-gone to school when they tried to make me, but I could take care o' her all a same. But she said it wasn't that—wasn't that.

"Red-boy," she said, "I couldn't be your wife, 'cause you—you don't know what you are. It wouldn't matter, but *I* am *African* and my blood is *royal!*"

She fell on my shoulder a-weepin', an' I understood. Her mother stamped it in her. Oroonoka! Wild blood an' fine.

I went away as far as I could get. I went back to the South, an' I went around the world two years, a-workin' on a ship, an' I saw fine ladies everywhere. I saw fine ladies, son, but I ain't seen none no finer than her. An' the same little song kep' a-singin' itself in my heart. I went to Africa, an' I saw a prince. Pride! Wild blood an' fine.

Thar was somethin' that made me go back where she was. Well, I went an' she was married, an' lived in the city. They told me her husband come from Morocco an' made translations for the gover'ment.

"Morocco," I thought to myself. "That's a man knows what he is. She's keepin' her faith with her mother."

I rented me a cottage. I wanted to wait till she come to visit. They said she'd come. I settled down to wait. Every night I listen to the March wind a-howlin' while I smoked my pipe by the fire. One night I caught sound o' somethin' that wasn't the wind. I went to my door an' I listen, an' I heard a voice 'way off, kind a-moanin' an' kind a-chantin'. I grabbed up my coat an' hat an' a lantern. Thar was a slow, drizzlin' rain, an' I couldn't see so well even with the lantern. I walked through the woods towards where I last heard the voice a-comin'. I walked for a good long time without hearin' anything a-tall. Then thar come all at once, straight ahead o' me, the catchin' o' breath an' sobs, an' I knew it was a woman. I raised my lantern high an' thar was Flo. Her head was back, an' she open an' shut her eyes, an' opened an' shut her eyes, an' sobbed an' caught her breath.

An', spite o' my wonderin' an' bein' almost scaired, that little song started up in me harder than ever. Son, you never seen nothin' lak that. A wild, helpless thing lak a thistle blowed to pieces—a wild, helpless thing lak a spirit chained to earth. Trampin' along in the woods in the night, with the March wind a-blowin' her along. Trampin' along, a-sobbin' out her grief to the night.

Thar wasn't no words for me to say; I just carried her in my arms to the fire in my house. I took off her coat an' her shoes an' put her by the fire, an' I wipe the rain out o' her hair. She was a-clutchin' somethin' in her hand, but I ain't said nothin' yet. I knew she'd tell me. After while she give the thing to me. It was a piece o' silk, very old an' crumpled. A piece of paper was tacked on it. Flo told me to read it. That time when we run away from the plantation she took a little jacket all braided with silk in her bundle. 'Twas the finest jacket her mother used to wear. This dreary night, when Flo come to visit, she start a-ransackin' her old trunk. She come across the jacket and ripped it up; an' she found the paper sewed to the linin'. An' when I read what was on the paper, I knew right off why I found her in the woods, a-running lak mad in the March night wind.

Her mother had a secret, an' she put it down on paper 'cause she couldn't tell it, an' she had to get it out—had to get it out. Thar was tears in every word an' they made tears in my eyes. The blood o' Oroonoka was tainted —tainted by the blood of his captor. The father o' her little girl was not Negro, an' the pride in her bein' was wounded. She was a slave woman, an' she was a beauty, an' she couldn't 'scape her fate. Thar was tears, tears, tears in every word.

I looked at Flo; her head was back. I never did see a time when her head wasn't back. It couldn't droop. She threw it back to laugh, an' she threw it back to sigh. Now she was a-starin' at the fire, an' the fire was a-flarin' at her. Wild thing lak a spirit—lak a scaired bird ready to fly. Oroonoka! Blood o' Oroonoka tainted.

"Red-boy," she said to me, an' she never look away from the fire. "Red-boy, I'm lookin' for a baby. I'm lookin' for a baby in the winter. How am I gonna welcome my baby? Anything else wouldn't matter so much—anything else but white. *That* blood in me—in my baby! Oh, Red-boy, I ain't royal no more!" I couldn't say much, but I took her hand an' I smoothed her hair, an' I led her back to the white house down the way.

Thar in the country she stayed on an' on, an' I stayed on too. Her husband come to see her every week, an' he look proud. He look proud an' happy, an' she look proud an' sad. She wandered in the woods an' she sang a low song. An' she stood at the gate an' she fed the birds. An' she sat on the grass an' she gazed at the sky. Wild thing, still an' proud—wild thing, still an' sad.

An' she stayed on an' on till the winter come. An' the baby come with the winter. She lie in the bed with the baby in her arm. Son, you never see nothin' lak that. A wild thing lak a flowerin' rose—lak a tired spirit. Flower goin', goin'; bud takin' its place. She said somethin' 'fore she died. She look at me an' said it.

"Red-boy, my blood is royal, but it's paled. Don't tell her,—yes tell her. Tell her about the usurpers o' Oroonoka's blood."

But I never did tell her, I went away again an' I stay twenty years. I just find out not long ago where her father went to live. I went to see 'em an' I make myself known. I didn't do so much talkin', so the miss entertain me. She played on the piano and forgot that she was a-playin'. Right then she was her mother. Yes suh, thar sat Flo. Wild thing! Royal blood! Paled, no doubt, but royal all a same.

Then she turned around, an' she wasn't Flo no longer. The brown skin was thar, an' the black, wild eyes, an' the curly dark hair. She spoke soft an' low, but she never did say, "*My* blood is royal! I am *African*." An' she never did say "Red-boy". Her father had never told her about Oroonoka —that was it. An' I come back too late to tell her.

Well it don't matter no how, I thought, so long as she can hold her head lak that, an' long as she can look so beautiful, an' long as she make her mark in the world with that music. But the little song started a-singin' itself in my heart, an' I could see the flower agin.

Tha's your material boy. 'Member how I told it to you, a-fishin' on the river edge. 'Member how you was a-singin' "Georgia Rose". Thar's your material. Georgia Rose. Oroonoka. A wild, young thing, an' a little song in an old man's heart.

DAYS

SECOND PRIZE, LITERARY ART AND EXPRESSION, 1927 CRISIS CONTEST

BRENDA RAY MORYCK

There was the day that Mrs. Randolph went to see about the apartment. —silver day.—A silver day in a silver month. Silver sunshine,—silver sky, —silver trees,—silver sidewalks,—and silver promises everywhere in the air.

The Greek real estate agent shrewdly eyed his client and rubbed his hands appreciatively over the dingy radiator in his grubby little office.— Not in appreciation of its faint heat however, no,—only in happy anticipation of securing at last a desirable tenant for his tiny, third-rate flat.

Mrs. Randolph was desirable, eminently so. In the first place she had money. Diamonds on her fingers,—not too many,—just enough to announce wealth and good taste,—furs around her neck,—elegant fur, —fine gloves which fitted hands that had never known work,—dainty shoes,—a soft, dark, silk dress occasionally disclosed between the flap of the handsome, heavy coat, and a small beautiful hat, very attractively tilted to the left side of the head.—And serene eyes and quiet hands.

The rent would never be late. Money.

And culture. Mrs. Randolph was a lady. The low, mellow voice accompanied by the swift, direct look out of kindly, yet experienced, dark eyes,—the rare, flashing smile,—the well-chosen word of her language, the deliberate manner, at once charming and practical, so easy and yet so elegant,—the whole general air about her bespoke the gentle woman. Such a fine-looking woman too. Tall, handsome, statuesque, with curling raven's-wing hair most unexpectedly streaked with gray, framing a face mature with worldly wisdom but still young in sympathy and outlook. Such magnificent bearing and carriage. Of course she was dark—very dark,—almost black: enough to be a nigger. French perhaps—or Spanish. Yes, that was it,—Spanish. That accounted for the slightly oriental expression in the eyes, and the high-bridged nose and the protruding white teeth gleaming between the small pretty mouth. Of course. Spanish.

A tenant like that would raise the value of property all around,—lift the whole tone of the neighborhood. He sighed and rubbed his hands again, this time with appreciation and regret. What a pity he had placed the rent at such a low figure since she particularly wanted to locate in that vicinity.

"Your husband is a lawyer, Mrs. Randolph?" he inquired ingratiatingly.

"Yes, he is a lawyer. His offices aren't far from here,—in the Lawyer's Building. That is why this is such a convenient location. We haven't been married very long," (this simply, and without any self-conscious smirking), "and I am a stranger here. I'd like to be near enough to his business that he can come home to lunch. Then, I too, this is near the Tubes."

Oh! of course. Five minutes walk—twenty-five cents taxi fare to the rapid transit line to New York. She would spend much time in New York. All fine ladies did. It would be some time before he discovered that the neighborhood was déclassé. By that dark time, the lease would be in operation and she would be used to the convenient nearness of all things desirable.

Yes, she could have the flat—have it at once.

"But I'd like to bring my husband first," Mrs. Randolph demurred as the agent prepared to bind the bargain immediately. "Perhaps you wish to talk with him."

"No need—no need." He waved his hands and laughed facetiously. "I know who is the hoss in any family when I see the lady, I don't need to see the husband. If you're satisfied, well,—the same here."

So Mrs. Randolph rented the apartment.—And went forth into the silver day, in the silver month, key in hand, to measure the windows for the dainty voile curtains she meant to put up, and to estimate the amount of old ivory enamel and floor stain and wax, and the number of rolls of imported paper she would need to make the little place over into her home,—her first home with her husband.

A silver day in a silver month,—and silver promises everywhere in the air.

There was the day that the neighbors went to demand satisfaction from the landlord who had rented to niggers.—A black day. A black day in a treacherous month. Treacherous skies, and black clouds,—black clouds too sullen to rain,—leaden mood, menacing, threatening, and hate everywhere in the air,—black looks and hate.

Outrageous, insulting, unendurable. The very idea! Niggers living on the street. Right next door and across the street, and down the street and around the corner! Niggers! They'd see about this thing. Those niggers would either move or they'd know the reason why. What did Rocci think they were anyway, a bunch of wops or sheenies that they'd live in the same row with niggers? Besides, they had their business interests to look out for. No paying roomers would take lodgings on, block with niggers, —not even the most undesirable. And Mr. Keenan had lost trade recently. The fellows and girls didn't come in any more in the day like they used to,_only at night. And Mrs. O'Hennessy's beaus sort of quit showing up before dark, and went out so quietly you couldn't hear them, which was a bad sign. They were always quiet when they didn't get what they wanted or quite *all* they wanted. Now it was niggers that had scared them. As for Mr. Schlitski and the still in his cellar—! All that good home brew! *Still* right since that damned nigger lawyer had moved into the block. Gosh! what was the country coming to? It must be darned hard up when it had to get a nigger for assistant district attorney.

They'd see.

"Rocci thought he was puttin' one over on us,—the damned skunk!" Mrs. Heery announced angrily to Mrs. O'Kelley as she jabbed a gaudy, brass hat-pin into a loud, cheap hat, and jammed it down rakishly over a somewhat bleary blue eye. "I smelt a rat the minute I put my peepers on the woman. I sez to Mick that night when he come home, 'Gosh, there's a swell-lookin' dame took Rocci's empty flat at 68.' 'Yeah' he answers, kind o' disinterested like. You know Mick. 'Any kids?' Mick's death on kids. 'Not so' you'd notice 'em,' sez I. 'I ain't seen nobody but *her yit*. But b'lieve me, Kid, somepun's wrong when a dame what kin wear them does an' has got them manners moves into a little flat like that in this here neighborhood.' "

"H'mph!" sniffed Mrs. O'Kelley. "This neighborhood ain't so bad. I've seen lots worse,—over in Jew town an' out in little Italy. When you look up an' down this here street an' don't know nuthin' about it, it looks swell as it ever was. That's why I like it. It looks class."

"Yea, *looks*!" Mrs. Heery gave a shrill guffaw and poked her companion familiarly. "But me an' you know diffrunt. We lives here. But ain't a-goner have the tone spoiled by niggers, I'll tell the world. Gosh! when I seen that nigger husband o' hers, I near died. An' Mick wanted to go right down an' knock Rocci's block off, only I wouldn't let him."

"Yea, this is much better. Do it dignified. All of us together,—a delegation like,—protestin' against insult. Jim fer callin' out the Ku Klux right away. He's Grand Goblin of the branch you know, but I sez we don't want to give this thing too much air. It'll hurt the roomers an' then,—well, we don't want the p'lice snoopin' around here. Sometimes they take up fer these niggers. Sure! An' since the coon's got a official position too. Jim sez he stands in down a the City Hall."

Mrs. Heery snapped shut the clasp on her yellow fur neck-piece and jerked aside the tawdry lace curtains screening her wide second-story window. "That's neither here nor there," she tossed over her sharp little shoulder. "I ain't half so mad at the niggers as I am at Rocci fer puttin' 'em in. My Gawd! was it midnight when he looked at the man? I kin see where he got took in on the woman, specially with them cloes and that air. Even Dutch says he can't believe she's a nigger. He says she talks an' acts just like them swells down on Clinton Avenue when he used to keep a hop down there before it went sheeney and she buys the same kind o' meat. But my Gawd! her husband! Come on,—Mrs. Keenan and Mrs. Stebbins and Mrs. Schmidt is all ready, an' the rest'll be there. All except that damn dago. Said he wouldn't join in. Said he saw them all the time and their company an' they was nice people,—kind and like fine ladies in his country. His country! Gosh, that's what comes o' lettin' scum o' the earth run all over the United States."

"He always did look simple to me. Always bowin' an' grinnin'. He did good work though, an' he's cheap.

"Yea, but nary a shoe o' mine will he ever remember fixin' fer me again. —Look they're goin'. Gosh! wait 'till we git through with Rocci, the rotten bum."

"What can you expect?" asked Mrs. O'Kelley with rhetorical airiness, as she flipped a dirty powder-puff against a thin turn-up oblong-tipped nose and gave final squirt of cheap perfume to me frizzled ash-blonde hair. "Rocci's nothin' but dirty foreigner hisself. Maybe he did it a purpose."

"Well, we'll see."

So the notice to move was angrily served.—And Mr. Randolph went blackly forth to court to battle about his lease while Mrs. Randolph remained at home and cried.—Her cozy little apartment which love and taste and money had made so beautiful,—her first home with her husband!

A black day. A black day in a treacherous month and hate and evil everywhere—black looks and hate.

Then there was the day that lovely Mr. Leighton came to call,—a golden day—and the neighbors decided that those colored people needn't move. A golden day in a glorious month. Golden sunshine,—pink-blue sky,—yellow-green buds, and glowing mood. Precious mood and radiant sky—and golden promises in the air.

And lovely Mrs. Leighton driving up to call. An exquisite woman altogether,—patrician from the start, little, black silk hat, covering the masses of glorious gold-brown hair with copper glints, to the daintily shod, higharched feet,—fair-skinned, wistful-eyed, sweet-mouthed,— sweet.

Mrs. O'Kelley, sweeping off the front; spied her first and rang Mrs. Heery's bell. And Mrs. Heery called up Mrs. Stebbins and left it to her to tip off the rest of the neighborhood as to the worthwhileness of suspending all regular afternoon operations in order to keep sharp look-out front, before she accepted the box seat next to Mrs. O'Kelley in the latter's parlor bay window.

Those colored people couldn't be just ordinary niggers after all. Not when they had elegant white people like that coming to see them. Of course, Mr. Leighton was white. Certainly. he had a nigger chauffeur and niggers didn't work for other niggers.

Then too, there was that time before when she came in the taxi and that grand looking man and another fine lady had come with her. The dago across the way had told them Mrs. Randolph had gone away,—he was always mixing himself up in other people's business, trying to please,— bowing and grinning from his shop window like illy ape. They had written a note and then walked leisurely away. Mr. Keenan had followed them and they had gone to the Robert Treat and had dinner. Nigger weren't allowed to put their peepers inside the door there,—not even as bell-hops. Mrs. Keenan had engaged the table next to theirs so she could hear them talk and gee! they were some swell. Of course, she was white. Cadillac car, nigger chauffeur, astrakan coat, kolinsky trimming! Some rich!

"They must be terrible intimate," Mr. O'Kelley smacked out as she wallowed the huge gaub of gum under her upper lip to the left jaw teeth and rocked to and fro complacently. "She comes here quite often. Noo Yawk license too."

"Yea," responded Mrs. Heery reflectively. "It's a swell car, sure. An' that fur coat! I priced 'em. Fifteen and eighteen hundred dollars. Salisbury— Jacobson's the only place that carries 'em in this burg."

"I mean the whole she-bang looks good, car standin' in the street,—coon sittin' on the front an' that swell dame on the stoop. 'Course, all her company's been good-lookin' an' some of 'em mighty near white, too, an' never nothin' dirty or suspicious-like about their actions either."

"Yea. It makes the street look good. Anyone comin' along an' seein' this here friend o' hers goin' in an' out so often would think all the swells that used to live here didn't move away after all.—Listen, Celia,—*look*, here they both come! Now ain't they a grand sight! Humph! Look at the coon hold open that door! My Gawd! see him touch his cap to *her*, too! Gosh! —I wonder where they're goin'."

"Noo Yawk, you bet cher life!"

"Yea—mos' likely."

Silence for some time afterwards. A slackening of the violent gum-chewing and a softening of the raucous squeaking of the rocker. Silence and much thinking.

Then:

"Say Celia,—listen," slowly from Mrs. O'Kelley. "I been thinkin' maybe Rocci wasn't such a dumb fool after all for puttin' 'em in. Maybe he was lyin' when he said he never seen the husband 'till afterwards, an' thought the woman was Spanish."

"Yea," in a squelched tone from Mrs. Heery. "I bin thinkin' the same thing. So's Mick."

"Maybe we was kind o' hasty-like when we made Rocci serve 'em notice," timidly ventured again by Mrs. O'Kelley. "Jim sez her husband knows O'Hara an' O'Toole an' Teeling down at the City Hall an' they all say he's a good fellow.—What d'ye say we tell Rocci—."

"Yea, let's."

So the Randolphs were told that they needn't go,—a golden day. A golden day in a glorious month. They needn't move because the neighbors had decided that high class colored people wouldn't ruin the block. Of course, they hadn't known what they would be like. Down where they came from niggers did nothing but wield razors and drink booze. The Randolphs were different. So clean and quiet and so refined.—Yes,—they might stay.

A golden day. A golden day in a lovely month, and radiance everywhere in the air,—radiance and tolerant feeling.

Then followed the day, that the Randolphs remained,—more golden days.—The day when Mr. Randolph came to have the time-o'day speaking acquaintance with his neighbors in the evening, and Mrs. Randolph came to give the children of the neighborhood piano lessens and receive their adoration and their little bunches of flowers in return. Days when the women learned to enjoy her music and admire her beautiful home and to marvel at her fine standards;—days when they tried to fix up their own places and copy her taste—days when the men came to respect Mr. Randolph, the man, as well as his name and power; —days when all was well.

All golden days—golden days in warm, golden months—and fulfilled promises everywhere—radiance and kindly feeling.

And then, finally, there was the day that the Randolphs moved,—a gray day. A gray day in a sultry month,—rain clouds,—misty air, drab sidewalks and gray mood. Gray mood and sorrow everywhere,—sorrow and regret.

Those nice colored people were moving away. What a shame! They wanted their own home, of course, but if Rocci hadn't been such a fool when he served the notice, they might have stayed,—one year anyway. Why, the rotter actually swore at Mr. Randolph when he told him that he couldn't possibly know that he wouldn't recognize her race. She had come from parts where one's face made no difference. in one's status, so it was honest and clean. She had wanted him to talk with her husband in the first place. The dirty rotten foreigner! Her husband couldn't forget that. You couldn't blame him.

Such lovely people,—so clean and nice. And such high class company. Just like white people. And that little, fat friend with the round, brown face and the big, black eves, who was always there, actually had her own car! And so many changes of clothes,—hats too, and never any men hanging about her, either. Gee! they made Mrs. O'Hennessy feel cheap. It was a shame the were leaving. Gee!

With avid and pitying interest the neighbors watched,—watched the men sling the pretty new furniture into the van and struggle under the beautiful baby rand piano,—watched until the rag man had scraped up the last choice debris,—watched until the last load left—watched until Mrs. Randolph gave a final gingerly pat to the many, many dainty dresses laid for safe-carrying on the rear seat of Bunny's coupe,—watched as she settled herself wearily against the little, fat brown friend as the latter shifted into gear.

Then:

Over came the Italian shoemaker,—the handsome, gentle, diffident shoemaker, with the big, beseeching, tragic, child-eyes and the soft, alluring voice and manners. Out came the neighbors.

"I sorry you go," ventured Tony shyly. "I so sorry. You fine lady. Your husband—he fine man. I sorry." (It is impossible to describe the inflection of his tone). "No more nice music."

His voice choked on the last phrase and water welled up in the gentle eyes. He shook his head dumbly and moved away.

"No more nice music.—I sorry you go."

"Aw, cheer up, Tony," Mrs. Heery attempted jocosely. "Come over an' git them tan shoes o' Mick's tonight an' you'll feel better. Mrs. Randolph ain't goin' so far away she can't come back sometime, huh?" But her own hard Irish eyes filled with moisture just the same. "It's a darn shame you're movin' away, Mrs. Randolph. We'll miss you."

"Yea, we will that," vouchsafed Mrs. O'Kelley honestly. "Seems like it' kind o' hard to part, we got so used to you."

"Maybe when you're down this way sometimes,—shoppin' or on your way to the Tubes or somethin' you'll stop in sometimes, huh?"

"Yea, an' play fer us a little, huh? I guess I could scare up a cup o' tea an' a little grub,—some o' them sausages an' a little o' that pickle you liked so much, yea?"

"Well, good-bye and good-luck to you!"

And all along the block, they waved and called good-bye as Mrs. Randolph kissed her hand to the charming nest which love had made so dear, and took a last look at her beautiful, little home,—her first home with her husband.

A gray day.—A gray day in a rainy month, mist and sadness everywhere, —sadness and regret.

———

Just days.

THERE NEVER FELL
A NIGHT SO DARK

SECOND PRIZE, SHORT
STORY, 1925 CRISIS CONTEST

MARIE LOUISE FRENCH

Dusk falling, slowly hovering over earth, as a veil being gently dropped. Birds twittered. A soft wind stirred—night would soon be here with its millions of stars. Night—brooding and sweet.

He wondered how long she would sit there. He looked at his watch—three hours—and more, perhaps. But he had watched her for three hours and still she sat. She was well dressed. He could not see her face, but he knew that she was not very young or very old—there was an air of desolation around her—he dared not leave her alone. He was afraid. Years ago, he had waited—in this same park—motionless—waited for night. He felt responsible for this woman—sitting there—at the edge of things waiting for the night to help her on across. He knew; Life could treat one badly, make one long for the eternal darkness and yet, if one could smile, one could endure. Well, he would stay on a while longer, and if she continued sitting there so still, so very still, he would approach her—even if she misunderstood.

He had taken her in for three hours, at least her clothes. Dark clothes. Her dress was blue and soft and dark. He liked dark blue—always made him think of "sensible" and "independent". Well dressed but so still, so statue like. Dusk had turned into darkness, night had stolen upon them.

He would have to say something to her, to break that desolate spell around her. He approached her quickly, so tall and self-assured, so used to living to the edge of loneliness and misery.

When he stood before her he was unprepared for what he had thought would never happen. In the darkness the dim outline of her face was beautiful but her eyes were cold, lifeless and black like black marble.

She scanned his face—and met eyes that were eternally young. A smile —pleading and irresistible. There was something vaguely familiar about this man—and yet,—he drew a breath and seemed to steady himself. He sensed her torture. It was going to be harder than he had thought it would be. He was disconcerted to realize how unemotional she was. Surely, ah, surely she could not miss the beauty of the night. The night with its vast stillness and stars and somewhere a pale moon hanging low.

It was hard to meet the misery in her eyes. She spoke unemotionally, dully.

"Do you believe in God?" she asked slowly. And on hearing her voice his heart almost stifled him.

"How can you doubt? You can't look at that moon and the stars and doubt. Is it as bad as that, my friend?" He answered and took a place beside her.

After all nothing mattered to her. She was at the end. Let him sit, let him talk. It would make her last night shorter, make the hours pass more quickly.

"Tell me about it, won't you?" he asked patiently. He knew. He had watched the night come on—years ago—alone.

Strange—she felt no fear of this tall man beside her and there was something about him, something indescribable, something that made her want to sob and sob her heartbreak aloud. His smile perhaps reminded her so vividly of some one; his voice was an echo of some one's she had heard dimly, an echo of the past.

"Yes," she said bitterly, "Life is beautiful, beauty all around us; but I can't believe that there is a Just God. If there is, why does He make us suffer like this?" She was decidedly intense, and he felt that there was depth to her sorrow.

"Like this?" he asked, staring at the woman beside him. "Whatever it is, don't lose faith in yourself. Life without faith is indeed deplorable. One needs faith to live, you know." His voice went on: "When sorrow touches us the first thing that we are so willing to believe is that there is no God, or that He is angry and will not

help—"

"But," she interrupted quickly, "suppose there were reasons that He should be angry, and suppose that His punishment was too severe, and suppose that one tried hard to make up for wickedness and finally found that it was useless—absolutely. What then?"

"You have lost your faith in yourself and life gets you on all sides. Unless," he paused for a second, "unless you smile, endure and go on and on. That's Life, you know."

"But I can't go on, I can't!" she said emphatically, in a low voice. Her lips trembled and he wished that she would cry, instead of fighting the sobs back.

"You have lost some one, I know," he said quietly. He knew.

She nodded. "And I cannot bear it; you don't know, unless you have lost all your own too. This loneliness is unbearable and there is nothing—nothing—to go on for."

"I understand," he said soothingly. "I have seen and felt frightful things too."

"But your God took them! I know one has to pay. I deserved some punishment but not this—not this!"

He lighted a cigarette; somehow he wanted desperately to help her, perhaps because he had known loneliness; perhaps because her voice did not seem strange. "You are pent up; tell me about yourself; it will help you to talk."

She did, she told him of the years of struggle, of work everlasting—no end; of the man that deserted her with two children, a boy and a girl; of the eternal grind to give them a good education. And after all those years of work and sacrifice the war claimed her boy—so splendid.

"And when the war took my boy, although something went out of me, out of my life, I kept my courage. That sorrow was made beautiful because of the way he went. Brave! He went west smiling. My sorrow was made glorious! And then, and then there was my girl; young, wonderfully sweet to me, happy. How she could sing—so young, so unafraid; ready to meet life—and I lost her! How," she said, "can you tell me that God is somewhere?"

Silence, nothing but the wind softly blowing through the trees. Lights were dotting the darkness of the city.

"Just as you see me now I went to her. She was at school, nearly finished. They told me that she could not live and I left to go to her. All the way on that hot train I prayed, I pleaded with God to let me see her alive; I promised I would dedicate my life to Him if I could just see her alive. Torture! Endless hours of riding—ah!—Merciful God!—If you have to take her only let her know that I am with her; let her eyes look into mine and let me know! He didn't hear. I was too late; she had gone; only a little while—such a short time—before I arrived. I was alone, utterly alone. Why, can you tell me, did He do that? Why could she not live a few hours longer? Tell me that, if you can!" She sobbed. At last she sobbed.

She thanked him inwardly for his silence. But he was thinking. "Of course," he thought to himself, "she cannot understand why, since this girl of her heart had to be taken, why she could not have been spared a while longer. That is where the real hurt is; the one is deeper than the other. Funny we can never remember that time has not the slightest regard for one individual and Death not one favorite."

"After all," he said quietly, "there are so many things worse than death, so many sorrows deeper than yours, my friend." Silence. He did not expect a reply so he continued, looking far out into the darkness. "You have lost courage. Sure, Life has treated you badly and it'll get you if you don't buck up, smile and endure." She opened her lips and was going to speak, but his voice went on.

"I once knew a man. His name was Jim, steady, slow moving, decent. Married a girl, the only girl he ever loved. To him there never could be any one like Sue. They were happy for a while. She soon tired of the monotony. The town was small. The work was hard. Days of loneliness, drab days of drudgery, and the inevitable happened. There was a man that had always wanted Sue. Fool that Jim was, he gave her the divorce because he wanted her happiness. Providing that she would never interfere with the children; he thought that he would touch her motherhood, but—she failed him. She left him and the kids, and went her way. He was sure that he could not endure days alone. Days with his kids wanting their mother, But—he did; he had to—for them, you know. He suffered. But the years passed on, as they do. Jim worked hard. He was proud of the boy; real pals, he and that boy of his. And the girl, his heart. Friends all of them and that is something, to be friends with one's children. But Jim's boy is in prison; innocent—consider that—innocent!"

The woman trembled. But she was silent. "Jim's boy worked for a rich man that had a good-for-nothing son, always in some kind of a jam. He gambled and lost. Was heavily in debt. And his father refused to help him longer. So his son came home one night to take what he claimed would be his own some day. They quarreled; Jim's boy heard and came to see what it was all about. Just in time to see the old man fall—and foolishly in his horror over what had happened, he picked up the smoking revolver and paid—and pays—for a crime that he did not commit.

"Jim was like a man fallen in a puddle. He knew not what to do. He couldn't eat; he couldn't sleep; he could do nothing but curse an unjust God. His boy—innocent—in prison—not for a day—not for a month—but for life. God!"

The woman's sobs had ceased; she drew her breath in shortly, but could say nothing. She was still, too still, like the night.

He went on in the same low voice. "Jim, of course, was unable to comprehend how such injustice could be meted out and he thought that he could not go on after that. But he did. Much worse that than the kindness of a death—a glorious death—is it not?" He turned to the silent figure beside him. "And the girl?" she asked, wiping her eyes.

"Ah! I am coming to her," he said. "The girl, as I told you, was sent to a good school and she came home, one day, unexpectedly. It was not long before he knew why. Insupportable calamity! Tragedy beyond realization! His boy, and now this—this—." The man bowed his head in his hands for a fleeting second and it seemed to the woman, so very still beside him, that she could see a garden and a Man of Sorrows long ago. But his voice went on doggedly.

"When her time was upon her one night, it was Jim that went down into some place of pain, some horrible place of darkness with his little one. She was so young, so frail to suffer so much. And it was then that he bargained with God, as you did. He must have been heard—because when the dawn came Jim's girl went, smiling and unafraid, taking back to Him the cause of all her suffering. And," he turned to the woman quickly, "your girl went without pain, didn't she?" he asked, a bit savagely she thought.

"Yes," she answered softly, "she went like a flower in the evening time. But Jim, what happened to him?" Her eyes were tear-dimmed.

"Jim," he said, clearing his throat. "Jim of course knew that God was a Myth. Nothing mattered. Life was at its lowest ebb and dark as dark could be. He decided that the quickest way out of the darkness would be the happiest. So he sat, one day, and watched for the sunset, and after the night came he knew what he was to do. It was winter and it was cold and Jim was sick, body and soul, so he turned to his little room which almost as cold as the night itself. Turned on the gas as he hovered between this world and some place of space, he was revealed to himself, he saw things he had never thought about. Darkness, one step on over, and he would be lost. And as he was wondering about the sweet coolness of that darkness, he seemed to hear some one say, 'How about that boy of yours that you are leaving, the years ahead of him with no one to care, no one to keep him smiling and help him through? Coward! Fight to get back!' And Jim tried as hard as he could to get back. He did not want to leave that boy of his alone, he wanted to help him live through the years that might be ahead, endless years of hopelessness. But try as he would, he was slowly being drawn on over—the blackness would soon envelop him. Only a miracle could save him. Oh, if God would only let him go back, and lo, when he raised his voice and cried aloud, 'Merciful God, let me go back, not for my wicked soul's sake but for the others that need me', the miracle happened. Slowly he came back, with his landlady and a doctor over him. The cold night wind that reached him through the small window was sweet and he knew that he had been very close to the easiest way out; had been on a precipice with just a step between himself and the twilight. But he did not forget why he had been permitted to come back and he has been merciful too. A restlessness drives him at times and it is then that he finds peace, only by searching for someone that finds loneliness unbearable. And so," he said, turning quietly to the woman, "Jim learned."

"But the boy?" she interrupted huskily. He could feel her fingers gripping his arm.

"Has reason to hope for freedom soon. But Jim has been able to help him endure these horrible years unto the end."

She gave him her hands and in the darkness he could read the pleading in her eyes. "Could you forgive me, Jim dear, could you?"

Taking off her hat he searched her face. Her voice he had known, but so long ago, so many years. How could it be possible? And yet it was. In his heart, he had known, from the beginning.

"My dear, need you ask?" He answered folding her hands in his own.

She was no longer unemotional and dead; her eyes were no longer eyes of black marble She was thrillingly alive.

"Jim," she said, "I have paid; teach me to smile and to endure. I have lost him and his children—yours and you; I know the thing that I did—to leave like that—is an injury irreparable; but my punishment for being wicked is more than I can bear. The days are so long and the nights—the nights—"

" 'There never fell a night m dark that it could put out the stars,' " he quoted. "And Life is big; but Love is great, and greater."

There were tears in her eyes of black, but as they stood together and he looked deep into them, to him they were sweet and there was something deeper than understanding, something indescribable in his slow smile, as he said: "Life gets you on all sides—if you lose courage; so smile, dear; there is so much for us to do—together." Triumphantly they passed into the night.

LETTERS

FIRST PRIZE (TIED), PERSONAL EXPERIENCE SKETCH, 1927 OPPORTUNITY CONTEST

IDABELLE YEISER

LETTER ONE

Algiers.

Dear Chum:

I know you will be astonished when you notice this postmark, but miracles never cease to happen. Truly I scarcely know how it all came about, except that being asked to come, I accepted the invitation before taking time for reflection. Our party is an odd one. There are three of us: —an Italian girl, a Norwegian fellow, and myself. We sailed from Port Vendres, a place you have doubtlessly never heard of, and probably won't even find on the map. It is on the French coast, very near the Spanish border. From the station at Port Vendres we were driven to the hotel in a queer rickety old coach, drawn by two half-fed, overworked horses. But a bit of beauty awaited us. Behind the hotel rose the mountains, before it stretched the sea,— and there, just within a three minute walk from the hotel was the boat—our boat. Sleep that night was almost impossible.

Our enthusiasm continued during the entire journey. The sea was calm and blue, the bluest blue possible. We drifted along peacefully for about twenty-four hours. The morning we landed, I was up about five o'clock, expecting to see land, but none was in sight. However to compensate, there was a sunrise. Picture the deep blue sea; then picture the sun, a huge red ball, rising above the horizon, casting its reflections in the water, and sending a golden path from the horizon to our boat. Wasn't that worth getting up for?

On entering the harbor a few hours later we were both impressed and a bit afraid. Impressed by the glaring whiteness of the city and chilled with fear at the sight that confronted us. There was every type of human being imaginable. And such shades! Every degree from the blackest black to the whitest white. Arabs, Africans that belonged in the jungles, and Europeans! Beggars, laborers, merchants! We welcomed the sight of our hotel where the cleanliness was in stark contrast to the filth at the dock.

After resting a bit and securing a guide we began our sight-seeing expedition. Being but little interested in the buildings of the European quarter, we took a tram to the Casbah in order to start there and walk back down through the Arabic quarter. The real meaning of Casbah is "a fortified place." In ancient times that section served as a fortification The building, where some of the former rulers used to have their harem is like a prison. The guide explained that the rulers' wives used to peer from each tiny grated window that adorned the third story. Now the place is used for soldiers.

Outside the walls of the Casbah were seated a group of Arabs intently listening to a native storyteller. This made me think of Arabian Nights and wonder if it was in this manner that some of the tales originated. From that elevation we had a good view of the native quarters. Noticing that some of the houses, monotonous in their whiteness, were painted here and there with blue, I asked why. The ones with the blue I learned, are the houses of the Jews. Being forbidden by religion to occupy the same houses as the others, they must designate their homes with a blue marking around the doors or windows. Upon closer inspection of the quarter, we found conditions abominable. The streets, no more than a series of steps, are very narrow—in fact so narrow that the tops of the houses almost touch, thus shutting out the sun and sky. Men in their white robes and turbans either lounged in the doorways or strolled through the streets. The veiled, white-robed women added a quaintness to it all.

In fact these natives in their costumes, mingled with the Turks and the Europeans, made Algiers quaint and picturesque. Some of the natives are beautiful, while others are so poverty-stricken and dirty that they give one the creeps.

We descended step after step, through these narrow streets, passed the Arabian University and continued until we came to a pretty park—Park Morengo. There was one path that was bordered on both sides with orange trees laden with fruit. How beautiful and fresh it seemed after the native quarter. Though there were many other places to visit, there was nothing of unusual interest.

A bientôt,
PAL

LETTER TWO

Biskra

Chum, dear:—

When we left France, we didn't plan to come as far south as Biskra but this city is the best starting-point for a trip to the Sahara Desert. Surely it would be a pity to be in Africa and not glimpse the desert. On the way here, however, we stopped through Constantine. Its chief interest is in its natural beauty—its ravine.

We visited a large Mosque there. An Arabian church or mosque is of special interest, perhaps because of its sharp contrasts to our places of worship. There are no scats; the altar always faces Mecca; there is always a row of shoes at the door—for worshippers and even visitors must leave their shoes on the threshold before stepping on the sacred rug. There is another odd religious observance which we noted while enroute from Constantine to Biskra. We stopped at one station about five o'clock and all the Arabs descended, faced Mecca and prayed. You might also be interested in knowing that the Arabian religion permits the men to have more than one wife. They may have as many as four, provided they are able to support them all. Often we encounter one with his several women. I don't believe I would like to belong to a harem, for I fear I should always be jealous of the other wives. I'm convinced, though, that any religion is acceptable as long as one follows it reverently.

But you must be impatient to hear about Biskra. Never visit Algiers without coming here. The city itself is a small, rather unattractive place but it contains a Treasure Island—the Garden of Allah. I am certain you have read Hutchinson's book, "The Garden of Allah." Read his description of the garden again and try to form a mental picture of this bit of paradise. Never have I seen such beauty. We walked through avenues of palms, then wandered through smaller lanes, too impressed to speak. The garden, with its tropical beauty, seems to have been made for lovers and dreamers.

As I said, Biskra is a good starting-place for a trip to the desert. Civilization has taken such strides as to permit travellers to see the desert in an automobile, but that method didn't appeal to us. Instead we secured a guide and camels and took a day's jaunt to the beginning of this immense sea of sand. We had to pass through "Vieux Biskra" with its old sun-baked houses and its curious old inhabitants. Once, we saw a group of women approach the guide, and point toward me while jabbering something in their Arabic dialect. I grew alarmed, and asked the cause. The guide said, smilingly, "They think you are one of them, so I told them you were taken away when a baby and had now come back to visit your native land." This story had evidently satisfied them for they hurried away to pass it on.

We jogged along and passed a nomad village. Here we stopped to snap a picture only to have curses heaped upon us for not paying for the privilege of taking the picture. Farther on we encountered a band of gypsies who tried to persuade us to have our fortunes told. Soon, however, we had left all signs of life behind us and there, stretched before us was the Great Sahara. We lingered till sunset and were well repaid for so doing. A sunset on the desert! Would that I were an artist to paint it, but even words fail me in trying to describe the beauty that clothed this barren expanse. Not even a rainbow can vie with such colorings. I shall let you form your own glorious images.

LETTER THREE

Tunis

Chum, dear:—

This morning, it was amusing! We had been trying to get rid of a guide for two days, but found it impossible. Today, when we thought we had lost him, we heard someone calling, "Monsieur! dames!" We turned and there was our guide. We didn't want him, for we had seen enough of native quarters to last a good while but it was much easier to take him than to lose him. We were, therefore, in for seeing another native quarter.

It proved interesting, however, and a little different from the others we had seen. The quarter is called the "Souks" and is a series of narrow streets occupied by merchants and craftsmen. The tiny shops are covered with arches so that the whole effect reminds one of the subway stations at home. Each trade occupies one or several streets to the exclusion of the others. For instance, in one street the natives were making shoes, weaving and embroidering. In another, we were interested in watching articles being made of beaten gold. The designs were hammered out with a hammer and chisel somewhat like sculptured work.

We had another amusing experience in a perfume shop. The guide must have been a friend of the owner, for before we had time to protest we found ourselves in the shop, examining different kinds of perfume. I managed to escape by saying "No" very emphatically in the beginning but my two companions were less fortunate. They emerged from the place with forty francs worth of perfume that neither wanted.

In order to avoid any more such experiences, we left the "Souks" and visited one of the palaces of the Bey. The Bey is the Arab ruler, a king of the Arabs. The palace is now devoted chiefly to business. The rooms are large and bare but the wood carvings and designs are well worth seeing. We then left the native quarters and were glad to get outside the gates and rid of our guide.

Yesterday, we visited Carthage. You remember Carthage of ancient fame and glory. It is one of those cities that existed long before the time of Christ and has been excavated. In fact, excavations are still going on. It is remarkable how things have been conserved. There are many huge cisterns that were used for water. One of them has even been used in recent years.

Perhaps the most interesting of all the ruins is the Amphitheatre. There has been erected in the center of this monument a column with a large cross in memory of the martyrs of Christianity, for here it was that many Christians were thrown to the ferocious beasts. Then there is the Roman theater and the ruins of a temple. The handsome marble forming the columns seems in perfect condition and some of the mosaic floor designs are still visible. There is also an interesting museum, "La Musee Lavigerie which contains many beautiful pieces of old Roman sculpture. Some of the skeletons are preserved here, showing how the ancients were buried with jewelry and enough money to pay their way to the next world. If you are a lover of antiquity you would be fascinated by Carthage.

Soon, these experiences will all be memories, for in a few hours our boat sails for Marseilles.

Adieu,
PAL

MASKS

HONORABLE MENTION, 1927
OPPORTUNITY VAN VECHTEN AWARD

ELOISE BIBB THOMPSON

Paupet, an octoroon and born free, was a man of considerable insight. That was because, having brains, he used them. The cause of Julie's, his wife's, trouble was no secret to him. Although it never dawned upon him fully until after she died. Then he dictated the words to be placed upon her tombstone. The inscription proved to be unique, but not more than the cemeteries themselves of old New Orleans. The motto written in 1832 read as follows: "Because she saw with the eyes of her grandfather, she died at the sight of her babe's face."

This grandfather, Aristile Blanchard, had been an enigma to the whole Quadroon Quarter of New Orleans. But he was no enigma to Paupet although he had never lain eyes upon him. Seeing him had not been necessary for Paupet had heard his whole life's history from Paul, Julie's brother, whom he met in Mobile before he had known Julie. Paul, although a ne'er do well who had left the home-fires early, admired his grandfather immensely. Hence he had found delight even as a youth in curing from the old man those facts of his life which had proved so interesting to Paupet.

Now Paupet, among other things, was a natural psychologist albeit an unconscious one. He was accustomed to ponder the motives of men, their peculiar mental traits and their similarity to those of their parents whom he happened to know. No one was more interesting to Paupet than Julie, his wife. So of course he gave much thought to her. But the occasion is always necessary for the knowledge of a soul, and the opportunity for really knowing Julie came only when she was expecting her offspring. But even then Paupet would not have known where to place the blame for her peculiarity had he not known, as we have said, all there was to know about old Aristile Blanchard.

That Aristile was a man to be pitied Paupet felt there was no question. For what man does not deserve pity who sees his fondest dream fall with the swiftness of a rocket from a starlit sky to the darkness of midnight? No wonder that hallucination then seized him. With such a nature as his that was to be expected. But that the influence of such a delusion should have blighted Julie's young life was the thing of which Paupet most bitterly complained.

Aristile, Paul told Paupet, had been a native of Hayti. Coming to New Orleans in 1795 when the slave insurrection was hottest, he had set up an atmosphere of revolt as forceful as the one he had left behind him. Of course when Julie entered the world, the revolution had long been over; Toussaint L'Ouverture had demonstrated his fitness to rule, had eventually been thrown in an ignominious dungeon and been mouldering in the grave some five years or more. But the fact that distressed Paupet was that Aristile lived on to throw his baneful influence over the granddaughter entrusted by a dying mother to his care.

Of all the free men of color in Hayti at the time none were more favored than Aristile. A quadroon of prepossessing appearance with some capital at hand, he had been sent to Bordeaux, France, by a doting mother to study the arts for which he was thought to show marked predilection. In reality he was but a dabbler in the arts, returning at length to his native land with some acquaintance with most of them, as for instance sculpture, painting, woodcarving and the like but with no very comprehensive knowledge of any one of them. There was one thing, however, that did not escape him—being there at the time when France was a hotbed of that revolt which finally stormed the Bastile—and that was the spirit of liberty. "Liberty, Fraternity, Equality" was in the very air he breathed. He returned from France with revolutionary tendencies far in advance of any free man in the island, tendencies that awaited but the opportunity to bloom into the strongest sort of heroism.

Although he burned to be of service to his race on returning to his native land he forced himself to resume his usual tenor of life. He sought apprenticeship to an Oriental mask-maker, a rare genius in his line where the rich French planters were wont to go in preparation for their masquerades and feast-day festivities. Masks had always had a strange fascination for Aristile. He would often sit lost in thought beside their maker, his mind full of conflicting emotions. But when the French slave-owners assembled at Cape Haitien to formulate measures against the free men of color to whom the National Assemble in France had decreed full citizenship, he forgot everything and throwing down his tools immediately headed the revolt that followed.

With Rigaud, the mulatto captain of the slaves, he gave himself to the cause of France, offering at the risk of his life to spy upon the English when they came to the support of the native French planters bent upon re-establishing slavery upon the island.

Making up as a white man as best he could, he boldly entered the port of Jeremie where the English had but recently landed. His ruse would have succeeded had it not been for a native white planter all too familiar with his African earmarks, who standing by at the time readily spotted him out. Without warning, Aristile was seized, flogged unmercifully and thrown into a dungeon to die. But he was rescued after a time by a good angel in the form of an octoroon planter identified with whites all his life because of a face that defied detection; not only rescued but shipped with his daughter in safety to New Orleans. Then the octoroon rescuer took up the work of spy upon the English which Aristile had been forced to relinquish. That he was successful is manifested in the subsequent work of Toussaint L'Ouverture who because of him was able before very long to drive in all the troops of the English, to invest their strongholds, to assault their forts, and ultimately to destroy them totally.

This incident had a lifelong effect upon Aristile. Full of despondency, disappointment over his failure in the work he had set himself to do with the enthusiasm and glow of a martyr, his mind dwelt wholly upon the facial lineaments that had brought about his defeat. "Cheated!" he would exclaim bitterly. "Cheated out of the opportunity of doing the highest service because of a face four degrees from the pattern prescribed for success. Fate has been against me.—Nature has been against me. It was never meant that I should do the thing I burned to do.—O, why did not Nature give me the face of my father?—Then all things would have been possible to me. Other quadroon have been so blessed. Hundreds of them —thousands of them! Save for a slight sallowness of the skin there was absolutely nothing to show their African lineage. But Nature in projecting my lips and expanding my nose has set me apart for the contumely of the world.—The ancients lied when they said the gods made man's face from the nose upwards, leaving their lower portion for him to make himself. Try as I may I will never be able to change the mask that Nature has imposed upon me."

Day and night these thoughts were with him. Paul described this state to Paupet declaring that his mother had feared for Aristile's mind. At length this mood suddenly changed to one of exultation and he rose from his bed a new man.

"I have found the formula for greatness!" he told those about him, "It reads, Thou shalt be seen wearing a white man's face.—But only a fraction being able to carry out this prescription it is left for me to create a symbol so perfect in its imitation of Nature that the remainder of mankind may likewise receive a place in the sun. My brothers and I shall no longer be marked for defeat. I shall make a mask that will defy Nature herself. There shall be no more distinct and unmistakable signs that will determine whether a man shall be master or slave. All men in future shall have the privilege of being what they will."

With this end in view he repaired to the Quadroon Quarter of New Orleans and set up a workshop that soon became the talk of the district because of the strange-looking objects it contained. Paupet could vouch for their strangeness for they were still in existence when he came to the place. Upon the walls of this room hung many attempts of the thing Aristile had set himself to do. There were masks of paper patiently glued in small bits together in a brave effort to imitate Nature in the making of a white man's face. Likewise masks of wood, of papier mache and of some soft, clinging, leaf-like material which is very likely he discovered in Louisiana's wonderous woods. Interesting-looking objects they were, every one of them, most of them, however, were far from the goal; but few in their skin-like possibility of stretching over a man's face might have been made perfect—who knows—greater marvels have been seen —had their completion not been suddenly broken off. There was about the whole of this room an unmistakable depression, an atmosphere of shattered hope as if the maker of these objects had set out with high purpose toward their completion then suddenly been chilled by some unforeseen happening that filled him with despair. And so it really had been. While Negro supremacy existed in his beloved country Aristile worked with ever-increasing enthusiasm toward his cherished dream. He had been unable, he told himself, to assist his brothers as a soldier because of the lineaments that Nature had imposed. But he would present them with a talisman like unto Aladdin's lamp that would work wonders for them in a world where to be blessed was to be white. But when the news reached him that Toussaint the savior of his race had been tricked and thrown into a French prison to die, he was plunged into the deepest sorrow and turned from his purpose in despair. Laying aside his implements for a long time he could not be induced to take interest in anything. At length when his funds began to dwindle, it was bourne in upon him that men must work if they would live. Then he turned to the making of those limp figures in weeping gowns that when Paupet saw them were no doubt of his own distorted mind, designed for standing in the farthest corner of the room—grotesque figures wearing hideous masks, the reflection, clowns and actors of the comic stage.

It was not very long before the place began to be frequented by patrons of the Quadroon Masques and of those open-air African dances and debaucheries known as "Voodoo Carousal" held in the Congo Square. Later action from the French Opera looked in upon him. Then he conceived the idea of having Clotile, his daughter, already an expert with the needle, prepare for his patrons of the masque and stage to be rented at a nominal fee, those gowns and wraps that were now fading behind the glass doors of yonder cabinets. But though he worked continuously it had no power, apparently, to change his usual course of thought. His mind ever dwelt upon the disaster that had blighted his life.

And then came Julie in the atmosphere of depression to take up in time the work which fate decreed Clotile should lay down. As apt with the needle as her dead mother had been she was able, when her grandfather through age and ill-health became enfeebled, to maintain them both. And those were formative years for the young Julie, obliged to listen to her grandfather's half-crazed tirade against Nature's way of fixing a man to his clan through the color of his skin. Unaccustomed to thinking independently she, however, could see something of the disastrousness of it all because of the stringent laws confronting her in New Orleans. As much as she longed to do so, for instance, she dared not wear any of the head-gear of the times, although much of it was made by her own fingers, because of the law forbidding it; a bandana handkerchief being decreed to all free women of color so that they might easily be distinguished from white ladies. And that was only one of the minor laws. There were others graver and more disastrous by far. So these conditions forced her to realize early that her grandfather had good reason for his lament. She too deplored the failure of his design—the making of a mask that would open the barred and bolted doors of privilege for those who knocked thereon. Without anything like bitterness for these conditions, she began to reason that color and not mental endowment or loftiness of character determined the caliber of a man. For did not color determine his destiny? He was rich or poor, happy or unhappy according to his complexion and not according to his efforts at all. And so the words superior and inferior were invariably dependent upon the color of his skin. She, a brunette-like quadroon, the counterpart of her grandfather, was far superior to the black slave-peddlers who sometimes came into the Quadroon Quarter begging a place to rest. And that was why the Quarter guarded the section so jealously from all black dwellers, however free they might be because they wanted only superior people in their midst.

One morning some months after her grandfather's death she awoke trembling with a great discovery, for years she reflected in wonderment her revered relative had tried to make a mask that when fitted to a man's face would change his entire future and had failed. And lo! the secret had just been whispered to her. "To me," she whispered to herself ecstatically, "to po' lil' me. An' I know it ees tr-rue, yes. It got to be tr-rue. 'Cause madda Nature, she will help in de work, an' w'at else you want?" For the life-mate she would choose for herself would be an octoroon, as fair as a lily. With her complexion and his she knew that she would be able to give to her children the mask which her grandfather had yearned. She saw now why he had failed. No doubt it was never meant for men to know anything about it at all. It must be in the keepings of mothers alone. "Now we will see," she told herself exultantly. "Ef my daughter got to wear a head handgcher lak me. Fo' me it ees notting. I cannot help. But jes' de same a son of mine goin' be king of some Carnival yet. You watch out fo' me."

And so when Paupet, the whitest octoroon that she had ever seen, came lo the Quarter, she showed her preference for him at once. When, after their marriage, in the course of time their first born was expected she was like an experimentalist in the mating of cross-breeds, painfully nervous and full of the greatest anxiety over the outcome of a situation that she had been planning so long. What preparations she made! She fitted up a room especially for the event. She was extravagance itself in the selection of the garments, buying enough material to clothe half a dozen infants. She literally covered the fly leaves of the Bible with male and female names in preparation for the Christening: and made so many trips to town for all sorts of purchases that Paupet became full of anxiety for the outcome of it all.

To him she talked very freely now of her readiness in marrying him—it was really for the good of the child that was about to come to them. Her trials would not be her infant's. She had seen to that. He would look like Paupet, and could therefore choose his own way in life unhampered by custom or law.

To the midwife too she communicated her hopes and expectations, dwelling at great length upon the future of the child the whiteness of whose face would be a charm against every prevailing ill. Such optimism augured ill to the midwife who rarely vouchsafed her a word. When at length the child was born, the midwife tarried a long time before placing it into Julie's arms. It was sympathy upon her part that caused the delay. But Julie could not understand it. In the midst of her great sufferings she marvelled at it, until at length she caught a glimpse of her child's face. Then she screamed. With horror she saw that it was identical with the one in the locket about her neck. It was the image of her chocolate-colored mother.

BATHESDA OF SINNERS RUN

FIRST PRIZE, THE CRISIS CHESNUTT
HONORARIA, APRIL 1928

MAUDE IRWIN OWENS

It was like reading the Books of Chronicles, to read in the Thornton family history of the attending succession of slave women that formed the single line of Bathesda's ancestry. The Thorntons had always boasted of their seven generations of slave housekeepers who had directly descended from the housekeeper of the first American Thornton. They would proudly point out the precious, faded entries, so faithfully recorded in the old genealogy. The paternal side of the issue was always politely ignored in strict accordance with the manners and customs of the South.

The scapegrace younger son of an English baron, Richard Thornton, was founder of the family. When gambling debts and foul dueling forced him to flee his native land, he decided upon the colony of George II under Governor Oglethorpe. His first slave purchase was written in two sentences, which seemed to wink and laugh up at the reader with its tan ink and old fashioned lettering. It read:

"On this day did I barter my gold hilted sword, some lace and several shillings to that villain from the Virginia colony whom I do sorely despise—for a black wench to cook my porridge, brew my tea and wash my linen. She is comely withal and methinks, the temper of a noble blooded colt; so I have named the vixen, Jezebel."

From this Jezebel on the issue became mulatto and less mulatto: for it was written that Jezebel foaled a likely mustard-colored filly whose father and master, with malicious humor, named for his King and the colony.

So Jezebel became the mother of Georgie; who begat Abigail; whose brat was Callie; whose offspring was Ruth; whose child was Viney; whose daughter was Anne; and twenty years after slavery, came Bathesda.

To the utter amazement and chagrin of her erstwhile master and mistress, when the bell of freedom tolled for those in bondage, Anne betook herself from under the Thornton roof, in spite of all the inducements and cajoleries the Thorntons offered.

She married Enoch Creek, a fusion of Creek Indian, Negro and white and who chose to select his surname from the Indian blood which dominated his being. He was a bitter man, having no faith or belief in mankind or the institutions and principles of mankind; a religion of hatred that banned all but Anne and much later, little Bathesda.

They founded a tiny home at Sinners Run, the Negro suburb of Thorntonville, Georgia, that had been called after a famous camp-meeting revival sermon preached there, years back. Their cabin was a little apart and elevated from the other huts and shacks of the Sinners Run people, so that they could look down upon the road which was alternatingly red clay or yellow mud and note the comings and goings of those who lived upon it.

Anne attended the Sinners Run Baptist Church regularly and prayed that her husband find salvation. Enoch traded at the store because it was necessary—but after that, all socializing with their neighbors ceased; unless in the case of illness, when Anne was administering angel and healer of the small community. Within her lean yellow hands was the strange, soothing power to allay pain, and from her husband, she learned much of the Indian mysteries of roots and herbs for medicinal use.

· · ·

They were thrifty and got along. For twenty years they worked, saved, improved their little two room home, and the acre upon which it stood. Anne was an expert needle-woman as Viney, Ruth and Callie had been before her; and she was in great demand in all the big houses down in Thorntonville. Enoch hired himself out as a plantation farmer, and in spite of his scowling silence, was known as a good hand.

Then, at the age of forty—when all hope of bearing the traditional one girl-child had flown from the heart of Anne, it happened; and Bathesda made her advent into the life of Sinners Run.

Enoch smiled for the first time—his squinting Indian eyes snapping with delight at the yellow gypsy-like Anne in the role of Madonna, with the robust little papoose that was his. Of course the Thorntons got wind of it, investigated and greedily annexed one more generation to old Jezebel's descendants, although the essence of reflected glory had lost its flavor since the inconvenient Emancipation. The distinction of being the first of her line born out of slavery, was the most disgraceful thing that could have been written about Bathesda, into the sacred Annals, according to Thornton opinion.

Two weeks later, Enoch stepped on a rusty spike. Blood-poisoning set in and, in spite of their combined knowledge of medicine and healing—his time had come to leave Anne and Bathesda, before Anne had convinced him there was a God.

Anne turned from the unmarked grave, and faced the world alone with her baby, unflinchingly—with that calm independence that asked no pity. She went about her sewing at the houses of her patrons, for a while, carrying her infant with her.

But as Bathesda began to toddle about, Anne realized her child should have home life, and be allowed to play in the vegetable patch and flower garden which Enoch had so painstakingly planted. So Anne took only work such as she could do at home, and her little daughter grew to be the marvel of the country side—a healthy, lovely child.

She attended the broken down school-house to be taught by a wizened old maid from Connecticut a few months a year, and she sat at her mother's knee, during the school period ... both struggling eagerly to master a clear fluent English. Anne, being ardently religious, insisted that the little girl read her Bible and attend church regularly, in which she was reluctantly obeyed.

Thus Bathesda grew up to woman-hood. Beautiful—of deep-rooted intelligence handicapped by inadequate schooling, a pagan love for the gorgeous wonders of Nature and a passion for all things artistic. She became adept at the fine French seams and hemming; learned to feather-stitch the picturesque quilts on the huge frame, to weave highly imaginative Indian designs out of the bright silken rags into rugs and mats, to make the difficult Yankee hook rug, the knowledge of which had been introduced South by a Yankee Thornton bride; and best of all, she became an expert copier of the old ante-bellum samplers. Anne's sampler embroidering frame looked worm-eaten—it was so old; and Bathesda considered it with great reverence.

They made a picture to be remembered, sitting together at their artistic labors—the older woman and her daughter. Anne invariably talked religion to Bathesda having sensed a silent indifference which bespoke much of Enoch's atheism. When at the stuffy little church, the sermon had become highly extortive, and the worshiper's down-trodden souls burst forth in howling primitive devotion to a God they desperately believed in—even when great tears spilled down her quiet mother's cheeks, Bathesda's sole reaction was a disdainfully cold squinting of her pretty black eyes.

"It's Enoch! It's Enoch!" mourned old Anne, as she watched the child of her old age flower into radiant womanhood with no change of heart.

"But Mother," Bathesda would say, "you take on so 'bout nothin'. Ain't we happy? We have always been different from them in our way of livin' and doin' things and so how can you expect me to be like them in their church doin's? You are not like them when you feel the spirit, Mother. You cry a little bit, but I have never seen you rear and tear and stomp and scream 'halleluliah' like someone crazy. ... I hate it! My church is the purple mist stealin' ahead of the red dawn—the chirpin' wood-chucks; wild wood blossoms! If I ever 'get religion' Mother 'twill be in that kind of church, and not among the sweaty, hysterical hypocrites of your church. Why! I believe to my soul, Mother, you are the only real Christian among them, and do the least testifyin'!"

"Child—you don't understand. It is as real with them as life itself! It is given to each to work out his own destiny in the Lord, in his own way. It is the feelin' that they are weak and sinful that overpowers them so—in their strivin' to follow the Good Book."

"I don't care 'bout them anyways, Mother. We are better colored folks ... that's all. It just ain't in them to be better. Look at their homes! Bare plank floors that all their scrubbin' and scourin' don't improve; walls plastered with newspapers full of pictures that they think are pretty; gunny-sacks tacked up to the windows ... ugh! Give them their winter supply of potatoes, rice and hog meat ... let them go to church and give chitterlin' suppers ... plenty of shoutin' and back-bitin' and they are happy all winter long, Mother. But—look at our home!"

She waved her pale brown hand proudly around the room in which they sat. The walls were whitewashed. The floor was covered with a huge rag rug rich with colorful stripes and the single square window was draped with deep rose curtains that fluttered happily in the breeze. They had been made from flour bags soaked in kerosene to remove the printing, and dyed with berry juice. There were two fine old pieces of colonial mahogany in this outer room—a gigantic highboy and a marble-topped medicine chest. The other articles of furniture were three rush-bottomed chairs and a table that Enoch had made, and carved all over with the weirdly grotesque totem-pole gargoyles. Upon the mantel over the fireplace were a brilliant basket and two odd potteries also relics of the Creek strain in the father of Bathesda. Small painted tubs and cans were in interesting groups about the room, filled with plants of various sorts.

"I don't suppose I should say I hate them, Mother dear," Bathesda continued, "but I can get along without them. I shall do as you have always done ... when they're sick, I'll make them well if they call upon me—but I don't ... I can't be one of them in religion or otherwise."

"Ah, my child," sadly smiled Anne, "you may have inherited the sense of medicine from Enoch, your father, but the Divine gift of healing can never descend upon a disbeliever ... and you are the first of us women who has not been born with the gift since Mother Jezebel. She, even in her early day, was a Christian convert."

At this, Bathesda would shake her head impatiently as if flinging aside the admonitions of her mother, and the two long black braids would flare about her arms and shoulders. Then, bowing earnestly over her work, she would concentrate upon the exact copying of probably old Viney's intricately designed sampler with the words—"Little flakes make the biggest snow", ordered by an antique dealer from Savannah.

Bathesda's mother died in her sixtieth year, and never had there been such a funeral in the history of Sinners Run. Unlike her husband who had only a faithful wife and new born babe to follow him to his grave— the entire countryside turned out to do honor to Anne Creek. All of the present generation of Thorntons came from their town house in Savannah, in full force, much to the awe of the Sinners Run folk. They even hinted about how appropriate and fitting it would be if Anne were buried beside Viney, in Thorntonville; but Bathesda was obdurate.

"Thank you, Mr. and Mrs. Thornton, but my mother's place is beside her husband. My father has been alone out there, long enough."

So the Thorntons had a second lesson in Negro independence.

"Promise me, my daughter, that you will seek Jesus!" gasped Anne in her last consciousness. "Go to the church—seek Him until you find Him ... and He will give you your birthright like he has given it to all the rest of us. Promise your poor old Mammy, Bathesda ... baby!"

And so she had promised to seek religion and the power to heal the sick.

Bathesda lived on, as the years rolled by, much as when Anne lived. She made beautiful things with her graceful slender hands, and more money than she needed in her simple mode of living. She lived alone with the spirit presences of her parents, except for the loyal protection of a watch dog. She cared for the gay little flower garden tenderly and kept her graves freshly decorated in flower season. She grew her vegetables, also the roots and herbs with which she concocted her famous medicinal recipes. She attended the Sinners Run Baptist Church and contributed to its support; but the Indian in her worshipped only the wonders of Nature and she put no other gods before the beauty of the earth.

The colored people of Sinners Run envied and hated her, yet maintained a deceitful courtesy that permitted them to call upon her when in need of intervention with white people, money or in sickness. Her ability to always smooth the way for them, in any form of distress, was known with a certainty that was uncanny to their superstitious minds. She could do all except smooth out actual pain like her mother had done. However, she did her all, in the name of Anne ... she herself caring little for these crude mean-hearted and petty people, who grinned in her face for favors, and hissed "half white bastard" behind her back. This last amused her, however, since her intelligence allowed her to see no difference between the black and yellow progeny of the illicit unions of slavery.

"What queer religion these folks have," laughed the woman, "it breaks forth in a certain place, and at a certain fixed time, then they lose it 'til the next time."

The women were especially incensed against her, because—if they married at all, they invariably married men who Bathesda had rejected. She allowed each suitor in his time, to visit her, sit as long as he pleased admiring her at the embroidering rack, while she, with serene indifference, hoped he would make his departure in time for her to take her dog and go to the crest for the sunset, or some such solitary jaunt. She could say "no" with a cool pleasantness that retained their goodwill; but the wives to whom she gave the men up, hated her venomously for so doing. Hated her for wrapping her long glossy braids around and around her head in a coronet which made her a queen among them. Hated her for appearing so youthful despite her forty-seven years. Hated her for not shouting at church, and for failing to testify or profess. Hated her for having the prettiest house and garden in the community—for making the medicine that cured them. Hated her for weaving and embroidering while they took in washing, or labored beside their men in the cotton and corn fields. Hated her for her chaste aloofness of man, while they bore large families in the morass of poverty and misery. Hated her for showing contempt for the edicts of fashions and mail order houses up North or the cheap stores in Thorntonville and Savannah and for wearing the simply made, richly embroidered garments which none could duplicate. For all these reasons, the women of Sinners Run despised Bathesda.

Among them, she had one sincere friend in the person of young Becky Johnson. The dark-skinned girl had sought Bathesda in a frenzy one stormy midnight. Bathesda had donned her cape and accompanied the wild young mother to the bedside of her baby who was strangling with dyptheria. It was a simple deed; the swabbing of the little throat with boiled vinegar and salt, with a few directions, but the brown girl had hugged Bathesda's knees and kissed her comfortably shod feet in feverish adoration. The father, too, had looked dumb gratitude with brimming eyes. After this incident, Becky took Li'l Jim up to see Bathesda regularly, and Bathesda became greatly attached to the small family, such devotion from Becky having awakened within her cold nature, something akin to affection.

Becky's sister, mother and grandmother, strongly disapproved of this friendship. The sister, whose name was Cisseretta, was somewhat of a belle, and when rigged up in the castoff clothes of the white people for whom she worked, was, for Sinners Run, quite elegant. She was light brown, with hazel eyes that were sly and coquettesh. Her hair was of that yellowish cotton-batten sort, known as riney. She meant to marry better than had her older sister, and scorned the field hands as prospective husbands, although she was not averse to keeping them from dancing attendance on the less discriminating girls of her set.

The mother, Eliza Lambert, was about Bathesda's age and a malicious "yes" woman to gossip and trouble making, although too stupid herself to even instigate a healthy lie.

· · ·

The grandmother, Granny Lou, was an ancient crone, black as pitch, who had lost trace of her age, but knew everything pertaining to a scandalous nature concerning the families of both races for miles around. She sat in one corner year in and year out, wrapped in filthy shawls and hoods summer and winter, smoking her foul clay pipe, and spitting snuff into the maw of the tumble-down stove, or gumming her vicious old tales. She was reputed to be the oldest woman in that section of Georgia, and to have borne more children than she herself knew; Eliza, being her youngest, to whom she had hitched herself. Just as most of the trouble making and under-current of evilness in the neighborhood could usually be traced to the chair of Granny Lou and Lambert household, so was she guilty of inciting most of the fierce antipathy among the women, against Bathesda.

One particular early autumn morning, she pursed and screwed her shrunken lips around to settle the snuff and saliva making a "Mpwhumnmpwhumn" noise, and began lisping to Eliza who was washing:

"Heh, heh! Ah sees whar dat-ar new ministah done gine sottin' up to Thesdy's already—heh, heh! 'Pears lak to me dat you 'omans ain't slaves no moah an' oughten't go fer to put up wid sich cayyin' on. Lize ... Yo' Cissy tryin' to sot huh cap foah him, but 'pears lak to me, effen she gits him, won't be twell dat Thesday's chawed 'im up an' spat him back at huh! Heh, heh!" and as if to suit the word with the action, she spat into the pink wood ashes which were falling out of the stove pit.

"Taint nothin' to them Jezebel 'omans, noways. De white folks make me sick cayin' on so high 'bout dem. Day all sold dere souls to de debbil. Don't dey fool 'round wid roots 'n things? ... mind how dey nebber show dere natchul age lak we'uns does?"

The silence that followed was broken by the sudsy slapping of wet clothes with home made lye soap. Eliza was too busy to bother about her old mother's chatter this morning, but Granny Lou was nothing loath to amusing herself.

"Becky, lak a li'l fool ... she run up dere case day yaller 'oman do foah dat brat ahern, jis what any of ussen coulda did. Ah knows, chal! Yo Granny Lou knowed dem f'om way back to Callie!"

"Kyah, kyah, kyah! Granny Lou—hush yo mouf," laughingly yelled Eliza above the suds, steam and slop, with perspiration dripping from her corn-rowed head into the tub.

Cisseretta, who had entered the room unnoticed, flared up angrily at the old hag's challenge—

"I wants Brother Parson Brown, and I's shore goin' to git him. 'Taint goin' to be after Thesday done chawed him, either, Granny!" So saying, she jammed her hands down upon her hips with her legs astride and frowned belligerently from her mother to her grinning grandmother.

The pine door swung open admitting Becky, resplendent in a soft white dress carrying Li'l Jim who was sportive in a blue smock and cap. The three women were aghast at the sudden picture. Poor Becky who was content to drudge in a one room cabin with her baby, for a husband who scarcely could pay for his fat back and meal down at the store,—what right had she to look nicer than Cisseretta, the acknowledged social leader of Sinners Run!

"Whar'd je git dem cloes?" darkly inquired Eliza of her daughter.

"Oh Mammy! Ain't dey jist swell? Miss Thesdy done made dis up special foh me out o' brand new goods case ah told huh 'twas my second year married, today! See Li'l Jim? Ain't he grand? I has a big suppah foh Big Jim when he gits home and thought I would run in an let you folks see us."

"Humph! 'Miss' Thesdy! Since whin did we start 'Missin' ' yaller niggers? Was Parson Brown anywhere bouts up there?" this from Cisseretta.

"Seems to me dat dose clo'es would scorch yo' skin, chal. Dat Thesdy is a woman wid no religion what-somever," exasperatingly sighed Eliza.

"Jes' gib yo all dose cloes fuh to git yo' wrapped up in huh, fudder—dan she gine conjuh yo ... heah me, now, heah me!" snapped old Granny Lou with a portentious shaking of her beshawled head.

. . .

Poor Becky! All her joyous happiness so quickly transformed to bitter antagonism.

"How come yo'all hates that pore woman so? What she done done aginst you? All I seed she done was good! She's up dere in huh own pretty li'l house, amindin' huh business, and you folks down heah hatin' huh! Cisseretta? You won't make no hit wid Parson Brown ... hatin' Miss Thesdy, 'case he thinks she is jest grand! As for me and Big Jim, she saved our boy's life which is moah dan you what's his own kin-folks done, and we loves huh, even ef she ain't done professed 'ligion. From what I seed of huh and knowed of younes, she's a heap sight nigh to God dan you folks who eat out yo hearts wid hatin' huh!"

She gathered the bewildered Li'l Jim up and left the scene of unsympathetic relatives, muttering to herself—"Gawd! Effen I stayed widdem any longer I would lose my own 'ligion. They's my own folks, but dey simply breed evilness, and I doesn't blame sweet Miss Thesdy from not minglin' wid 'em, 'ceptin' when she has to."

In the Lambert cabin, Granny Lou was grunting—"See dat? She done got dat chal tu'ned agin huh own folks already ... an de preachuh eatin' out ob huh hand,"—with a cunning glance at Cisseretta.

"For two cents, Granny—" whined Cisseretta, petulantly, "I'd git the women together and go up to her ol' house and beat her up!"

"Kyah kyah! Lawsy me! Hush yo' mouf, chal!" elaborately guffawed her mother.

"Go hade, den ... go hade! Do moah—an' talk less, honey!" huskily whimpered the old woman to her infuriated grandchild.

The day had been a busy one for Bathesda. She had contracted to make reproductions of the old samplers for an important Jewish antique dealer of Atlanta. Little Alice Thornton, quite grown up, and home from college, had motored out to see her, bringing with her her fiancé from Boston, an artist. He had begged for the privilege of painting Bathesda in all the glory of her little cottage and embroidering frames. To please

Alice, she consented, on condition that it wouldn't interfere with her work.

"Like one of Millet's peasant women," he had said—"and that interior! Worthy of the old Dutch masters."

The young minister had sat awhile, explaining his well meant plan of progress for his congregation, which she knew would never be accepted by the deluded Sinners Run folks, the present pastor being their first seminary man. They understood only the old fashioned untrained "called-but-not-sent" type of ministering.

Becky and Lil Jim dropped in with the new things she had made for them, and the sight of the mother and child transformed by her handiwork, thrilled her deeply.

She bent her queenly head over the crimson, green and purple threads she was interweaving so intricately into the words—"Heart within, God without" on the square of yellow, and smiled the smile of the middle-aged who had all they wanted in life—peace, pleasant labor, and contentment. Why should she be sad because of a God who withheld Himself, or the doubtful power of healing a people who despised her?

She decided to pick a fresh cabbage for her supper, and going to the door, was surprised to see Cisseretta Lambert approaching. With shifting eyes, and lowered brow, she informed Bathesda they had come to fetch her for a friend. At the little picket gate stood an old rickety home-made cart with ill matched wheels, drawn by a sorry nag whose hips punctured his skin in miss-meal significance. Eliza was driving and perched beside her for all the world like a bundled up mummy, sat Granny Lou.

"We kin fotch you there and back in no time, Thesdy. New folks jest come to Sinners Run, and powerful sick."

Bathesda hurriedly threw a light shawl around her shoulders with a strong sense of foreboding which she forcibly thrust out of her mind, and joined the trio at the cart.

She and Cisseretta rode backwards with their feet swinging, and nothing was said by the four women as the half dead animal faltered along the lonely road pulling the unbalanced, lurching, wabbling vehicle behind him.

Then Eliza …

"Kyah kyah! Heah we all is, folksies! Kyah kyah! Lawdy, Lawdy, Lawd!"

Bathesda turned from the back end of the wagon and saw glaring malevolently at her, the dark faces of ten or twelve women. They were as a pack of hungry hounds eager to be off on the chase. Cisseretta leaped from her seat on the wagon and rudely grabbed Bathesda, causing her to stumble to the ground on her knees. As if waiting for the initiative action from their leader, they pounced upon her, dragging her by the arms up the sloping hill side. The decrepit conveyance with the beswaddled old woman, was left standing on the road.

The maddened women yelled violent invectives—brandished whips, twigs and sticks aloft, dragging her roughly uphill, not allowing her to regain her foothold or the freedom of her arms.

"Thought you'd git yo claws. on Revern Bro Brown, didn't you? We see 'bout dat, won't we? Cain't feed him none o' yo hoodoo vittles … nuh-uh!"

"Yes indeedy. We is gwine to see 'bout all dis heah monkey business yo been cayin' on all dese yeahs wid de men folks. …"

"Think you better dan ussens, doesn't you? Humph! Old half white niggers make me sick … caint be white an' caint be black!"

"Naw! We niggers don't want you and de white folks won't hab you!"

"Lawdy, Lawdy, Lawd today! Yeowh!"

"Pull huh ol' plaits down! Make me tiahd wid huh ol' dawg har! Wouldn't have straight har, mahself—Revelations say as plain as day—'har lak lambs wool' like ussen got. …"

"Sis Grenn? Dis is shoah a holy deed Cisseretta done called on us to do ... to pertect ouah poah pastor from de wiles ob dis sinner woman. ..."

"Kyah kyah! Lawd today!"

They reached the summit of the hill which was capped with a small patch of woods. A few of the trees had recently been chopped down, judging by the fresh stumps. The several women in whose clutches Bathesda had fallen, suddenly released their hold on her and jumped back out of her reach. But Bathesda merely stomped the caked dirt from her shoes and torn skirt, thru a quiet searching glance around the semi-circle of women, and made to swing her loosened braids around her head.

This action galled Cisseretta, who saw in it a self assurance, a composure that was shaking the courage of her vigilance committee. She sprang at Bathesda heavily with an angry snarl, pushing her back into a tree which instantaneously crashed to the earth, sideways, sending Cisseretta and all the women scrambling and yelping down the hill.

"Conjuh woman! conjuh ... Lawd ah's feared!"

"Hoodoo stuff! Told yo'all we oughten to bother wid huh!"

"Lawd! Jist 'low me to git home oncet moah ... please!"

"Cisseretta done got ussen into dis mess ...!

From the opposite direction came two white men, hurrying toward Bathesda who stood arranging her hair beside the fallen tree.

"Anybody hurt, Auntie? We are clearing these here woods for Ben Lovett who has bought the strip, and my buddy here—he sprained his joint while chopping down that 'un a few minutes ago. We went up to my shack after some liniment and we didn't 'reckon anyone would come along before we got back. The tree was nearly cut thru and I 'spec a slight jostle knocked her over."

"No one was hurt. It fell to the side," murmured the yellow woman absently—eyes searching into the distance.

A delicate tenderness played over her face, and kindly wrinkles appeared about her mouth and forehead. Like Haggard's "She", Bathesda unexpectedly looked her age, all at once. She had dropped the cloak of a hardened, held-over youth, and taken on the ethereal robe of an inner beauty—a soul transformation had taken place.

She, for the first time, turned directly to the lumberjacks, and asked of the one with the bandaged arm—

"Is it bad?"

"Hurts mightily and swellin' every second."

She unwrapped the crude bandage, wiped away the stench of liniment, cupped her two hands about the swollen arm and gazed upward—her thin lips moving almost imperceptibly while the men stood transfixed. She finally withdrew her hands, clenched them into tight fists and then shook them open and away from her, as if throwing off the contamination of alien flesh.

"Now ... it is well!"

"Bill! Honest to John! She's right! The dadburned misery has gone completely, and look! The swellin' is goin' down right before my very eyes!"

"Good God! 'tis a miracle we've just witnessed! The woman's a saint." And he hastily crossed himself, while the other man tested his healed arm by swinging an ax.

Bathesda went down the hill with wide masculine strides—the light winds causing her snagged skirt and white apron to billow and flurry. Her eyes were two muddy pools of tears. She was testifying.

"Up Calvary's rugged brow did I go, this day with Thee, dear Lord ... To the very foot of the Cross ... and I saw the bloody nails in Thy precious feet ... the cruel thorns ... and the bitter cup was spared me ... me, a worthless worm ... but Thou didst drink it to the dregs!"

And she went home with a new power—with understanding, tolerance and forgiveness; to be one of her people; to take care of Becky with her

Lil Jim and Big Jim; and the fragrant drops of rain pelted her in gentle benediction.

THE FOOLISH AND THE WISE

SALLIE RUNNER IS
INTRODUCED TO SOCRATES

LEILA AMOS PENDLETON

Mrs. Maxwell Thoro (born Audrey Lemere) tiptoed down the spacious hall toward the kitchen of her dwelling whence issued sounds, not exactly of revelry but—perhaps jubilation would be a better fit. For in a high soprano voice her colored maid-of-all-work, Sallie Runner, for the past half-hour had been informing to the accompaniment of energetic thumps of a flatiron, whomsoever it might concern that she had a robe, a crown, a harp and wings.

Mrs. Thoro moved quietly for, enjoyable as was Sallie's repertoire, one could never tell when she would do some even more enjoyable improvising, and her employer knew from long experience that Sallie's flights were much freer and more artistic when she was unaware of an audience.

Just as Mrs. Thoro reached the kitchen door the soloist started off on the verse, "I gotta shoes," so she stood quietly listening until the verse ended:

> "I gotta shoes, yo' gotta shoes,
> All a Gawd's chillun gotta shoes;
> Wen I getto hebben goin' to put on my shoes
> An' skip all ober Gawd's hebben.
> Hebben, Hebben! Ever'buddy hollerin' 'bout hebben

Ain't goin' dere."

Hebben, hebben, goin' to skip all ober Gawd's hebben."

As the singer ceased she whirled around upon her employer with a loud laugh. "Ha, ha, Miss Oddry!" cried she. "I knowd yo' was dere. I sho is glad yo' done come, 'cause I'se mighty lonesome an' powerful tired. Jes' was thinkin' to myseff dat I'se goin' to try to swade Brother Runner to move away fum Starton. Nobuddy don't do nothin' here but git bornd, git married an' git daid, an' wurk, wurk, wurk! Miss Oddry, I'se goin' to tell yo' a secret."

"What is it, Sallie?" inquired Mrs. Thoro.

"I don't lak to wurk. Nuvver did."

"Why, Sallie! That is a surprise," replied her employer. "I should never have guessed it, for there is not a more capable maid in town than you are."

"Yassum, I guess dat's right. I wurks wid my might an' I does whut my hands finds to do, but taint my nature doe. Muss be my Ma's trainin' an' mazin-grace-how-sweet-de-sound mixed togedder, I reckon. Miss Oddry, does yo' know whut I'd ruther us do dan anything? I'd ruther know how to read an' write dan anything in de whole, wide world, an' den I'd nuvver do nothin' else but jes' dem two."

"Well, Sallie, I'm sure you would get very tired of reading and writing all the time; but you're not too old to learn."

"Nome, not too ole, mebbe, but too dumb an' too sot in de haid, I reckun. Miss Oddry, couldn't yo' read to me or talk to me on ironin' days 'bout sumpin' outside uv Starton? Cose I woulin't want yo' round under my feet on wash-days, but ironin' days is fine fur lissening."

"Why yes, Sallie, I'd love to do that. Why didn't you ask me before? Mr. Thoro and I are re-reading an old school course, just for the fun of it, and I'll share it with you. I'm sure you would enjoy hearing about some of earth's greatest characters. How would you like to have me tell you about Socrates?"

"Sockertees? Huh! Funny name! Sockertees whut?"

"Well, in his time men seldom had more than one name, Sallie. He was the son of Sophroniscus and Phaenarete. He was a sculptor and a philosopher."

"Gosh!" cried Sallie. "A sculpture an' a lossipede! Wusser an' mo' uv it! But go on, Miss Oddry, tell me mo' 'bout him."

"Socrates was born about 469 years before our Lord, and died at the age of seventy. He is said to have had thick lips, a flat nose, protruding eyes, bald head, a squat figure, and a shambling gait."

"Why!" exclaimed Sallie. "He was a cullud gentmun, warn't he? Musta looked jes' lak Brudder Runner, 'cordin' to dat."

"Oh no, Sallie, he wasn't colored."

"Wal, ef he been daid all dat long time, Miss Oddry, how kin yo' tell his color?"

"Why he was an Athenian, Sallie. He lived in Greece."

"Dar now! Dat settles it! Ever'buddy knows dat my cullud folks sho do lak grease."

"Oh Sallie! 'Greece' was the name of his country, just as 'America' is the name of ours." Sallie grunted.

"Socrates," continued Mrs. Thoro, "was a very wise, just, and a good man, and he loved his country and his countrymen very much. He used to delight in wandering through the streets of Athens, conversing with those whom he met, giving them the benefit of the truths he had discovered and seeking to obtain from each more truth or new light. He spent the whole day in public, in the walks, the workshops, the gymnasiums, the porticoes, the schools and the market place at the hour it was most crowded, talking with everyone without distinction of age, sex, rank or condition. It was said that 'as he talked the hearts of all who heard him leaped up and their tears gushed out.' "

"Hole on, Miss Oddry," interrupted Sallie, "Jes' wanta ax yo' one queshun. While ole Sockertees was runnin' round the streets, shootin' off his lip an' makin' peepul cry, who was takin' keer uv his fambly? Sounds mo' an' mo' lak Brudder Runner to me."

"Well, Sallie, he had a very capable wife who bore him three sons and whose name was Xanthippe. No doubt she managed the household. The only fault Socrates found with her was that she had a violent temper."

Sallie slammed the flatiron down and braced herself against the board, arms akimbo, eyes flashing with indignation.

"Vilent temper?" cried she. "Vilent temper? Whut 'oman wouldn't had a vilent temper in a fix lak dat? I sho do symperthize wid Zantipsy an' I doesn't blame her fur gittin' tipsy needer, pore thing. I betcha she was es sweet es a angel befo' she got mahred, 'cause whut it takes to change yo' disposition, a man lak dat sho is got. It's jes' es much es a 'oman kin do to take keer uv her house right an' raise her chillun right wen her husband is doin' all he kin to hepp her, less mo' wen he ain't doin' nothin' but goin' round runnin' he mouf. Dis ain't de fust time I'se met a gentmun whut loves he kentry mo' dan he do he home folks. Go on, Miss Oddry, dear, tell me some mo' 'bout Reveral Eyesire Runner's twin brudder."

"Of course, Sallie," said Mrs. Thoro laughing, "Socrates was human and had his faults, but all in all he was a noble character."

"I hopes so, Miss Oddry, but I'll have to hear mo' fo' I 'cide."

"Socrates," resumed Mrs. Thoro, "believed in signs and omens and in following warnings received in his dreams; he also claimed that there was an inner voice which had guided him from childhood."

"Miss Oddry," expostulated Sallie, "yo' keep on tellin' me Sockertees warn't cullud, but yo' keep on tellin' me cullud things 'bout him. Wen we all b'lieve in signs. an' dreams yo'-all allus says, 'It's jes' darky superstishun an' ignunce.' How yo' splain dat?"

"Well, Sallie, in those days the most learned people were very superstitious. Of course we know better now."

"How yo' know yo' knows better, Miss Oddry? How yo' know yo' don't know wusser? Dere's one thing I done found fur sho, an' dat is dat de mo' folks knows de less dey knows. I b'lieves in dreams an' wen I follers dem I goes right. Cose I ain't nuvver heerd no cujjus voice, but ef ole Sockertees say he heerd it I b'lieve he heerd it. Nobuddy can't prove he didn't."

"Very true, Sallie, but,—"

"Jes' one minute, Miss Oddry, please. Dere's sumpin' I been thinkin' a long time, an' now I knows it. An' dat is dat wen ye' come right down to de fack-trufe uv de inside feelin's, peepul is all alak; black ones is lak white ones an' dem ole ancienty ones lak Sockertees is jes' lak dese here ones right now."

"I believe there is some truth in that, Sallie, but shall I go on shout Socrates?"

"Oh, yassum, Miss Oddry, I do love to hear 'bout him."

"He tried most earnestly to make people think, to reason out what was right and what wrong in their treatment of each other. He constantly repeated, 'Virtue is knowledge; Vice is ignorance', while to the young his advice was always, 'Know thyself.' "

"Humph!" interrupted Sallie. "Mighty good advice, Miss Oddry, but it's some job, b'lieve me. I'se es ole es Methusalum's billy goat now an' I ain't nuvver found myseff out yit. Dere's some new kink comin' out ev'ry day. How 'bout you, Miss Oddry?"

"I think you are right, Sallie. But don't you think we are better off if we study ourselves than if we just blunder along blindly?"

"Oh, yassum, I guess so. But how did ole Sockertees come out wid all his runnin' round an' talkin'?"

"Very sadly, I am sorry to say. Very sadly. Most of the Athenians entirely misunderstood him."

"Bound to," said Sallie.

"He made a great many unscrupulous enemies."

"Bound to," said Sallie.

"They accused him of being the very opposite of what he was."

"Bound to," said Sallie.

"And finally they tried him and condemned him to death."

Sallie set down the flatiron and folded her arms, while her eyes flew wide open in astonishment. "What?" she exclaimed. "Jes' fur talkin'? Wal I-will-be-swijjled!"

"Yes," continued Mrs. Thoro. "They imprisoned him and sent him a cup of hemlock, which is deadly poison, to drink."

"But he had mo' gumption dan to drink it, I hope?"

"It was the law of his country, Sallie, and Socrates was always a law-abiding citizen."

"Wal, fur gosh sake!" cried Sally. "Whut in de world was de use uv him havin' all dat tongue ef he couldn't use it to show dem people wherein? He mouts well been es dumd es a doodlebug!"

"But," explained Mrs. Thoro, "he had spent his whole life in trying to make the Athenians love and honor and obey their laws and he was willing to die for the same cause. He had many friends who loved him truly and they tried to persuade him to escape, but by unanswerable arguments he proved to them how wrong they were."

"Humph!" grunted Sallie. "Tonguey to de last! An' in de wrong way to de wrong ones."

"Plato, who was a friend as well as a pupil," continued Mrs. Thoro, "tells how beautifully Socrates died. He took the cup of hemlock quite calmly and cheerfully and drained it to the dregs. When his friends could not restrain their sorrow for the loss they were about to sustain, he reproved them and urged them to remember that they were about to bury, not Socrates, but the shell which had contained him, for he, himself, was about to enter the joys of the blessed. He tried to the last to make them see that unless they honored and obeyed all the laws, their country could not survive, because lawlessness was the same as suicide."

"Miss Oddry," said Sallie, solemnly, "don't yo' wisht we had one million of dem Sockertees down here in ower sunny Soufland?"

MAMMY

ADELINE F. RIES

Mammy's heart felt heavy indeed when (the time was now two years past) marriage had borne Shiela, her "white baby," away from the Governor's plantation to the coast. But as the months passed, the old colored nurse became accustomed to the change, until the great joy brought by the news that Shiela had a son, made her reconciliation complete. Besides, had there not always been Lucy, Mammy's own "black baby," to comfort her?

Yes, up to that day there had always been Lucy; but on that very day the young Negress had been sold—sold like common household ware!—and (the irony of it chilled poor Mammy's leaden heart)—she had been sold to Shiela as nurse to the baby whose birth, but four days earlier had caused Mammy so much rejoicing. The poor slave could not believe that it was true, and as she buried her head deeper into the pillows, she prayed that she might wake to find it all a dream.

But a reality it proved and a reality which she dared not attempt to change. For despite the Governor's customary kindness, she knew from experience, that any interference on her part would but result in serious floggings. One morning each week she would go to his study and he would tell her the news from the coast and then with a kindly smile dismiss her.

So for about a year, Mammy feasted her hungering soul with these meagre scraps of news, until one morning, contrary to his wont, the Governor rose as she entered the room, and he bade her sit in a chair close to his own. Placing one of his white hands over her knotted brown ones, he read aloud the letter he held in his other hand:

"Dear Father:—

"I can hardly write the sad news and can, therefore, fully appreciate how difficult it will be for you to deliver it verbally. Lucy was found lying on the nursery floor yesterday, dead. The physician whom I immediately summoned pronounced her death a case of heart-failure. Break it gently to my dear old mammy, father, and tell her too, that the coach, should she wish to come here before the burial, is at her disposal.

"Your daughter,

"SHIELA."

While he read, the Governor unconsciously nerved himself to a violent outburst of grief, but none came. Instead, as he finished, Mammy rose, curtsied, and made as if to withdraw. At the door she turned back and requested the coach, "if it weren't asking too much," and then left the room. She did not return to her cabin; simply stood at the edge of the road until the coach with its horses and driver drew up, and then she entered. From that time and until nightfall she did not once change the upright position she had assumed, nor did her eyelids once droop over her staring eyes. "They took her from me an' she died"—"They took her from me an' she died"—over and over she repeated the same sentence.

When early the next morning Mammy reached Shiela's home, Shiela herself came down the road to meet her, ready with words of comfort and love. But as in years gone by, it was Mammy who took the golden head on her breast, and patted it, and bade the girl to dry her tears. As of old, too, it was Mammy who first spoke of other things; she asked to be shown the baby, and Shiela only too willingly led the way to the nursery where in his crib the child lay cooing to itself. Mammy took up the little body and again and again tossed it up into the air with the old cry, "Up she goes, Shiela," till he laughed aloud.

Suddenly she stopped; and clasping the child close she took a hurried step towards the open window. At a short distance from the house rolled the sea and Mammy gazed upon it as if fascinated. And as she stared, over and over the words formed themselves: "They took her from me an' she died," — "They took her from me an' she died."

From below came the sound of voices, "They're waiting for you, Mammy,"—it was Shiela's soft voice that spoke—"to take Lucy—you understand, dear."

Mammy's eyes remained fixed upon the waves,—"I can't go—go foh me, chile, won't you?" And Shiela thought that she understood the poor woman's feelings and without even pausing to kiss her child she left the room and joined the waiting slaves.

Mammy heard the scraping as of a heavy box upon the gravel below; heard the tramp of departing footsteps as they grew fainter and fainter until they died away. Then and only then, did she turn her eyes from the wild waters and looking down at the child in her arms, she laughed a low, peculiar laugh. She smoothed back the golden ringlets from his forehead, straightened out the little white dress, and then, choosing a light covering for his head, she descended the stairs and passed quietly out of the house.

A short walk brought Mammy and her burden to the lonely beach; at the water's edge she stood still. Then she shifted the child's position until she supported his weight in her hands and with a shrill cry of "Up she goes, Shiela," she lifted him above her head. Suddenly she flung her arms forward, at the same time releasing her hold of his little body. A large breaker caught him in its foam, swept him a few feet towards the shore and retreating, carried him out into the sea—

A few hours later, two slaves in frantic search for the missing child found Mammy on the beach tossing handfuls of sand into the air and uttering loud, incoherent cries. And as they came close, she pointed towards the sea and with the laugh of a mad-woman shouted: "They took her from me an' she died!"

DOOR-STOPS

MAY MILLER

Green Willow Street never boasted of virgins; not, of course, that one could be certain that such did not exist within its narrow confines but rather that one would never have associated such an anomaly with such a street. Indeed, the reputation of this little section was due entirely to ladies who plied a most distinctive trade, nor would the casual passerby have hesitated to add to the long list of artful traffickers the plump brown girl who sprawled indolently over the stoop at number __. She herself did not expect anyone to believe the truth; moreover did not want anyone to. With unnatural horror she dreaded the disclosure of the fact—so much did she desire to be like all the others.

Spring had stolen up the street so insidiously that few recognized it. There were no trees to herald its coming and the closely laid bricks of the pavements and cobblestones of the street brooked no intruding grass. Tonight, however, one knew of the season's arrival. The stoops were cluttered with lounging figures—thermometers were not needed in Green Willow Street so well did the appearance of the stoops register changes in weather. At number __ the feeble cries of Nannie Bowen's new baby (it was her fourth fatherless brat) could be heard through the open window. Next door Easy Jones began to pump the pedals of his new pianola, and in the streets the children were mimicking life—choosing and losing lovers to rhythmic clapping and tuneful repetition of the barely intelligible words,

"That ol' man ain't got no wife, Mis Liza Jane,
Shouldn't have mine to save his life, Mis Liza Jane.
Oh, Mis Liza, Mis Liza Jane."

A slender, dark form towering for an instant above the enthusiastic singers, a gruff exchange of greetings with the half-dozing stoop-loungers, an unusual alertness on the part of the plump brown girl—Joe had arrived.

"Hey, Irma, you ready? We ain't got much time; it's after ten now," was the youth's abrupt greeting.

"Uh huh, what's yo' hurry?" the girl rejoined.

"We want seats; don't we? The place was crowded when I come past."

"Be wid you in a minute." Irma rose and went into the house.

It was a gala night at the Bucket of Blood. Count and his far famed troubadours from Atlantic City were the visiting artists and the cabaret was delightfully crowded. Smoke ascended to the low ceiling and returned to sting the eyes and mingle with the products of fresh cigarets. Gracefully draped half-pint, pint, and quart bottles were furtively produced from the most unexpected places. A stout, dark diva was crooning in a deep contralto voice, "I can't give you anything but love, baby."

Irma, a tingling warmth stealing over her, surveyed the sea of black, brown, and yellow faces. They harmoniously blended into one effective background from which the only real visage that emerged was the one that stood out in bold relief, face to face with hers. The smoke from Joe's cigaret circled their heads and inclosed them in a little paradise of their own. She leaned dizzily over the rickety table.

"Love me, Joe?" she asked thickly.

"How do I know?" the youth grumbled.

"You don' know? How come you don' know? I knows I loves you."

"I ain't sayin' nothin' 'bout you; I'se talkin' 'bout mahself an' I ain't got no ways of tellin' yit."

The youth reached down beside the table leg, brought up a bottle and filled the two glasses with a clear liquid which the proprietors called gin and sold at sixty-five cents a half-pint. Irma drained her glass and persisted.

"Whatcha mean, Joe?"

"You know damned well what I mean, but this ain't no time to talk 'bout that. Let's dance."

Joe gulped down the liquor, pushed his chair back violently and lurched toward Irma. She rose unsteadily. Joe's arms encircled her and they swayed to the saxophone's wail. After five minutes of movement in which they had progressed merely five feet from their table, they realized that the selection had ended and stumbled back to their places. Joe filled the glasses again. Irma drank and questioned anew.

"Joe, you ain't meaning you ain't lovin' me an' count of that?"

"I ain't said that yit, but I been goin' wid yuh foh two weeks now an' I guess we'd better be gittin' somewheres."

"Somewheres!" Irma opened her heavy eyes in alarm.

Joe sensed another explanation. "Forgit it, kid," he retorted harshly and emptied his glass.

And so a new day was born and grew older with the same round repeated—a drink, a question, a dance—a question, a dance, a drink. At two Joe muttered something about that ride to Sparrow's Point in the morning, kicked the empty bottle, grabbed his hat from the table and started toward the door. Irma snatched her threadbare black coat from the back of the chair and staggered after him.

The fresh air cleared her eyes and cooled her brow, but she clutched desperately at Joe's arm as he strode rapidly toward her home. Why couldn't they go on like this—just Joe and her—her and Joe—liquor warming her body and April's breeze in her face? But he was waiting— just waiting—and when the time came, she had nothing to say. She could not talk of that; it had been so long ago she had forgotten—forgotten—there was no forgetting that. She shuddered and tightened her grasp on Joe's arm.

They had reached her stoop and Joe's voice cut in on her reverie.

"Listen, Irma," he was murmuring "am I goin' in wid you tonight or not?"

"Joe, tonight?" she floundered helplessly.

"Yes, tonight. Ise tired of this tomorrow—tomorrow. I ain't takin' no mo' chances."

"But————"

"There ain't no but. We lef' yo' ant down at The Bucket an' there ain't no one else to kick. Aw, come on, kid."

Joe reached out and with hands as gentle as a mother's and drew Irma into his arms. She went willingly and nestled close. He covered her forehead, face, and neck with hot, hurried kisses. Irma was limp in his arms. She closed her eyes in a dizzy whirl.

"Come on, let's go in." Joe had turned the knob and kicked the door open. They were half way over the sill.

Irma was sober in a minute. She jerked herself away stammering, "Joe, you know—you know—"

"Sure, I knows," he interrupted harshly, "You don' like me an' you don' like mah kisses. Gawd, Irma, what does you 'spect of a feller?"

"I don' know, Joe. Hones' to Gawd, I loves you—I loves you better'n anythin' else, but I jus' can't now."

"Now! It's been two weeks."

"Yes, I knows, but somethin'—somethin' happened once an'—"

"Somethin' happened! What happened?" Joe was frankly puzzled.

"Somethin'—somethin'—Oh, I can't talk 'bout it, but I ain't never been like all the others since."

"Ain't like all the others! What you mean?" The boy eyed the girl with open suspicion.

Irma drew back as if to hide herself from her sweetheart's scrutiny. "No, not that but—but—" She stopped, attempted once more to explain, then ended in a burst of tears.

"Tears ain't helpin' none," Joe cried exasperated. "Ise been 'bout as decent as any feller could be an' this is what I gets foh it. You'se jus' the queerest gal I ever met. You makes believe you loves me an' then you acts like this. 'Course you'se been good company, I don' know a better sport; but there's a time when a feller wants a girl,. an' you don' know how to be a girl. Ise quittin'. Understan' I likes you awright but you gotta learn." He concluded his statement with air of finality and turned sullenly away from Irma.

"Joe! Joe!" the girl cried brokenly and clutched at his arm, but he swung himself violently away, walked down the steps and up the street without a backward glance. Regretfully she followed his retreating form until the shadows swallowed it, then bewildered passed through the open door.

She made no light but groped her way to the staircase and mounted wearily. Behind the dowdy cretonne curtain that divided her own sleeping quarters from those of her aunt and her mate, Irma jerked her red dress over her head and flung it carelessly over the back of a chair.

She dropped to her knees beside the sagging bed and muttered half audibly the Lord's Prayer. Her lips moved as she repeated the words, but her mind was sauntering down Green Willow Street with the departing Joe. The prayer was ended; Irma, however, unconscious that her lips had made the "Amen," remained crouched there with her head buried in her arms. Finally she realized that her duty to God had been executed and started to rise, then sank back again. A new thought had come. She did as much for God every night; maybe God could help her. No longer were lips alone moving to the words of memory; a teeming brain was driving them to some greater being who could chain wayward men and convert virgins to adultery. If God would only answer this plea, she'd go to church every Sunday—every Sunday, honest to God—and she'd sing and shout louder than all the rest, if God would only bring Joe back.

A load lifted. Irma climbed contentedly into the bed, confident of Joe's hasty return, for hadn't she promised God what she would do? Now a new dress to charm him when he sulked shamefacedly back. She thought with satisfaction of the three dollars she had been hoarding for a butterfly skirt that she had seen in the window at the corner of Biddle and the Avenue for two ninety-eight. She'd hang on Joe's arm as she went down the street, both alike rejoicing in the sneering glances of its envious residents. Irma smiled drowsily, nestling contentedly under the disarranged cover. Then with a start and a dull emptiness that was almost physical pain, she returned to consciousness.

The glorious creature in a red checkered butterfly skirt had vanished. In her place stood a cringing ten-year-old girl trying hard to remember everything that the big white man with the thundering voice commanded. Oh, if only God would help her forget the little of it she did remember!

It had been a morning seven years ago that her mother had started to work. Irma had always wanted to cry when her mother left for work, partially because she, Irma, hated to be left alone but more because her frail mother had never seemed strong enough to work. Irma had felt particularly sorry for her that hot summer morning because she was sick. Her face was black and swollen where Steve had hit her and she walked with a limp. Steve always quarreled and beat her when he had been drinking; but that last night the quarrel had seemed more violent and lengthy and the beating, more severe. Then, too, it was strange that her mother, who usually left at six, had waited until Steve had departed at seven before going to work. Irma and she had stood in the doorway together and watched him scuffle down the street.

"An' foh Gawd's sake, Steve, don' git no mo' of that kind of licker," her mother hollered after him.

"Shut yo' damned mouth an' git yo' lazy self tuh work," he retorted thickly.

"Yes," her mother half muttered as she drew Irma gently over the threshold, "I wasn't fixin' tuh leab this chile in no house alone wid you, wid all that licker in you an' another pint on yo' hip. She ain't the worse lookin' creature an' you ain't got no sense. I been watchin',"

"Watchin' what?" the child in curiosity questioned and forgot to wait for an answer. It came shortly after noon. (It wasn't hard for Irma to remember that, for the whistles of all the factories had announced in chorus the hour.)

The answer was Steve. About twelve-thirty he thrust his head warily in the door and asked gruffly, "Yo' mother gone?"

"Uh huh," the child replied noticing that Steve was uglier than usual. He shut the door as cautiously as any sober man could have but reeled as he caught at the edge of the table and sank in a chair.

"Come here," he mumbled.

"Whatcha want?" she asked.

"Damn you, don' cha hear me say come?" Irma was silent in her confusion. "Don' make me come fah you," Steve added harshly and glowered at her threateningly.

Irma now thoroughly frightened retreated toward the back door. Steve rose with an oath and flung himself between her and the door. She sought the corner. He followed. She didn't know this Steve. His eyes were red and bulging; his mouth was open and his nostrils moved with labored breathing. Heavy hands moved over her body and she felt smothered in her corner. The hands moved swiftly; she must evade them. She sank to the floor as the outer door flung open. Her mother stood there—a woman she did not know.

After that, things happened quickly—things that the man of the booming voice and the large, hushed court room waited to hear. That heavy iron lion that had held the front door back—they had thrust it in front of her face—and asked if she had ever seen it before. How had her mother grasped it when she hit Steve?

Why did they think she knew? She had thrown her arm before her face and not until a heavy thud, her mother's shriek and an awful silence had alarmed her, had she uncovered her eyes. She opened them then to a picture she had never forgotten—a frail, little woman bending over a huge form stretched still on the floor—a bloody Steve who could not answer a pleading voice that wailed, "I ain't never meant to, Steve, but you ought n' had of touched her. Steve! Steve——"

Irma did not remember much, but others did. The whole street seemed to know that her mother and Steve had quarreled the night before, and a number of quiet men listened as they told what they knew. Especially did Martha Lewis remember and once she shook her finger in Irma's mother's face to help her remember.

The men went out. There were twelve of them, for Irma, proud of her number work and anxious to do something, counted them as they filed past. Evidently everyone had forgotten a child of ten who sat cramped between two towering men. An age passed—an age filled with the restless walking back and forth of men, the hushed whispers of women, and the periodic sobs of her mother.

"Come on, kid. They're waitin' fer you." An officer stood over her and spoke in a gruff, not unkindly voice. She must have been sleeping, for she opened her eyes on a room that was practically deserted.

Martha Lewis, state's witness, rushed up to her and encircling her with fat, motherly arms, sobbed, "How'd I know they'd send her up? Gee, honey, I'm sorry."

Irma looked at her in bewilderment. "Where's Ma" she asked.

"That's what I jus' said. She's gain' away an' might not never come back no mo'. I'm goin' be yo' ant from now on an' take care of you."

"Yes," Irma persisted, "but where's Ma?"

"She's gone," Martha sobbed audibly. Irma had never seen her mother again. Years later Martha told her how her mother had fainted on hearing the sentence and had been carried unconscious from the room. Prison routine had soon put an end to a frail, unhappy life.

Irma had grown up much as all of Green Willow Street's illegitimates, living under the protection of first one and then another of Martha's lovers whom the street called husbands. She was one of the group of ragged children who bare-foot raced madly up and down the cobble-stones. In "Miss Liza" she sang louder and swayed more energetically to the rhythm than all the other participants, On the cluttered stoops at night it was Irma who told the most frightful ghost story or out-argued the wisest boy. The only sport from which she apologetically, almost shamefacedly, excused herself was the secret ceremony which was conducted under the door-steps and in the narrow passage-ways between the houses. From these mystic rites she fled precipitantly driven by a very vivid memory.

The same vivid memory that haunted her now as she pulled the ragged sheet almost over her head to shut out the picture of a ten-year-old girl cringing in a corner, a twelve-year-old barred from the holy councils, and a maid in her teens losing sweethearts to less attractive but more fortunate rivals.

The cover over her head, however, did not smother her thoughts and the endless torture continued. Suppose Joe did return, it would only mean that he would leave again unless—. There her imagination failed her as she realized the hopelessness of the situation. It was like getting out of bed in the morning. No matter how long you delayed, you still had to get up. The thing just waited. Once up, however, it was over. One might as well arise at once then, and have it over since delay brought only dreaded anticipation and no less effort in the end. If Joe left her now, at least it would be ended; but if he returned——. Thus she thought and having resigned herself to a Joe-less tomorrow fell into a heavy slumber.

The morrow held no such resignation. She woke conscious of a lack and with a heaviness which at first puzzled her; then with an indefinable ache she realized anew that Joe had left her. The day brought its usual routine but no forgetfulness for Irma. She worked swiftly and efficiently at her tasks for Mrs. Davis on Madison Avenue trying to hide from her own thoughts. She scrubbed the marble steps with vengeance as his features outlined themselves there. She rubbed vigorously on the silver service to blot out a familiar visage that shone from its lustrous surface. Joe was everywhere.

Evening again—childhood at its sportive pranks—youth at nature's eternal game of love-making and sleep coming to tired old age. Alone on her stoop Irma slouched defiantly. Nobody had to know. She'd just lounge rather indifferently like all the others waiting for their fellows. Of course, she knew Joe was not coming, but the others need not know. She slouched more carelessly on the steps.

In the medley of street sounds she heard a strumming. Her body quivered in response as if those practiced fingers were playing on its nerves. Irma jerked herself to an upright position and listened tensely. She did not need the feeble rays of the street lamp to distinguish his figure on Bessie Briggs' stoop. No one could miss Joe's uke—certainly not Irma. Even Easy's heartiest rendition could not drown altogether the strain. Throbbing and passionate it ran, a seductive undercurrent. God! why didn't Easy stop just a minute? She might hear what Joe was playing. At last a break! Easy was changing the roll. Now she could hear plainly. The clear, unmistakable tenor of Green Willow Street's bard unashamed cried its love message to the street,

> *"Say gal, say gal,*
> *Ain't you mine—*
> *Ain't you mine?"*

Why had she listened? Joe and Bessie—Bessie and her Joe! It wasn't fair. Bessie with all her knowledge of hospital clinics—Bessie who had all the street's fellows—and now her Joe, God! how she hated her. No, that wasn't hatred; it was just envy. Wouldn't she change places with Bessie tomorrow—didn't she wish that she could die and be born again, a Bessie? She crouched lower on the step, her ear alert to every sound and her body unrelaxed.

No, she couldn't blame Joe either. He played the game as he saw it. He was only seeking the kind of love he understood. No use talking to Joe; he couldn't see—others had not understood. Sometimes Irma wondered if she herself understood. Even in her confusion, however, there was one fact that she did understand with unusual perception—she must have Joe back.

He had said she had to learn to be a girl. Very well, she would learn. Slumped there on the stoop with his song ringing in her ears she made the resolution. Almost triumphantly she raised her head and watched them. The song was ended. Bessie rose and took Joe's uke. She went into the house and returned almost immediately. Together they went down the street arm in arm. Irma smiled at their retreating backs. They were going to the Bucket. Let Bessie make good of this night; it would be her last. Tomorrow belonged to her, Irma.

Irma outlined her plan of attack carefully as she lay in bed. The next day she executed it without faltering. She worked until six as usual. By six-thirty she had visited the department store and had procured the much desired butterfly skirt. She added to her list, moreover, a new item—a black and red slip-on sweater. At home she brushed vigorously on a rebellious bob and heightened her rich brown complexion with dabs of rouge, At last she donned the butterfly skirt and slip-on sweater and mumbling something about a movie date fared forth on her adventure.

Seven o'clock found her walking rather aimlessly back and forth on the Avenue between McMechen and Wilson Streets, avidly eyeing every prospect. An early show was ended and the crowd issued from the theatre joyous, nonchalant. Delayed dinners and more pressing engagements called a limited number who rudely zig-zagged through the crowd; but the majority leisurely wended their way letting the spell of April and the shrieking melodrama, which they had just seen, take effect. They passed one apparently nervous girl whose eyes eagerly sought theirs without recognition or surprise.

Substituting disgust for misgiving she abruptly decided that a Green Willow Street virgin seeking prey would work more successfully below Dolphin Street. These hinkty folks uptown didn't even pause for a swell outfit like hers. She didn't want to go down among Joe's crowd; but then she had to learn. A little discouraged but none the less determined, she mingled with the south bound line of pedestrians. So intent was she on her newly decided territory and its prospects that she hardly felt a body that brushed hers so gently that she should have doubted the accident of the contact. A husky, pleasant voice burst so suddenly on her consciousness that she wheeled abruptly to look into the smiling face of a stout brown man.

"'Scuse me please, Miss, but ain't you—" He had caught her steps and was walking close by her side.

"You know damned well I ain't," Irma responded in a not unfriendly voice giving the stranger a sly side glance.

"Sho, I knew you wasn't no Miss ah ___ but how's a feller goin' to meet a good lookin' girl if he don' asx is you Miss ___". He looked Irma frankly in the face now and grinned an infectious grin. Irma found it easy to respond.

"Can't be that you ain't got nothin' to do a nice evenin' like this?"

"Nothin' particular," Irma answered thoroughly at ease.

"I don' see why we can't git together." He grinned again in his good natured ease.

"I don' neither."

"Oh, I almost forgot to asx you yo' name."

"Irma," she replied simply.

He was satisfied. In this world where lives touch and pass Christian or nicknames alone are required. It never occurred to him to question further and in turn he answered without cunning. "An' they calls me Chubby."

The rest was managed swiftly and efficiently—a pint and a two dollar room in a nearby hotel. Irma thought learning might be easier than she had anticipated, but she drank little of the liquor. Liquor did something to you that got your mind turned upside down and she needed more sense than she usually had without the liquor. She encouraged her companion to drink freely, however, gaily joking as he drank. Once she even essayed a song. There was little time for selection and Irma shocked even herself when she heard herself singing,

> *"Say gal, ain't you mine,*
> *Ain't you mine?"*

That was Joe's song and she must not think of him until this other was over. Joe had said "Until you learn." The song was ended. Irma, still a little uneasy that her thoughts would not be controlled, sauntered to the open window. April's breeze in her face; liquor warming her body and ——. She looked toward the bed. Chubby, half stupified from the bad liquor, had kicked off his shoes and stretched himself at full length.

"Come on, girl." The inevitable grin mocked the haste of the man's words.

"Awright, Chubby," Irma answered calmly. Chubby was good-natured. Maybe after all it was not going to be as horrible as she had anticipated. If all men were only like Chubby ——. Bessie needn't any longer feel superior and Joe needn't stop there because Bessie understood. She, Irma, would understand hereafter.

How would she tell Joe? Maybe she could get Chubby to take her to the Bucket, In this new outfit and with a strange fellow, she would most certainly attract Joe to her table. Again, it might be better just to sit on the stoop tomorrow night and when Joe started past on his way to Bessie's, to call him rather half-heartedly. She could hear him even now asking in surprise, "Yeah, kid, what cha want?"

Then she would answer, "Nothin' only you."

"Oh no, you ain't wantin' me 'cause I wants a girl."

"Well, can't I be yo' girl?"

"You don' know how."

"Oh, don't I? "An almost beatific expression illumined Irma's features for a minute as she reviewed the reconciliation that would follow.

"Oh, come on," Chubby called again bringing Irma back to the realization of the present.

"Uh huh," she grunted distractedly and turned away from the window. She stumbled and cursing her own awkwardness looked down. Only a heavy iron lion that held a door (hundreds had once been cast in the same pattern) but Irma stopped as still as the figure over which she had tripped.

MORE STORIES

BLACK

THIRD PRIZE, PERSONAL EXPERIENCE
SKETCH, 1927 OPPORTUNITY CONTEST

NELLIE R. BRIGHT

Have you ever longed to go to Hankow, or Nice, or Scheveningen, but you never went because your shekels were too few? That often happens to me, but last summer I went to Scheveningen on the North Sea.

Getting passage is quite an adventure.

As I wanted to get accommodations in the tourist third cabin, I went to the steamship office six months before sailing. The clerks looked at me in great amazement over the shining black counter. Then, they looked at each other. As I continued to stand, one arose and came to me. "What can I do for you?" he asked doubtfully.

"I should like to get passage on one of your steamers carrying tourist third accommodations."

"They're all booked," he said, eyeing me in a strange way.

"But this is February and I don't want to sail until July. Are you sure there's nothing left?"

At this unexpected sally, another clerk came to his assistance. "You see," he began suavely, "this is one of the oldest and most popular lines and we book early. We really have nothing left."

"Thank you," I breathed, and headed for an office on the opposite corner. The force must have seen me enter the rival office, for as I went in every clerk was on his feet. One stood expectantly looking in my direction. In my handbag was an advertisement that I had cut from the morning paper. "Now you are permitted more than a dream of the old fame of Europe." Go the "new way," by "tourist third." "In the first place, of course, it is really intended for students and teachers, writers, artists, and people of this class on both East-bound and West-bound sailings."

This was just what I wanted. As I turned from closing the door, a clerk said, "Well—?"

I repeated my query as to accommodations on their tourist third to Europe. "We haven't any tourist third. I suppose that we're the only line that doesn't have it."

"But," I began, taking the ad from my bag, "here is your announcement giving dates for these accommodations."

"Some mistake. We don't—." I waited to hear no more.

That morning I went to five steamship offices, making the same request, and was looked at in great consternation, answered glibly or curtly, but always with the flat denial that there were any bookings left. I had no idea what a tremendous business steamship offices carried on six months before sailings!

Perhaps the —— Line had a berth left. When I entered, all of the clerks became so suddenly entranced with their typing or 'phoning that none saw me. I waited, the blood pounding at my temples, my heart beating at such a pace that when a little boy was sent to ask me what I wanted, I could only gasp.

"The manager wants to know why you're waiting in here."

"I'm waiting here to get information concerning your bookings to France," I answered loudly enough to be heard by the office force and the clerk at the rear behind a screen.

No one lifted his eyes from his work. There was a stillness as if fingers had suddenly forgotten the keys of the typewriters. After a brief conference, during which I heard the rasping voice of the manager, and saw the screen move, then return to its former position, the boy came to me and said "We don't sell tourist third to Negroes."

"Sacre bleu!"

———

Then, that was it. It wasn't that it was a curse to be poor, but in my case it was a curse to be a Negro. My skin was brown. In my excitement in planning for the adventure, I had committed a new crime. I had forgotten that I was a brown girl. Now, I saw clearly how foolish I had appeared to those Nordic clerks. I was too eager to be "permitted more than a dream of the old fame of Europe." I was a "student," but brown. A brown "student," a brown "teacher" should not "wish to make a trip to Europe at moderate cost, in comfort, and with a minimum expenditure for the ocean passage." God!

I had always wanted to go to Europe. When a few years old I had gone with my father and mother. As I grew, I never wearied of re-traversing the scenes dear to my father, as he described our first service in Westminster, or a sail down the Thames, as he told of the ivy-covered walls of Christ Church, or a jaunt to the island of Marken. I must go to the "Cheshire Cheese," to Anne Hathaway's cottage, to the Louvre.

Then, in those years I had become a student. I was even now engaged in writing a thesis and I must go to Bodley and to the British Museum to search out old manuscripts for myself. I, a brown girl, would reveal to the world of literature knowledge that has lain secret for centuries. But, since they did not want to give me passage, I wondered if, after all, the trip would be worth the effort. Wouldn't I be meeting Nordics everywhere? I was going to the north of Europe. Wouldn't the American students tell the librarians what a despicable creature I was because my skin was brown, and would they, because of this, say, "We can't register any more students to search records. You see 'this is one of the oldest and most popular' libraries and we 'register' 'early'."

And, when I went to Bodley, would the keeper of the manuscripts look at me queerly when I asked to see the original "Roland," which I had translated the year before from photostats, and say, "You are permitted no more than a dream of the old fame of the "Roland". We don't expose it to the gaze of Negroes"? And, when I stood at the end of that long corridor in the Louvre with the vision of the Venus de Milo luring me from the velvety shadows, would an attendant come silently to me and say, "You must go no nearer; you see the Venus is dazzling white, and her beauty would be marred by the blackness of your visage. We must protect our masterpieces for the white men of the earth." And, being so near, would I withdraw in confusion without steeping my soul in the loveliness of that statue, because I was black?

Thus debating the question, I threaded my way thru the traffic like one bearing a life apart, and entered another steamship office. How alert they were in that last output, and how busy. They must be too busy to see me, I thought. But, after waiting five minutes, a woman came forward and asked, "What do you want?"

"I should like to book passage on your tourist third for Liverpool," I ventured. Without a word, she turned and called to Mr. Johns, who evidently did the booking. I told him my errand and he proceeded to take out a huge book. As he turned the leaves, he shook his head. Before he could say, "We're full," I asked him for two dates and told him that I could make the first payment immediately. "Have a seat and I'll tell you in a few minutes."

Mr. Johns consulted three other clerks then, "Here's something that will suit you," he said. We settled the dates and the first payment. He took my name and address. This surely looked as if I were going to Europe. But I was weary with their subterfuges and thot as soon as I was out of the office "That's only a bluff, too. I suppose he took my address so as to be able to identify that audacious person who wanted to go on a holiday with the "best youth of America."

I had seen enough of American youth in the schools and at the University. I knew only too well how the "best" would smile with their faces and draw their skirts aside at my coming. What I wanted was the cleanliness, the wholesome food, deck space, comforts that I would not get in the steerage. While the American youths smirked and smoked and babbled of Freud and Ford, I should be wrapped in my blanket, my thots racing with the waves.

Sailing day came! I was rushed down, down, down into the hold of the ship. My father, who knows ships, would not look at me. He did not want me to see the hurt in his eyes. I didn't have tourist accommodations after all. This ship didn't carry student tours. Black! What did it matter?

That night I sat upon a roil of hawsers. There were no chairs for steerage passengers. At my back, the winches black with shining grease. The soft night wind caressed my cheek and my breath came quickly as I watched for the first star. I had eaten no supper. When I emerged from my stateroom in the hold of the ship, I felt that I would never eat again, so choked was I with the echoes of the voices of lily white liars in steamship offices.

Gradually my fellow passengers came up from the dining saloon. There was the ruddy-cheeked, black-haired woman who had embarked so stylishly dressed with her husband and two boys. She now wore a loose sweater over an ill-fitting blue dress. She sat moodily, her family near her. The red-lipped girl whom I had fancied a Paquin model came on deck, her raven locks hidden beneath a somber scarf. The Welsh woman who had put her babies to bed chatted with the old Spaniard. He had come aboard in a dapper blue suit and yellow shoes but now had a red kerchief knitted at his throat and his feet encased in knitted bedroom slippers.

An elderly man, graying hair at his temples, sat beside me. I kept my gaze fixed upon the deepening sky for should he see even in the dusk the black of my face he might leap away. And I was too lonely to have a fellow creature shun me just then. Voices babbled incessantly. Everybody talked but me. They were talking about themselves. Two English boys, having made a fortune, were returning to care for their mother. I heard the Irish girl say that she was being deported because she had no wealth save her fur coat.

Presently, a voice beside me asked, "And what of you, lass? Are you going home too?"

"No," I answered, "America is my home." The muscles of my throat tightened. "I'm off on a holiday." At the mention of holiday, several forms loitered nearer. Some had never had a holiday. What a joyful thing it must be to go just where one wanted and to do the things one liked best. The Englishman became eloquent. "You must go to the cheese market at Shrewsbury. Shop in 'petticoat alley' on a Sunday morning. Don't miss the changing of the horse guard at Whitehall. Go to Kew and to the Tower. I'll make a list of the places that you must visit."

"You 're very kind," I murmured, skeptical at his enthusiasm. He surely hadn't seen my face. How could he know that the word "holiday" had made my voice husky, that my holidays were honey drained from crystal cups with jagged edges?

As we talked, the lights came on. They looked full upon my face. I looked straight at them, a challenge in my eye. None even winced. Then, they knew—and didn't care? I pondered this while they chatted.

The Spaniard, his face gashed with wrinkles, wondered if his family in Madrid would recognize him after forty years. He was darker than I. Perhaps they talked to me because they thot me a Spaniard, too. Odd! Anything but a Negro.

One day, the social worker (she knew) came to me, her eyes wet. "Do go over and talk to that poor boy by the railing. He's a Nigerian and was brought to America by missionaries. But he seems so depressed and he won't tell me what troubles him. Perhaps he'll tell you."

"I didn't know that such a person was on board," I replied. "Where has he been all this time?"

"They've had him locked in his cabin for fear that he would injure himself," she explained. "But, go to him, now."

The boy, a youth of eighteen, stood gazing fixedly at the horizon, much as I had done that first night at sea. Already, I knew his sorrow, I thot. He is suffering as I did. I stood near him for a moment, then made a casual remark about the speed of the vessel as is the way with fellow passengers.

"It can't fly too swiftly for me," replied Oojoula, looking at me almost fiercely.

"Where are you going?" I asked.

"To my home, five hundred miles from the Gold Coast, where my father is chief and where the white man has never set foot."

"How long were you in America?"

"Four long years."

"Were you in school?"

"Yes, civilized, educated, Christianized. They made me a Christian. Think of it—a Christian! I was but a child then. I even believed in their Christ until I felt their hatred for us. My people are more loyal to their gods than Christ's followers to Him. I would have killed myself, but I must go back to the jungle. I go to my people. I shall warn them against the white man. I would record their history. It is necessary. The world must know how noble black men are." Oojoula turned his eyes from mine. I was forgotten.

How could I help him? This poor, disillusioned boy? He hadn't grown up with them as I had. He didn't know that equal opportunity for us meant denial of opportunity, or a struggle for opportunity that is so bitter that, when the end is realized, our strength and enthusiasm are spent. How was he to know that these people whom he hated with an intensity greater than the blackness of his skin, felt it their duty to prevent a Negro from enjoying the simplest of pleasures, from having the barest comforts. I could never make him understand.

We were too different. He had lost his faith in man suddenly. I had been losing mine all thru my childhood, all thru my time of dreams, all thru my college days. It was simply this: I had been born in a country where a man was good or evil according to the color of his skin. Oojoula had not.

When the ship's orchestra dropped down the ladders from the second class to entertain us that afternoon, the first and second class passengers crowded the rail. To look down upon the steerage passengers was quite a diversion. Oojoula, unable to bear the amused stare of the "superior" group, pointed out to me the priest and his wife who were taking him back to Africa. Then he locked himself in his cabin.

That night, while the ship's orchestra played in the first class saloon, a fiddler from Lisconnel, perched himself upon a capstan and drew his bow across the strings. Forms rose from the shadows, swaying. There was the click of heels, the clap of hands. They were "stacking the barley." A rollicking dance. One of the English lads held out his hands to mine. "Come, jig with me," he urged, his feet beating a tatoo to the rhythm. The blood tingled in my veins. I drew away. How could I, a brown girl, dance with him? I loved to dance—but—with an English lad! He must be joking. I was a Negro. I had only danced with boys of my own race. All the inhibitions that had grown up with me forbade me to put my hand into his and swing with him in the sheer enjoyment of the dance.

"No," I said, my heart contracted with fear—the fear that he had chosen me to play the fool because I was black.

"No?" he repeated; "I don't take 'no' for an answer. I just know that you dance. You're like a willow. Won't you try it? Look, it goes like this." He showed me the steps. He was in earnest. I mustn't be rude. He was simply being kind. But, why? Wasn't he white and I—? Queer!

He insisted. What could I say? I was confused. "I do dance," I stammered, "but not the Irish folk dances, so you'll have to get another partner."

"No, I don't," he persisted. "I'll teach you to 'stack the barley' in a trice. Come!" He seized both my hands in a firm grip, drawing me to my feet. My body, singing with the music, danced one round. As the fiddler laid by his bow, I fled to my cabin.

What had I done? I had danced, a joyful thing in itself, but I had degraded myself by dancing with a Nordic.

As I lay in my berth, I marveled at many things. I thot of what I had done, of Oojoula, of my fellow passengers. They were Nordics, to be sure, but they had seemed kind. They had treated me as a human being. But, perhaps, that was only the camaraderie of the traveler. We would soon land in old England. Would they perchance know me if they spied me on the pier? If we should pass each other in Piccadilly, would they see me?

At times as I sat silent in black isolation for fear of inviting insult, they had come to me and chatted of the merits of farming in Poland, or of Yeats' poetry, or of their families. Sometimes, I found myself holding the Portuguese baby while its mother took her turn about the deck. Again, I was the center of a group swapping yarns. They hadn't seemed to notice. Perhaps, after all, these people were different from Americans in that they did not despise my color. My doubts would soon be quelled for we were nearing Queenstown, our first stop; then England, Belgium, and France.

The next day there was a perceptible restlessness among the passengers and crew. Gulls began to follow the ship. As sailors walked the deck they would stop, lean far over the port rail and peer toward the horizon. Toward sunset, I discerned an opalescent mist low in the sky. Knots of passengers began to watch the cloud. Field glasses were eagerly borrowed. The mist remained, began against the sky. There was no cloud. Land! The wild, rocky coast of Ireland. There was a cry of joy That thrilled from every deck. There came a Shout, and a song of Erin floated across the waves to Killarney.

The people with whom I had lived for eleven days embraced each other and some wept for joy. They rushed below and returned, dressed in their stylish American clothes. Once more they saw their beloved Ireland. They were going home. I rejoiced with them. Oojoula looked on from his cabin. He, too, was going home. He was thinking of the kindly black faces that would greet him.

At eleven o'clock that night, we set off two flares. In the wavering ribbon of light picking out a path of quicksilver from Queenstown to our steamer, glided the pilot's tiny boat. I drew my coat close against the cold. There was the roar of the propeller as we swung round toward the city. There was the tang of green hills in the air. Shrill cries and deep laughter mingled with the clanking of chairs and the bustle of passengers. Two tenders chugged along side. My fellow passengers beamed upon me. As soon as the mail had been taken off, they would go. As they went across the bridge to the second class deck, I went with them. Irish women who had just come on board with huge baskets were selling lace and shawls of soft silk. I stooped to look, then fled down the deck as the order came, "Steerage passengers not debarking, go below."

I must bid my friends goodbye as they went down the gangplank to the waiting tender. It began to rain, a sharp, drenching shower. Lights flowed from the city across the harbor to us. Those that were leaving wrung my hands, smiled wistfully, and were gone. I followed with my eyes and smiled as the steamer was lost in the thick night. I was weeping.

Was it because I should never see those kindly faces again, or because I had thot them kind when they only thot of me as black?

THE PINK HAT

THIRD PRIZE, PERSONAL EXPERIENCE SKETCH, 1926 OPPORTUNITY CONTEST

CAROLINE BOND DAY

This hat has become to me a symbol. It represents the respective advantages and disadvantages of my life here. It is at once my magic-carpet, my enchanted cloak, my Aladdin's lamp. Yet it is a plain, rough, straw hat, "pour le sport," as was the recently famous green one. Before its purchase, life was wont to become periodically flat for me. Teaching is an exhausting profession unless there are wells to draw from, and the soil of my world seems hard and dry. One needs adventure and touch with the main current of human life, and contact with many of one's kind to keep from "going stale on the job." I had not had these things and heretofore had passed back and forth from the town a more or less drab figure eliciting no attention.

Then suddenly one day with the self-confidence bred of a becoming hat, careful grooming, and satisfactory clothes I stepped on to a street car, and lo! the world was reversed. A portly gentleman of obvious rank arose and offered me a seat. Shortly afterwards as I alighted a comely young lad jumped to rescue my gloves. Walking on into the store where I always shopped, I was startled to hear the salesgirl sweetly drawl, "Miss or Mrs.?" as I gave the customary initials. I heard myself answering reassuringly "Mrs." Was this myself? I, who was frequently addressed as "Sarah." For you see this is south of the Mason and Dixon line, and I am a Negro woman of mixed blood unaccustomed to these respectable prefixes.

I had been mistaken for other than a Negro, yet I look like hundreds of other colored women—yellow-skinned and slightly heavy featured, with frizzy brown hair. My maternal grand-parents were Scotch-Irish and English quadroons; paternal grand-parents Cherokee Indian and full blooded Negro; but the ruddy pigment of the Scotch-Irish ancestry is my inheritance, and it is this which shows through my yellow skin, and in the reflection of my pink hat glows pink. Loosely speaking. I should be called a mulatto—anthropologically speaking, I am a dominant of the white type of the F^3 generation of secondary crossings. There is a tendency known to the initiated persons of mixed Negro blood in this climate to "breed white" as we say, propagandists to the contrary notwithstanding. In this sense the Proud Race is, as it were, really dominant. The cause? I'll save that for another time.

Coming back to the hat—when I realized what had made me the recipient of those unlooked for, yet common courtesies, I decided to experiment further.

So I wore it to town again one day when visiting an art store looking for prints for my school room. Here, where formerly I had met with indifference and poor service, I encountered a new girl today who was the essence of courtesy. She pulled out drawer after drawer of prints as we talked and compared from Gritto to Sargent. Yet she agreed that Giorgione had a sweet, worldly taste, that he was not sufficiently appreciated, that Titian did over-shadow him. We went back to Velasquez as the master technician and had about decided on "The Forge of Vulcan" as appropriate for my needs, when suddenly she asked, "but where do you teach?" I answered, and she recognized the name of a Negro university. Well—I felt sorry for her. She had blundered. She had been chatting familiarly, almost intimately with a Negro woman. I spared her by leaving quickly, and murmured that I would send for the package.

My mood forced me to walk—and I walked on and on until I stood at the "curb-market." I do love markets, and at this one they sell flowers as well as vegetables. A feeble old man came up beside me. I noticed that he was near-sighted. "Lady," he began, "would you tell me—is them dahlias or peernies up there?" Then, "market smells so good—don't it?"

I recognized a kindred spirit. He sniffed about among the flowers, and was about to say more—a nice old man—I should have liked to stop and talk with him after the leisurely southern fashion, but he was a white old man—and I moved on hastily.

I walked home the long way and in doing so passed the city library. I thought of my far away Boston—no Abbey nor Puvis de Chauvannes here, no marble stairs, no spirit of studiousness of which I might become a part. Then I saw a notice of a lecture by Drinkwater at the women's club—I was starved for something good—and starvation of body or soul sometimes breeds criminals.

So then I deliberately set out to deceive. Now, I decided, I would enjoy all that had previously been impossible. When necessary I would add a bit of rouge and the frizzy hair (thanks to the marcel) could be crimped into smoothness. I supposed also that a well-modulated voice and assurance of manner would be assets.

So thus disguised, for a brief space of time, I enjoyed everything from the attentions of an expert Chiropodist, to grand opera, avoiding only the Restaurants—I could not have borne the questioning eyes of the colored waiters.

I would press on my Aladdin's lamp and presto, I could be comforted with a hot drink at the same soda-fountain where ordinarily I should have been hissed at. I could pull my hat down a bit and buy a ticket to see my favorite movie star while the play was still new.

I could wrap my enchanted cloak about me and have the decent comfort of ladies' rest-rooms. I could have my shoes fitted in the best shops, and be shown the best values in all of the stores—not the common styles "which all the darkies buy, you know." At one of these times a policeman helped me across the street. A sales-girl in the most human way once said, "I wouldn't get that, Sweetie, you and me is the same style and I know." How warming to be like the rest of the world, albeit a slangy and gum-chewing world!

But it was best of all of an afternoon when it was impossible to correct any more papers or to look longer at my own Lares and Penates, to sit upon my magic-carpet and be transported into the midst of a local art exhibit, to enjoy the freshness of George Inness and the vague charm of Brangwyn, and to see white-folk enjoying Tanner—really nice, likable, folk too, when they don't know one. Again it was good to be transported into the midst of a great expectant throng, awaiting the pealing of the Christmas carols at the Municipal Pageant. One could not enjoy this without compunction however, for there was not a dark face to be seen among all of those thousands of people, and my two hundred bright-eyed youngsters should have been there.

Finally—and the last time that I dared upon my carpet, was to answer the call of a Greek play to be given on the lawn of a State University. I drank it all in. Marvellous beauty! Perfection of speech and gesture on a velvet greensward, music, color, life!

Then a crash came. I suppose I was nervous—one does have "horrible imaginings and present fears" down here, sub-conscious pictures of hooded figures and burning crosses. Anyway in hurrying out to avoid the crowd, I fell and broke an anklebone.

Someone took me home. My doctor talked plaster-casts. "No," I said, "I'll try osteopathy," but there was no chance for magic now. I was home in bed with my family—a colored family—and in a colored section of the town. A friend interceded with the doctor whom I had named. "No," he said, "it is against the rules of the osteopathic association to serve Negroes."

I waited a day—perhaps my foot would be better—then they talked bone-surgery. I am afraid of doctors. Three operations have been enough for me. Then a friend said, "try Christian Science." Perhaps I had been taking matters too much in my own hands, I thought. Yes, that would be the thing. Would she find a practitioner for me?

Dear, loyal daughter of New England—as loyal to the Freedmen's children as she had been to them. She tried to spare me. "They will give you absent treatments and when you are better we will go down." I regret now having said, "Where, to the back door?" What was the need of wounding my friend?

Besides, I have recovered some how—I am only a wee bit lame now. And mirabili dictu! My spirit has knit together as well as my bones. My hat has grown useless. I am so glad to be well again, and back at my desk. My brown boys and girls have become reservoirs of interest. One is attending Radcliffe this year. My neighborly friend needs me now to while away the hours for her. We've gone back to Chaucer and dug out forgotten romances to be read aloud. The little boy next door has a new family of Belgian hares with which we play wonderful games. And the man and I have ordered seed catalogues for spring.

Health, a job, young minds and souls to touch, a friend, some books, a child, a garden, Spring! Who'd want a hat?

IN HOUSES OF GLASS

HONORABLE MENTION, SHORT STORY, 1926 CRISIS CONTEST

ETHEL R. CLARK

The soft, languid voice of Mrs. Langford, wife of a middle-class merchant in Xville, Georgia, interrupted the awkward, sorrowful silence.

"There, there, "Honey", don' take on so! Y'all must have some kin-folk back where you came from an' when they read of yo' mothah's death, they'll sure come fo' you. While you're waitin', you just stay right heah with Willie Mae. We all 're right glad to have you."

"Honey" Davis, the girl addressed, made a forlorn-looking picture as she sat huddled on the top step of the Langford home, eyes swollen from weeping and bobbed curls in tousled disorder. There was something uncommonly attractive, wistfully appealing, about her. She wore a trig little sport dress of mystical mauve, set off by soft collar and cuffs of friendliest yellow. But it was the unlooked-for beauty of face in a child only fourteen years old that fastened one's attention. The summer's sun had poured a rich brown tint over the velvety olive skin, against which the appealing blue eyes and dark brown hair stood out in challenging contrast.

"But I feel so lonesome without Mothah! Y'all are powerful good to me (caressing the hand of Mrs. Langford), but you don' know how it feels to be all alone. You reckon folks will see that notice in the papah, sure 'nough? O, I wish I knew where Mothah's people are!"

"Didn't she ever tell you where y'all come from? Nor anything 'bout her folks? Y'all always looked like foreigners to me an' I set out several times to ask yo' mothah, but she was so sort o' tight-mouthed, a body didn't 'low to ask her many questions."

At the reference to her mother's much-discussed failure to talk about herself or her family, Honey's full lips disappeared into a stubborn, set line and her eyes flashed a warning not unheeded by the woman. In a conciliatory tone of voice she bade "Honey" make herself comfortable while she, Mrs. Langford, returned to the house to superintend the preparations for supper.

Left to herself, "Honey" resumed her mournful, tearful meditation, from which state, she was rudely roused by the sound of wild, hilarious laughter and rythmical, racing feet. As she hastily peered over the railing, a ten or twelve-year old boy rounded the corner near the Langford home, running at top speed and followed by a yelling, pelting trio of colored boys. No sooner did the runner catch sight of "Honey" than he dashed up the steps in search of refuge. "Honey" rushed the boy into the house. Returning immediately to the porch, she faced the chasing, barefoot trio who now stood defiantly bunched on the edge of the sidewalk.

"Go 'way from heah, you good-for-nothing niggers! How dare you chuck stones at a white boy? Y'all orter be skinned alive! Go on 'way from heah! Go on, I say! How come y'all don' move?"

"He beat up mah li'l brothah what "wasn' both'rin' him a 'tall an we all gonna fix him," bravely spoke the oldest, aged eight.

"I don' believe it," shouted "Honey". "Leastways if he did, y'all ain't got no call to hit him. You're nothin' but niggers, nohow. Get away from heah!"

With which shrill command she reached for some nearby stones, but the dusky trio had already decided in favor of "safety first" and were retreating precipitately, with many a backward glance. When all was once more restored to tranquility, the white boy emerged in answer to

"Honey's" call, curtly thanked her for her assistance and continued on his way.

Scarcely was he out of sight when the unusually animated form of Willie Mae dashed up the steps.

"O, "Honey", look what I just got fo' you from the Post Office!"

"A letter? Sure 'nough! O, I do hope it's from some of Mothah's folks! Maybe they did see the notice in the papah after all. I'm so excited I can't open it and besides I've just had a time with these nasty, dirty nigger boys that live two streets back yonder in Sawdust Bottom. Mothah always scolded me for calling 'em 'nigger' but they are and I just can't help calling 'em that. I hate 'em all with their smelly black skins. Ugh! I nevah could see how she could take up fo' 'em so. I'm so nervous I can't read this letter. Read it fo' me, Willie Mae?"

"Sho'. Mighty pretty handwriting an' yes! it's signed 'Your loving Aunt, Etta Philips'. Goodness, "Honey", I reckon she's rich as anything! Now listen:

—————— Hospital,

Boston, Mass.

Aug. 12, 1921.

My dear Niece:— I can scarcely hold my pen for I am so excited, so anxious to see you. I have just read an overlooked copy of *The Blade*, the one in which your mothers death is announced and your search for relatives. I am your mother's sister, but we have neither seen nor heard from each other for more than fourteen years.

O! my little niece, how I long to go to you, but I am temporarily indisposed, the result of an automobile accident—nothing serious. So I have arranged for you to go to a boarding school for girls at ——————, N. C., until such time as I can make the trip and fetch you home with me. Miss Mabel Whitely, the principal, is a personal friend and knew your mother many years ago. I am enclosing a check to cover your expenses. Meanwhile, be a good girl and bear up bravely.

Your loving Aunt,

ETTA PHILIPS.

"My, but you're a lucky girl, "Honey"!"

During the reading of the letter "Honey's" eyes had grown positively luminous. As Willie Mae ceased speaking, the little motherless girl sprang to her feet, threw both arms around Willie Mae with boundless enthusiasm, then pulling Willie May by the hand, ran into the house calling to Mrs. Langford in high, exultant tones.

The train had deposited "Honey", three other passengers and some baggage at their mutual destination, a rural station in North Carolina. The three passengers and most of the baggage had disappeared. Only a small group of colored bystanders, men and a half-grown boy, remained within "Honey's" range of vision. As the girl remained standing there, the boy started toward her bearing a covered basket in one hand and a large pot of steaming coffee in the other.

When he was within hailing distance, he thus offered his wares:

"Fried chicken, fried chicken,
Right out'n de pan!
Fresh coffee, hot coffee,
Bes' in de lan'."

"Honey" was too full of anticipation and anxiety even to think of eating, so shook her head impatiently and walked toward the section of the waiting room designated for the whites. Ere she reached the threshold, one of the blacks, an elderly man who had detached himself from the idle group, accosted her hesitantly, hat in hand. " 'Scuse me, Missy, but is yo' name Davis?"

"Reckon 'tis. Did Miss Whitely send, y'all fo' me?" appraisingly.

"Yes, Miss, but I 'lowed 'twarnt you at fus'. Dis heah y'all's baggage? Jes' follah me. Heah's owah cyah."

"Owah cyah" proved to be a much-battered, mud-besmeared Ford and as the journey to the school progressed, the unsightly appearance of the car was amply justified by the terrible condition of the roads, most of which were deep, red mud. After what seemed to be the longest three miles in "Honey's" experience, the school was finally sighted.

As the Ford ground its familiar course up the driveway, the girl became a human whirlpool of conflicting emotions. Colored girls all over the campus! What was the driver taking her here for? Could he have mistaken her for some other person by the name of Davis? Had her Aunt made a mistake in the name and location of the school? Surely not, for she had specifically said the principal and she were friends.

Feverishly she extracted her Aunt's letter from the handbag and re-read the instructions, comparing the name of the school given in the letter with the name written over the main doorway of the building they were approaching. The names were identical!

What could it mean? What was the trouble? Why was her Aunt sending her, "Honey", a white girl, to a colored school? There was some terrible, hideous mistake. She would see the principal!

"Welcome to our fold, dear! So this is the little niece of whom your Aunt wrote me? We are indeed glad to have you. Yes, I am Miss Whitely Walker, please see that her baggage is taken to Room 8. Have you the trunk check?"

All this from a dark-skinned, portly woman. "Honey's" face had gradually been assuming the color of poppies. As Miss Whitely reached in the car to help the girl to alight, she could restrain herself no longer. Wild eyed, she wrenched herself free and literally screamed at the woman:

"Take yo' black hands off me! Take 'em off I say! Don't you dare touch me! Do y'all heah? Send those black devils away! Send them away, I tell you ! I'll—I'll—Leave me alone! Let go! Don't you push me! Stop it, I say! Stop! Just wait till I—"

Only by sheer force, violent struggling, did Miss Whitely finally manage to get the biting, scratching, kicking girl into the office and close the door. She was as one insane. The scuffle had drawn a crowd of curious, eager onlookers, whose proximity served but to incense her the more.

At first the older woman had been frankly stunned by the outburst, but only for a moment. Intuitively she understood. Now taking from the wall a group photograph and looking intently at "Honey", the principal inquired whether the girl had ever seen her Aunt. Upon receiving a sullen shake of the head, Miss Whitely singled out a woman of pleasing appearance in the group and pointing to her said,

"There is your Aunt."

Amazement, incredulity, lastly fear, passed in swift succession over the face of "Honey". This woman with brown skin and curly black hair her Aunt! What a joke! What a silly, cheap, degrading lie! What was the matter with this woman, anyhow? How dare she! Her Aunt a nigger! Well I reckon not! Wasn't her Aunt her mother's own sister? And wasn't her mother white?

Wasn't her mother white? That phrase began to repeat itself automatically in her mind until with each successive repetition a hellish doubt began to take form. First one remembered trait of her late mother, then another doubtful characteristic suggested itself in embryo. Evidence of the growth and torture of these reflections was plainly visible on "Honey's" countenance. Mechanically she retreated step by step to the opposite side of the room, eyes riveted alternately on the photograph and Miss Whitely as if she would educe from the one or the other the truth of this terrible accusation.

It was a lie! Of course! Of course! This Negro, this dark-skinned woman, her Aunt!

Now the hysterical laughter! Again the sudden contraction of the mouth and the dilating of the pupils as a seeming doubt once more entered the portals of thought. How Miss Whitely longed to go to her and clear away the vacillating look of terror! Now it was Miss Whitely's turn to question. Why had this girl been kept in deliberate ignorance of her racial identity? Yet even as she asked herself the question she knew only too well the answer. To enable "Honey" to receive the best in education and advantages, of course. But oh! the penalty of the awakening!

Now "Honey" was sitting down, still absorbed, verily hypnotized by the photograph. Suddenly she sprang to her feet, ran to a mirror in the corner of the room and gazed scrutinously at herself. What torture to watch her! Demented with fear. Hunted, hounded, by an invisible enemy which chased her in never-ending circles of doubt, broken only by fragmentary intervals of approaching hysteria.

At length, turning abruptly from the mirror, she advanced toward the principal and looked her full in the eye.

"Tell me honestly, is she really mah Aunt? mothah colored, too? Am I— Am I—a—n—n—nigger?"

O, the pathos, the quivering agony voiced in that query!

For reply, Miss Whitely inclined her head and extended two gracious hands. With a smothered shriek and a visible crumpling of the body as though a burden too heavy to be borne had suddenly been placed upon it, "Honey" sank to the floor, senseless.

For two long weeks, a motherless, raceless girl battled with delirium and soul-destroying humiliation. Eventually youth won. The period of convalescence over, she was permitted to leave her room the third week but remained a willfully solitary figure on porch or campus.

A month dragged slowly by, a month of unrealities, of searing pain and readjustments. The awful shame of it! She, "Honey" Davis, one of those things, a nigger! O dear God! Why hadn't someone told her before! What would her white friends say when they knew?

It was all so clear now. Mother's reticence! Their solitary existence! Mother, whom she had almost worshipped, only a nigger! O, well, maybe the dreadful sting of it would wear away after a while. Already she was beginning to like Miss Whitely.

What had happened to her. "Honey", anyhow? How had she changed? Wasn't she the same girl now that she had always been? Did her mind, her body, function any differently now than in former times? No and yes! To all outward appearance she was the same. But the inner self! Funny how just thinking a thing could change one so! Maybe that was all that really made things different anyway. Just thinking so.

Another change had been effected, too. Whereas, heretofore. she had always thought of colored people as "niggers", the term now filled her with abhorrence and uncontrollable revulsion. Applied to herself it was intolerable!

How it must have hurt Mother to hear her, "Honey", use it! Mother! How she yearned for that presence now! Mother wouldn't have hurt her so! There! That was it! Mother had kept the knowledge from her to keep from wounding her.

"Honey" had wandered on during her silent soliloquy until now she found herself on the edge of the campus boundary with acres of ripening fields stretching before her. In the distance, Walker, general man-of-all-work, was busily working in the garden. As he worked he sang and the words of the song came floating brokenly to her:

"Although you see me goin' 'long so,
O, yes, Lord!
I has my trials heah below,
O, yes, Lord!"

With a brave little smile of resignation, she slowly recrossed the campus and, with determined mien, approached a group of girl-strollers, and timidly asked to join them.

Here was the opportunity for which the girls had been waiting! They would show the stuck-up thing that they were just as good as she! Forthwith, they proceeded to demonstrate the old Mosaic law by turning their backs upon her and walking away in high, sarcastic glee. The deliberate

rebuff to her overt act of conciliation was the last straw. "Honey" took refuge behind the nearest tree trunk and burst into convulsive sobbing.

At this unexpected turn of affairs the girls stood stark still, looked at each other in unfeigned amazement, then, as if by common consent, made a simultaneous dive toward "Honey". Ere the girl could collect her scared and scattered wits, she was surrounded quite by an affectionate, chattering bunch of repentant who began at once to prove to her that the slate was wiped clean.

Later in the evening, Miss Whitely thought she heard a sound as of singing on the front porch. Going noiselessly to the door, she beheld "Honey" seated alone in the porch-swing, eyes gazing into space and singing with a conviction that could be felt:

"And He walks with me and He talks with me,
And He tells me I am His own;
And the joy we share as we tarry there,
None other has ever known."

Hastily wiping away her tears, Miss Whitely stepped onto the porch.

"Come, dear, I think you have been long enough in the night air. Perhaps you would like to come into my office and read a nice, long, interesting letter I received today from your Aunt."

Smiling acquiescence, "Honey" graciously accepted the presence of Miss Whitely's arm about her waist and together they reentered the building.

"Honey" Davis "belonged",—belonged to that great human race whose members form one brotherhood, acclaim one Father—God!

HIGH FALUTIN'

HONORABLE MENTION, SHORT STORY, 1926 OPPORTUNITY CONTEST

PEARL FISHER

Lew Haskins, porter and soda fountain attendant in Greene & Scott's Pharmacy, was in his glory. Both Doctor Greene and Doctor Scott were out, the errand boy was off for the afternoon, and Lew was in charge. He looked around the store. Yes, everything was in order. The cases had been dusted, the fountain was spotless, the chairs and tables were arranged with geometric precision. Assuring himself that nothing was amiss, he turned to survey his own lordly person in the mirror.

He liked himself hugely, did Lew. His white coat was exactly like Dr. Greene's. Yes, it was quite possible that customers might mistake him for the proprietor, or at any rate for the chief clerk. He was certain that none would suspect him of being merely a porter. He almost made himself believe that he was in fact the chief clerk helping out at the fountain in an emergency. With the thought, he straightened his narrow sloping shoulders, and smiled approvingly at the reelection of his yellow-brown, heavy-featured face topped with a mass of crinkly black hair stocking-capped into a semblance of a brush back.

The entrance of two white men interrupted Lew's self-admiration. They asked for the proprietor. With a skill born of experience, he classified them as salesmen and, in his most proprietary manner, invited them to wait, whereupon the men ordered refreshments and seated themselves at a rear table. Having served them condescendingly, Lew was again left free to muse on his own sartorial impeccability.

"Hello, Lew!"

Lew wheeled, his slouching figure suddenly rigid, eager—

"Hello, Ossie!" When did you get back?"

"Oh, the other day."

Oscreola Pitts, known as Ossie, tall, white-skinned, blue-eyed, and blonde, insinuated herself on a high stool before the fountain. She was distinctly personable and knew it. Her silk frock fitted her with an air of careless, expensive elegance. True, her crossed legs displayed an undue amount of silken hosiery, her nails were rather too sharply pointed and too highly polished, and perhaps a trifle less rouge might have been used with better effect, but Lew saw only perfection—a perfection that he desired above all else to possess.

"What's it to be this time?"

"Oh, per usual."

Lew proceeded to make the sundae, piling in a double portion of ice-cream and serving the final concoction with elaborate care. He leaned over the counter towards the girl.

"Missed you while you was away."

"That so?"

"Yeah. Be home this evening?"

"Got a date."

"To-morrow then?"

"Sorry Lew."

"When, Sunday?"

"Can't say, Lew. I'm kinder busy these days and I'm always away over the week-ends," parried Ossie.

"Oh, that's what you always tell me here lately."

Lew became conscious of the fact that the two white men at the table in the rear were watching him. Certain that they couldn't hear, he smiled broadly, glad of the effect that his familiarity with the girl was producing.

Ossie finished her sundae, but Lew held her in conversation, trying to enveigle from her an open date. Laughing, the girl evaded, backing slowly toward the door. Suddenly, by some telepathic medium she became aware of eyes upon her. Other eyes—not Lew's. Suddenly found herself staring into a tense, tight-lipped face, with eyes hard as spear points and as sharp—eyes that seemed to pierce through the present to some well remembered past. Eyes that questioned while they defied her to deny. A moment, speechless, confused, she stared back, then turned and hurried into the street.

Lew, puzzled, watched her out of sight, then slowly began putting the counter to rights.

"I wonder," he muttered under his breath.

The men arose and approached Lew.

"Sorry we can't wait any longer," said one. "We'll be back another time."

Still he hesitated. Leisurely he lighted a cigarette and flicked the match away.

"Who's the beautiful blonde?" he began, trying to seem casual. Lew was instantly on the alert.

"Huh?"

"Who's the blonde beauty who just left?"

"Oh, a customer."

"You seem to know her pretty well."

"Oh, I know 'em all. They all kid with me."

"White?"

"Huh?"

"White or colored?"

"How do I know?"

"You know damn well."

Lew noted the loss of self-control and dared.

"How do I know what she is or anybody? What are you? How do I know? I only know what you look like. Same with her."

Off his guard, the speaker blurted out, "Damn your insolence. But I'm hanged if I wouldn't like to know."

"Why you so interested?"

"Because I hate my best friend to have a raw deal put over on him, even if he is—. If she's a —. Well." He left off short and followed his companion out of the store.

Lew stood still a long time.

"I wonder," he said again.

Two hours later, Lew still pondering on Ossie's hasty retreat, saw her come in and enter the telephone booth.

Stealthily he slid behind the counter and up near the booth. She had not closed the door entirely. He heard her give the number, Calvert 4683. He moved away and busied himself ostensibly about the shelves.

Ossie came out of the booth and stood before him.

"Say Lew," —

"Oh, 's that you Ossie?"

Ossie gave a nervous laugh.

"Lew, er, did you see that ofay in here this afternoon?"

"Huh?"

"You know—when I was in here. He was sittin' back there."

"Oh, yeah."

"Did he—did he say anything about—ask anything about me?"

"No," lied Lew. "What would he be askin' me 'bout you?"

"Oh, nothin'. I thought maybe—that is he looked at me so hard—I thought maybe he took me for somebody else. He didn't say nothing?"

"Nothin' 'tall."

Ossie looked relieved.

"So long, Lew!"

"S'long Ossie."

At nine o'clock Lew changed the white coat for a dark one, straightened his polka dot tie, put on his hat, and swaggered into the street, trying to stroll with the air of a gentleman of leisure out taking the air.

Lew always walked the length of the Avenue before going home. The street was lined with rows of tall, red brick houses still retaining some remnants of a former glory. Houses once the abode of aristocrats, now become the dwelling place of their servitors. People sat on the low, white stone door steps, making the most of the occasional breezes that sifted through the sultry air. People sauntered along talking, laughing, whistling snatches of popular tunes. Lew was enjoying himself immensely. He idled on his way, peering at the strollers so as not to miss a chance of speaking. He liked to appear to know everybody, and was in no way disturbed that some to whom he bowed responded coldly and others not at all.

From a house a short distance ahead came fragments of syncopation, the wail of a saxophone, the strumming of mandolins, the thumping of a piano—

"Everybody loves mah baby,
But mah baby don't love nobody but me,"
sang a husky voice above the instruments.

Lew noted the house where the party was in progress, and stopped to glance through the open windows at the dancers clasped tight in each others arms, their bodies scarcely moving, their feet keeping up a rhythmic shuffle on the bare floor. None of the faces inside was sufficiently familiar for Lew to risk "breaking in" on the party. Disappointed, he was about to pass on, when a man and a woman mounted the steps and rang.

The door opened, and a wedge of light split the darkness. The man and woman were clearly visible to the watching Lew before they passed inside. His face hardened. He dug his nails into his palms.

"Had a date eh?" he muttered. "A date with that damn black Matt Hicks. I ain't good enuf fo' you any mo' since you got to wearin' good clothes and goin' roun' with the high flyers. Matt Hicks eh! Who's Matt Hicks any mor'n me? Nothin' but a railroad porter crazy 'bout every good lookin' high yaller he sees. And they fall for him cause he's good lookin' and wears swell clothes and spends dough on 'em." Even in his jealous rage Lew remembered with envy the stalwart figure, the broad shoulders, the air of easy grace and poise that made Matt Hicks so popular with the women in spite of vague unsavory rumours concerning his amorous exploits.

"Turned me down for Matt Hicks," he muttered.

Lew continued his way up the Avenue but he no longer smiled nor bowed.

Saturday morning found Lew on hand at the store a half hour earlier than usual. He set to work at once, and before anybody else arrived he had finished his morning chores. He changed his blue porter's apron for the white coat, and taking the telephone directory began laboriously scanning its pages, all the while mumbling a number over and over. But there were frequent interruptions, and it was past noon before his search was rewarded. Taking a worn memorandum from his vest pocket he wrote—

Hugh Middleton,
The Wellington Arms,
Charles Street.

Then he waited his chance. When the store was empty he slipped into the telephone booth. Nervously he gave the number, Calvert 4683, and waited. A woman's voice answered. Lew's heart pounded at the familiar sound. He couldn't be wrong. That smoky softness was rather uncommon.

In a high falsetto he asked for Mrs. Middleton.

"Mrs. Middleton speaking," came the response.

Lew's story was ready. All day he had rehearsed what he would say. Hurriedly he went on. Would Mrs. Middleton care to look at a group of imported gowns that he was showing only to a few customers who had been recommended? His supply was limited. He'd like her to see them before the choice ones had been sold.

The soft smoky voice was answering. If he came at seven o'clock she would be in. She was going out at eight. She'd be glad to look at the gowns.

Lew hung up and mopped the perspiration from his face and neck. There was a malicious glint in the black eyes as he returned to his place at the fountain.

When the errand boy started out, Lew handed him an envelope. "Leave this while you're out," he directed. The envelope was addressed to Mr. Matthew Hicks.

But the boy had barely gotten out of sight when Lew began to have misgivings. He wished he hadn't sent the note. Suppose he had been mistaken? He had worked on such a slight clue. He had heard her call a number, had spent hours searching for that number, until he had located it and the name under which it was listed. He could think of no reason why Ossie should be calling an exclusive white apartment house —no reason except—. He had taken a chance on calling up the number and she had answered. Ossie had answered. He had been sure at the time that it was she, but suppose he was wrong! That note. True it was unsigned and the handwriting disguised—.

"If you want to know where your high falutin' high yaller gets her swell clothes and where she spends her week-ends go to the Wellington Arms, Charles Street at 8 o'clock," he had written.

Lew knew Matt's boast that no nigger could get a woman away from him. Well, let Matt see her with an ofay. She would be going out about eight she had said. Lew knew Matt would follow the clue—would try to find out what it meant. Well let him feel what he, Lew, had felt. Matt was such a smart guy. He wouldn't fly so high after he knew. And Ossie,—maybe, with Matt out of the running, Ossie might not be so uppish with a drug store porter.

Evening came. Greene & Scott's Pharmacy always did a rushing business on Saturday night. Refreshments were not much in demand, and Lew was pressed into service to cater to the wants of the stream of customers that came in search of means for improving either health or pulchritude. They asked for every known tonic and pill; every cream, lotion, powder, pomade, and perfume on the market, and some that weren't. Lew usually enjoyed his Saturday prestige, but tonight he was ill at ease. How the time lagged! Nervously he watched the door and the clock longing for closing time.

Then, vaguely in the penumbra of his consciousness, was borne the sense of a commotion outside. A woman screamed. People went running in the direction of the sound. Lew strode to the door. Half-way down the block a taxi had stopped. People crowded around it. Lew, straining eyes and ears to catch the meaning of it all, dimly saw a form being carried into a house. At length the bystanders began to move away. Stray snatches of comment floated to him.

"Oh boy!

"Tell you 'bout cheat'n!"

"Kinder bowled the old lady over."

"Wonder how bad she's hurt."

"Old Matt sho' did get her."

"Did he make a get-a-way?"

"He didn't miss."

The errand boy emerged from the crowd. Lew grabbed him by the shoulders.

"What's the matter down the street?"

"Miss Ossie Pitts is been hurt and old lady Pitts is tryin' to die."

"Hurt? Miss Ossie?" Lew's throat was dry. "Hurt? How?"

"Some guy saw her out walkin' with an ofay and slashed her with a razor."

"Slashed Ossie Pitts?"

"Uh huh."

"Bad?" Lew tried to hide his agitation.

"Oh, they say she ain't hurt bad, but she's sho marked for life. He got her right across the face. They give her treatment at the hospital but when they found she was colored they sends her home. When her Maw sees 'em bringin' er in all bandaged up she yells blue murder."

Lew's hand fell heavily from the boy's shoulders. Slowly he shambled out of the door and down the street. Only a few people now stood looking curiously at the Pitt's house. From inside came a woman's sobs. Lew slouched against a lamp post, staring blankly at the lighted second story windows, oblivious of the presence of the by-standers—of their abortive attempts at humorous comment on the fracas. Ossie—marked for life—he hadn't thought—he hadn't meant—God! His face worked painfully.

The sobbing ceased. The lighted windows grew dark. Inside all was quiet. Outside only Lew kept watch. The Avenue had forgotten.

GOLDIE

ANGELINA WELD GRIMKÉ

He had never thought of the night before as so sharply black and white; but then, he had never walked before, three long miles, after midnight, over a country road. A short distance only, after leaving the railroad station, the road plunged into the woods and stayed there most of the way. Even in the day, he remembered, although he had not traveled over it for five years, it had not been the easiest to journey over. Now, in the almost palpable darkness, the going was hard, indeed; and he was compelled to proceed, it almost seemed to him, one careful step after another careful step.

Singular fancies may come to one, at such times; and, as he plodded forward, one came, quite unceremoniously, quite unsolicited, to him and fastened its tentacles upon him. Perhaps it was born of the darkness and the utter windlessness with the resulting great stillness perhaps—but who knows from what fancies spring? At any rate, it seemed to him, the woods, on either side of him, were really not woods at all but an ocean that had flowed down in a great rolling black wave of flood to the very lips of the road itself and paused there as though suddenly arrested and held poised in some strange and sinister spell. Of course, all of this came, he told himself over and over, from having such a cursed imagination; but whether he would or not, the fancy persisted and the growing feeling with it, that he, Victor Forrest, went in actual danger, for at any second the spell might snap and with that snapping, this boundless, deep upon deep of horrible, waiting sea, would move, rush, hurl itself heavily and swiftly together from the two sides, thus engulfing, grinding, crushing, blotting out all in its path, not excluding what he now knew to be that most insignificant of insignificant pigmies, Victor Forrest.

But there were bright spots, here and there in the going—he found himself calling them white islands of safety. These occurred where the woods receded at some little distance from the road.

"It's as though," he thought aloud, "they drew back here in order to get a good deep breath before plunging forward again. Well, all I hope is, the spell holds O. K. beyond."

He always paused, a moment or so, on one of these islands to drive out expulsively the dark, black oppressiveness of the air he had been breathing and to fill his lungs anew with God's night air, that, here, at least, was sweet and untroubled. Here, too, his eyes were free again and he could see the dimmed white blur of road for a space each way; and, above, the stars, millions upon millions of them, each one hardly brilliant, stabbing its way whitely through the black heavens. And if the island were large enough there was a glimpse, scarcely more, of a very pallid, slightly crumpled moon sliding furtively down the west.—Yes, sharply black and sharply white, that was it, but mostly it was black.

And as he went, his mind busy enough with many thoughts, many memories, subconsciously always the aforementioned fancy persisted, clung to him; and he was never entirely able to throw off the feeling of his very probable and imminent danger in the midst of this arrested wood-ocean.

—Of course, he thought, it was downright foolishness, his expecting Goldie, or rather Cy, to meet him. He hadn't written or telegraphed.— Instinct he guessed, must have warned him that wouldn't be safe; but confound it all! this was the devil of a road.—Gosh ! What a lot of noise a man's feet could make couldn't they?—All alone like this?—Well, Goldie and Cy would feel a lot worse over the whole business than he did.— After all it was only once in a lifetime, wasn't it?—Hoofing it was good for him, anyway.—No doubt about his having grown soft—He'd be as lame as the dickens tomorrow.—Well, Goldie would enjoy that—liked nothing better than fussing over a fellow.—If (but he very resolutely turned away from that if).

—In one way, it didn't seem like five years and yet, in another, it seemed longer—since he'd been over this road last. It had been the sunshiniest and the saddest May morning he ever remembered.—He'd been going in the opposite direction, then; and that little sister of his, Goldie, had been sitting very straight beside him, the two lines held rigidly in her two little gold paws and her little gold face stiff with repressed emotion. He felt a twinge, yet, as he remembered her face and the way the great tears would well up and run down her cheeks at intervals.—Proud little thing!—She had disdained even to notice them and treated them as a matter with which she had no concern.—No, she hadn't wanted him to go.—Good, little Goldie!—Well, she never knew, how close, how very close he had been to putting his hand out and telling her to turn back— he'd changed his mind and wasn't going after all.

He drew a sharp breath.—He hadn't put out his hand.

—And at the station, her face there below him, as he looked down at her through the open window of the train.—The unwavering way her eyes had held his—and the look in them, he hadn't understood then, or didn't now, for that matter.

"Don't," he had said. "Don't, Goldie!"

"I must, Vic, I must—I don't know—Don't you understand I may never see you again?"

"Rot!" he had said. "Am I not going to send for you?"

—And then she had tried to smile and that had been worse than her eyes.

"You think so, now, Vic,—but will you?"

"Of course."

"Vic!"

"Yes."

"Remember, whatever it is—it's all right. *It's all right.*—I mean it.—See! I couldn't smile—could I?—if I didn't?"

And then, when it had seemed as if he couldn't stand any more—had leaned over, even to pick up his bag to get off, give it all up—the train had started and it was too late. The last he had seen of her, she bad been standing there, very straight, her arms at her sides and her little gold paws two little tight fists.—And her eyes!—And her twisted smile! God! that was about enough of that—He was going to her, now, wasn't be?

—Had he been wrong to go?—*Had* he?—Somehow, now, it seemed that way.—And yet, at the time, be had felt he was right.—He still did for that matter.—His chance, that's what it had meant—Oughtn't he to have had it?—Certainly a colored man couldn't do the things that counted in the South.—To live here, just to live here, he had to swallow his self-respect —Well, he had tried, honestly, too, for Goldie's sake, to swallow his.— The trouble was he couldn't keep it swallowed—it nauseated him.—The thing for him to have done, he saw that now, was to have risked everything and taken Goldie with him.—He shouldn't have waited, as he had from year to year, to send for her.—It would have meant hard sledding, but they could have managed somehow.—Of course, it wouldn't have been the home she had had here with her Uncle Ray and her Aunt Millie, still.—Well, there wasn't any use in crying over spilt milk.—One thing was certain, never mind how much you might wish to, you couldn't recall the past.

—TWO YEARS AGO—Gosh! but time flew—when her letter had come telling him she had married Cy Harper.—Queer thing, this life! —Darned queer thing!—Why he had been in the very midst of debating whether or not he could afford to send for her—had almost decided he could.—Well, sisters, even the very best of them, it turned out, weren't above marrying and going off and leaving you high and dry—just like this.—Oh! of course, Cy was a good enough fellow, clean, steadygoing, true, and all the rest of it;—no one could deny that—still, confound it all! how could Goldie prefer a fathead like Cy to him.— Hm!—peeved yet, it seemed!—Well, he'd acknowledged it—he was peeved all right.

Involuntarily he began to slow up.

—Good! since he was acknowledging things—why not get along and acknowledge the rest.—Might just as well have this out with himself here and now.—Peeved first, then, what?

He came to an abrupt stop in the midst of the black silence of the arrested wood-ocean.

—There was one thing, it appeared, a dark road could do for you—it could make it possible for you to see yourself quite plainly—almost too plainly.—Peeved first, then what?—No blinking now, the truth.—He'd evaded himself very cleverly—hadn't he?—up until tonight?—No use any more.—Well, what was he waiting for? Out with it.—Peeved first; go ahead, now.—Louder!—*Relief!*—Honest, at last.—Relief! Think of it, he had felt relief when he had learned he wasn't to be bothered, after all, with little, loyal, big-hearted Goldie.—Bothered!—And he had prided himself upon being rather a decent, upright, respectable fellow.—Why, if he had heard this about anybody else, he wouldn't have been able to find language strong enough to describe him.—A rotter, that's what he was, and a cad.

"And Goldie would have sacrificed herself for you any time, and gladly, and you know it."

To his surprise he found himself speaking aloud.

Why once when the kid had been only eight years old and he had been taken with a cramp while in swimming, she had jumped in too!—Goldie, who couldn't swim a single stroke!—Her screams had done it and they were saved. He could see his mother's face yet, quizzical, a little puzzled, a little worried.

"But what on earth, Goldie, possessed you to jump in too?" she had asked. "Didn't you know you couldn't save him?"

"Yes I knew it,"

"Then, why?"

"I don't know. It just seemed that if Vic had to drown, why I had to drown with him.—I just couldn't live *afterwards*, Momsey, if I lived *then* and be drowned."

"Goldie, Goldie!—If Vic fell out of a tree, would you have to fall out too?"

"Proberbly." Goldie bad never been able to master "probably," but it fascinated her.

"Well, for heavens' sake, Vic, do be careful of yourself hereafter. You see how it is," his mother had said.

And Goldie had answered—how serious, how quaint, how true her little face had been—:

"Yes, that's how it is, isn't it?" Another trick of hers, ending, so often, what she had to say with a question.—And he hadn't wished to be bothered with her!—

He groaned and started on again.

—Well, he'd try to even up things a little, now.—He'd show her (there was a lump in his throat) if he could.

For the first time Victor Forrest began to understand the possibilities of tragedy that may lie in those three little words, "if I can."

—Perhaps Goldie had understood and married Cy so that he needn't bother any more about having to have her with him. He hoped, as he had never hoped, for anything before that this hadn't been her reason. She was quite equal to marrying, he knew, for such a motive—and so game, too, you'd never dream it was a sacrifice she was making. He'd rather believe, even, that it had been just to get the little home all her own.

—When Goldie was only a little thing and you asked her what she wanted most in all the world when she grew up, she had always answered:

"Why, a little home—all my own—a cunning one—and young things in it and about it."

And if you asked her to explain, she had said:

"Don't you know?—not *really*?"

And, then, if you had suggested children, she had answered: "Of course, all my own; and kittens and puppies and little fluffy chickens and ducks and little birds in my trees, who will make little nests and little songs there because they will know that the trees near the little home all my own are the very nicest ever and ever."

—Once, she must have been around fifteen, then—how well he remembered that once—he had said:

"Look here, Goldie, isn't this an awful lot you're asking God to put over for you?"

Only teasing, he had been—but Goldie's face!

"Oh! Vic, am I?—Do you *really* think that?"

And then, before he could reply in little eager, humble rushes:

"I hadn't thought of it—that way—before.—Maybe you're Right—If—if —I gave up something, perhaps—the ducks—or the chickens—or the— birds—or the kittens—or the puppies?"

Then very slowly:

"Or—the—children?—Oh!—but I couldn't—I *couldn't!*—Not any of them.—Don't you think, perhaps,—just, perhaps, Vic,—if—if—I'm— good—always—from now on—that—that—maybe—maybe— sometime, Vic, sometime—I—I—might? Oh! don't you?"

He shut his mouth hard.

—Well, she had had the little home all her own. Cy had made a little clearing, she had written, just beyond the great live oak. Did he remember it? And did he remember, too, how much Cy loved the trees?

—No, he hadn't forgotten that live oak—not the way he had played in it —and carved his initials all over it; and he hadn't forgotten Cy and the trees, either.—Silly way, Cy had had, even after he grew up, of mooning among them.

"Talk to me—they do sometimes.—Tell me big, quiet things, nice things."

—Gosh! after *his* experience, *this* night among them. *Love* 'em!—Hm!—Damned, waiting, greedy things!—Cy could have them and welcome.

—It had been last year Goldie had written about the clearing with the little home all her own in the very "prezact" middle of it—They had had to wait a whole year after they were married before they could move in —not finished or something—he'd forgotten the reason.—How had the rest of that letter gone?—Goldie's letters were easy to remember—had, somehow, a sort of burrlike quality about them. He had it, now, something like this:

She wished she could tell him how cunning the little home all her own was, but there was really no cunning word cunning enough to describe it.—Why even the very trees came right down to the very edges of the clearing on all four sides just to look at it.—If he could only see how proudly they stood there and nodded their entire approval one to the other!

Four rooms, the little home—all her own, had.—Four!—And a little porch in the front and a "littler" one in the back, and a hall that had really the most absurd way of trying to get out both the front and rear doors at the same time. Would he believe it, they had to keep both the doors shut tight in order to hold that ridiculous hall in? Had he ever, in all his life, heard of such a thing? And just off of this little hall, at the right of the front door, was their bedroom, and back of this, at the end of this same very silly hall was their dining room and opposite, across the hall again—she hoped he saw how this hall simply refused to be ignored —opposite was the kitchen.—He was, then, to step back into the hall once more, but *this* time he was to pretend very hard not to see it. There was no telling, it's vanity was so great, if you paid too much attention to it, what it might do. Why, the unbearable little thing might rise up, break down the front and back doors and escape; and then where'd they be, she'd like to know, without any little hall at all?—He was to step, then, quite nonchalantly—if he knew what that was, back into the hall and come forwards but this time he was to look at the room at the left of the front door; and *there*, if he pleased, he would see something really to repay him for his trouble, for here he would behold her sitting room and parlor both in one. And if he couldn't believe how perfectly adorable this little room could be and was, why she was right there to tell him all about it.—Every single bit of the little home all her own was built just as she had wished and furnished just as she had hoped. And, well, to sum it all up, it wasn't safe, if you had any kind of heart trouble at all to stand in the road in front of the little home all her own, because it had such a way of calling you that before you knew it, you were running to it and running fast. She could vouch for the absolute truth of this statement.

And she had a puppy, yellow all over, all but his little heart—she dared him even to suggest such a little thing!—with a funny wrinkled forehead and a most impudent grin. And he insisted upon eating up all the uneatable things they possessed, including Cy's best straw hat and her own Sunday-go-to-meeting slippers. And she had a kitten, a grey one; and the busiest things he did were to eat and sleep. Sometimes he condescended to play with his tail and to keep the puppy in his place. He had a way of looking at you out of blue, very young, very innocent eyes that you knew perfectly well were not a bit young nor yet a bit innocent. And she had the darlingest, downiest, little chickens and ducks and a canary bird, that Emma Elizabeth lent her sometimes when she went away to work, and the canary had been made of two golden songs. And outside of the little home all her own—in the closest trees, the birds were, lots of them, and they had nested there.—If, of a morning, he could only hear them singing!—As if they knew—and did it on purpose —just as she had wished.

How happy it had all sounded—and yet—and yet—once or twice—he had had the feeling something wasn't quite right. He hoped it didn't mean she wasn't caring for Cy.—He would rather believe it was because there hadn't been children.—The latter could be remedied—from little hints he had been gathering lately, he rather thought it was already being remedied; but if she didn't care for Cy, there wasn't much to be done about that.—Well, he was going to her, at last.—She couldn't fool him—couldn't Goldie;—and if that fathead, Cy, couldn't take care of her, he was here, now. Just let somebody start something.

—That break ahead there, in the darkness, ought to be just about where the settlement was.—No one need ever tell him again it was only three miles from the station—he guessed he knew better.—More like ten or twenty.—The settlement, all right.—Thought he hadn't been mistaken. —So far, then, so good.

The road, here, became the main street of the little colored settlement. Three or four smaller ones cut it at right angles and, then, ran off into the darkness. The houses, for the most part, sat back, not very far apart; and, as the shamed moon had entirely disappeared, all he could make out of them was their silent, black little masses. His quick eyes and his ears were busy. No sound broke the stillness. He drew a deep breath of relief.

He did not pause until he was about midway of this settlement. Here he set his bag down, sat on it and looked at the illuminated hands of his watch. It was half past two. In the woods he had found it almost cold, but, in this spot, the air was warm and close. He pulled out his handkerchief, took off his hat, mopped his face, head and neck, finally the sweatband of his hat.

Queer!—but he wouldn't have believed that the mere sight of all this, after five years, could make him feel this way. There was something to this home idea, after all.—Didn't feel, hardly, as though he had ever been away.

Suddenly he wondered if old man Tom Jackson had fixed that gate of his yet. Curiosity got the better of him. He arose, went over and looked. Sure enough the gate swung outward on a broken hinge. Forrest grinned.

"Don't believe over much here, in change, do they?—That gate was that way ever since I can remember.—Bet every window is shut tight too. 'Turrible' the night air always used to be.—Wonder if my people will ever get over these things."

He came back and sat down again. He was facing a house that his eyes had turned to more than any other.

"Looks just the same.—Wonder who lives there, now.—Suppose someone does.—Looks like it—Mother sure had courage—more than I would have had—to give up a good job in the North, teaching school to come down here and marry a poor doctor in a colored settlement. I give it to her.—Game! Goldie's just like her—she'd have done it too."

—How long had it been since his father had died?—Nine—ten—why, it was ten years and eight since his mother.—They'd both been born there —he and Goldie.—What was that story his mother used to tell about him when he had first been brought in to see her?—He had been six at the time.

"Mother," he had asked, "is her gold?"

"What, Son?"

"I say, is her gold?"

"Oh! I see," his mother had said and smiled, he was sure, that very nice understanding smile of hers. "Why, she *is* gold, isn't she?"

"Yes, all of her. What's her name?"

"She hasn't any, yet, Son."

"Her aint got no name?—Too bad! I give her one. Hers name's Goldie. Cause."

"All right, Son, Goldie it shall be." And Goldie it had always been.

—No, you couldn't call Goldie pretty exactly.—Something about her, though, mighty attractive.—Different looking!—that was it—Like herself.—She had never lost that beautiful even gold color of hers.— Even her hair was "goldeny" and her long eye lashes.—Nice eyes, Goldie had, big and brown with flecks of gold in them—set in a little wistful, pointed face.

He came to his feet suddenly and picked up his bag. He moved swiftly, now, but not so swiftly as not to notice things still as he went.

"Why, hello!" he exclaimed and paused a second or so before going on again. "What's happened to Uncle Ray's house?—Something's not the same.—Seems larger, somehow.—Wonder what it is?—Maybe a porch. —So they do change here a little.—That there ought to be Aunt Phoebe's house—but she must be dead—though I don't remember Goldie's saying so.—Why, she'd be way over ninety.—Used to be afraid of the dark or something and never slept without a dim light.—Gosh! if there isn't the light—just the same as ever!—And way over ninety.—Whew!—Wonder how it feels to be that old.—Bet I wouldn't like it.—Gee! what's that?

Victor Forrest Stopped short and listened. The sound was muffled but continuous, it seemed to come from the closed faintly lighted pane of Aunt Phoebe's room. It was a sound, it struck him, remarkably like the keening he had heard in an Irish play. It died out slowly and though he waited it did not begin again.

"Probably dreaming or something and woke herself up," and he started on once more.

He soon left the settlement behind and, continuing along the same road found himself (he hoped for the last time) in the midst of the arrested wood-ocean.

But the sound of that keening, although he had explained it quite satisfactorily to himself had left him disturbed. Thoughts, conjectures, fears that he had refused, until now, quite resolutely to entertain no longer would be denied. They were rooted in Goldie's two last letters, the cause of his hurried trip South.

"Of course, there's no *real* danger.—I'm foolish, even, to entertain such a thought.—Women get like that sometimes—nervous and overwrought.—And if it is with her as I suspect and hope—why the whole matter's explained.—The letter didn't seem like Goldie, though, not a bit like her.—Why it had really sounded *frightened!*—and parts of it were—hm!—almost incoherent—The whole thing's too ridiculous however, to believe.—Well, when she sees me we'll have a good big laugh over it all.—Just the same, I'm glad I came—Rather funny—somehow—thinking of Goldie—with a kid—in her arms.—Nice, though—."

—Lafe Coleman!—Lafe Coleman!—He seemed to remember dimly a stringy, long white man with stringy colorless hair, quite disagreeably underclean; eyes a pale grey and fishlike.—He associated a sort of toothless grin, with that face.—No, that wasn't it, either.—Ah! that was it!

—He had it clearly, now.—The grin was all right but it displayed the dark and rotting remains of tooth stumps.

He made a grimace of strong disquiet and loathing.

—And—*this*—*this*—*thing* had been annoying Goldie, had been in fact, for years.—She hadn't told anybody, it seems, because she had been able to take care of herself.—But since she had married and been living away, from the settlement—it had been easier for him, and much more difficult for her. He wasn't to worry, though, for the man was stupid and so far she'd always been able to outwit him.—What she feared was Cy. It was true Cy was amiability itself—but—well—she had seen him angry once.—Ought she to tell him? She didn't believe Cy would kill the creature—not outright—but it would be pretty close to it. The feeling between the races was running higher than it used to.—There had been a very terrible lynching in the next county only last year.—She hadn't spoken of it before—for there didn't seem any use going into it—As he had never mentioned it, she supposed it had never gotten into the papers. Nothing, of course, had been done about it, nothing ever was. Everybody knew who were in the mob.—Even he would be surprised at some of the names.—The brother of the lynched man, quite naturally, had tried to bring some of the leaders to justice; and he, too, had paid with his life. Then the mob, not satisfied, had threatened, terrorized, cowed all the colored people in the locality.—He was to remember that when you were under the heel it wasn't the most difficult of matters to be terrorized and cowed. There was absolutely no law, as he knew, to protect a colored man. That was one of the reasons she had hesitated to tell Cy, for not only Cy and she might be made to pay for what Cy might do, but the little settlement as well. Now, keeping all this in mind, ought she to tell Cy?

And the letter had ended:

"I'm a little nervous, Vic, and frightened and not quite sure of my judgment. Whatever you advise me to do, I am sure will be right."

On the very heels of this had come the "Special" mailed by Goldie in another town.—She hadn't dared, it seems, to post it in Hopewood.—It had contained just twelve words, but they had brought him South on the next train.

"Cy knows," it had said, "and O! Vic, if you love me, come, come, come!"

Way down, inside of him, in the very depths, a dull cold rage began to glow, but he banked it down again, carefully, very carefully, as he had been able to do, so far, each time before that the thoughts of Lafe Coleman and little Goldie's helplessness had threatened anew to stir it.

—That there ought to be the great live oak—and beyond should be the clearing, in the very "prezact" middle of which should be the little home all of Goldie's own.—

For some inexplicable reason his feet suddenly began to show a strange reluctance to go forward.

"Damned silly ass!" he said to himself. "There wasn't a thing wrong with the settlement. That ought to be a good enough sign for anybody with a grain of sense."

And then, quite suddenly, he remembered the keening.

He did not tum back or pause, still his feet showed no tendency to hasten. Of necessity, however, it was only a matter of time before he reached the live oak. He came to a halt beside it, ears and every sense keenly on the alert. Save for the stabbing, white stars above the clearing, there was nothing else in all the world, it seemed, but himself and the heavy black silence.

Once more he advanced but, this time, by an act of sheer will. He paused, set his jaw and faced the clearing. In the very center was a dark small mass, it must be the little home. The breath he had drawn in sharply, while turning, he emitted in a deep sigh. His knees felt strangely weak.—What he had expected to see exactly, he hardly knew. He was almost afraid of the reaction going on inside of him. The relief, the blessed relief at merely finding it there, the little home all her own!

It made him feel suddenly very young and joyous and the world, bad as it was, a pretty decent old place after all. Danger!—of course, there was no danger.—How could he have been so absurd?—Just wait until he had teased Goldie a plenty about this. He started to laugh aloud but caught himself in time.

—No use awaking them.—He'd steal up and sit on the porch, there'd probably be a chair there or something, and wait until dawn.—They shouldn't be allowed to sleep one single second after that—And then he'd bang on their window, and call out quite casually:

"O Goldie Harper, this is a nice way—isn't it?—to treat a fellow; not even to leave the latch string out for him?" He could hear Goldie's little squeal now.

And then he'd say to Cy:

"Hello, you big fathead, you!—what do you mean, anyhow, by making a perfectly good brother-in-law hoof it the whole way here, like this?"

He had reached the steps by this time and he began softly to mount them. It was very dark on the little porch and he wished he dared to light a match, but he mustn't risk anything that might spoil the little surprise he was planning. He transferred his bag from his right to his left hand, the better to feel his way. With his fingers outstretched in front of him he took a cautious step forward and stumbled over something.

"Clumsy chump!" he exclaimed below his breath, "that will about finish your little surprise I am thinking." He stood stock-still for several seconds, but there was no sound.

"Some sleepers," he commented.

He leaned over to find out what it was he had stumbled against and discovered that it was a broken chair lying on its side. Slowly he came to a standing posture. He was not as happy for some reason. He stood there, very quiet, for several moments. Then his hand stretched out before him, he started forward again. This time, after only a couple of steps, his hand came in contact with the housefront. He was feeling his way along, cautiously still, when all of a sudden his fingers encountered nothing but air. Surprised, he paused. He thought, at first, he had come to the end of the porch. He put out a carefully exploring foot only to find firm boards beneath. A second time he experimented with the same result. And then, as suddenly, he felt the housefront once more beneath his fingers. Gradually it came to him where he must be. He was standing before the door and it was open, wide open!

He could not have moved if he had wished. He made no sound and none broke the blackness all about.

It was sometime afterwards when he put his bag down upon the porch, took a box of matches out of his pocket, lit one and held it up. His hand was trembling, but he managed, before it burned his fingers and he blew it out automatically, to see four things—two open doors to right and left, a lamp in a bracket just beyond the door at the left and a dirty mud-trodden floor.

The minutes went by and then, it seemed to him, somebody else called out:

"Goldie! Cy!" This was followed by silence only.

Again the voice tried, a little louder this time:

"Goldie! Cy!"—There was no response.

This other person who seemed, somehow, to have entered into his body, moved forward, struck another match, lit the lamp and took it down out of the bracket. Nothing seemed to make very much difference to this stranger. He moved his body stiffly; his eyes felt large and dry. He passed through the open door at the left and what he saw there did not surprise him in the least. In some dim way, only, he knew that it affected him.

There was not, in this room. one single whole piece of furniture. Chairs, tables, a sofa, a whatnot, all had been smashed, broken, torn apart; the stuffing thrown, scattered here, there and everywhere. The piano lay on one side, its other staved in.—Something, it reminded him of—something to do with a grin—the black notes like the rotting stumps of teeth. Oh! yes, Lafe Coleman!—that was it. The thought aroused no particular emotion in him. Only, again he knew it affected him in some far off way.

Every picture on the walls had been wrenched down and the moulding with it, the pictures, themselves, defaced and torn, and the glass splintered and crushed under foot. Knick-knacks, vases, a china clock, all lay smashed and broken. Even the rug upon the floor had not escaped, but had been ripped up, torn into shreds and fouled by many dirty feet. The frail white curtains and window shades had gone down, too, in this human whirlwind; not a pane of glass was whole. The white woodwork and the white walls were soiled and smeared. Over and over the splay-fingered imprint of one dirty hand repeated itself on the walls. A wanton boot had kicked through the plastering in places.

This someone else went out of the door, down the hall, into the little kitchen and dining room. In each room he found precisely the same conditions prevailing.

There was one left, he remembered, so he turned back into the hall, went along it to the open door and entered in.—What was the matter, here, with the air?—He raised the lamp higher above bis head. He saw the same confusion as elsewhere. A brass bed was overturned and all things else shattered and topsy-turvy. There was something dark at the foot of the bed. He moved nearer, and understood why the air was not pleasant. The dark object was a little dead dog, a yellow one, with a wrinkled forehead. His teeth were bared in a snarl. A kick in the belly had done for him. He leaned over; the little leg was quite stiff. Less dimly, this time, he knew that this affected him.

He straightened up. When he had entered the room there had been something he had noticed for him to do. But, what was it? This stranger's memory was not all that should be.—Oh! yes, he knew, now. The bed. He was to right the bed. With some difficulty he cleared a space for the lamp and set it down carefully. He raised the bed. Nothing but the mattress and the rumpled and twisted bed clothing. He didn't know exactly just what this person was expecting to find.

He was sitting on the steps, the extinguished lamp at his side. It was dawn. Everything was veiled over with grey. As the day came on a breeze followed softly after, and with the breeze there came to him there on the steps a creaking, two creakings!—somewhere there to the right, they were, among the trees. The grey world became a shining green one. Why were the birds singing like that, he wondered.—It didn't take the day long to get here—did it?—once it started. A second time his eyes went to the woods at the right. He was able to see, now. Nothing there, as far as he could make out. His eyes dropped from the trees to the ground and he beheld what looked to him like a trampled path. It began, there at the trees; it approached the house; it passed over a circular bed of little pansies. It ended at the steps. Again his eyes traversed the path, but this time from the steps to the trees.

Quite automatically he arose and followed the path. Quite automatically he drew the branches aside and saw what he saw. Underneath those two terribly mutilated swinging bodies, lay a tiny unborn child, its head crushed in by a deliberate heel.

Suddenly something went very wrong in bis bead. He dropped the branches, turned and sat down. A spider, in the sunshine, was reweaving the web some one had just destroyed while passing through the grass. He sat slouched far forward watching the spider for hours. He wished the birds wouldn't sing so.—Somebody had said something once about them. He wished, too, he could remember who it was.

About midday, the children of the colored settlement, playing in the road looked up and saw a man approaching. There was something about him that frightened them, the little ones in particular, for they ran screaming to their mothers. The larger ones drew back as unobtrusively as possible into their own yards. The man came on with a high head and an unhurried gait. His should have been a young face, but it was not. Out of its set sternness looked his eyes, and they were very terrible eyes indeed. Mothers with children hanging to them from behind and peering around, came to their doors. The man was passing through the settlement, now. A woman, startled, recognized him and called the news out shrilly to her man eating his dinner within. He came out, went down to the road rather reluctantly. The news spread. Other men from other houses followed the first man's example. They stood about him, quite a crowd of them. The stranger, of necessity, came to a pause. There were no greetings on either side. He eyed them over, this crowd, coolly, appraisingly, contemptuously. They eyed him, in turn, but surreptitiously. They were plainly very uncomfortable. Wiping their hands on aprons, women joined the crowd. A larger child or two dared the outskirts. No one would meet his eyes.

Suddenly a man was speaking. His voice came sharply, jerkily. He was telling a story. Another took it up and another. One added a detail here; one, a detail there. Heated arguments arose over insignificant particulars; angry words were passed. Then came too noisy explanations, excuses, speeches in extenuation of their own actions, pleas, at tempted exoneration of themselves. The strange man said never a word. He listened to each and to all. His contemptuous eyes made each writhe in turn. They had finished. There was nothing more, that they could see to be said. They waited, eyes on the ground, for him to speak.

But what he said was: "Where is Uncle Ray?"

Uncle Ray, it seemed was away—had been for two weeks, and Aunt Millie with him. No one had written to him for his address was not known.

The strange man made no comment.

"Where is Lafe Coleman?" he asked.

No one there knew where he was to be found—not one. They regretted the fact, they were sorry, but they couldn't say. They spoke with lowered lids, shifting their bodies uneasily from foot to foot.

Watching their faces he saw their eyes suddenly lift as if with one accord and focus upon something behind him and to his right. He turned his head. In the brilliant sunshine, a very old, very bent form leaning heavily on a cane was coming down the path from the house in whose window he had seen the dimmed light. It was Aunt Phoebe.

He left the crowd abruptly and went to meet her. When she was quite sure he was coming she paused where she was, bent over double, her two hands, one over the other, on the knob of her cane, and waited for him. No words, either, between these two. He looked down at her and she bent back her head, tremulous from age, and looked up at him.

The wrinkles were many and deep-bitten in Aunt Phoebe's dark skin. A border of white wool fringed the bright bandana tied tightly around her head. There were grey hairs in her chin; two blue rings encircled the irises of her dim eyes. But all her ugliness could not hide the big heart of her, kind yet, and brave, after ninety years on earth.

And as he stood gazing down at her, quite suddenly he remembered what Goldie had once said about those circled eyes.

"Kings and Queens may have *their* crowns and welcome. What' s there to *them?*—But the kind Aunt Phoebe wears—that's different. She earned hers, Vic, earned them through many years and long of sorrow, and heartbreak and bitter, bitter tears. She hears with her the unforgetting heart.—And though they could take husband and children and sell them South, though she lost them in the body—never a word of them, since—she keeps them always in her heart.—I know, Vic, I *know!*—And God who is good and God who is just touched her eyes, both of them and gave her blue crowns, beautiful ones, a crown for each. Don't you see she is of God's Elect?"

For a long time Victor Forrest stood looking down into those crowned eyes.

No one disturbed these two in the sun drenched little yard. They, in the road, drew closer together and watched silently. And then he spoke:

"You are to tell me, Aunt Phoebe—aren't you?—where I am to find Lafe Coleman?"

Aunt Phoebe did not hesitate a second. "Yes," she said and told him.

The crowd in the road moved uneasily, but no one uttered a word.

And, then, Victor Forrest did a thing he had never done before, he leaned over swiftly and kissed the wrinkled parchment cheek of Aunt Phoebe.

"Goldie loved you," he said and straightened up, turned on his heel without another word and went down the path to the road. Those, there, made no attempt to speak. They drew closer together and made way for him. He looked neither to the right nor to the left. He passed them without a glance. He went with a steady, purposeful gait and a high head. All watched him for they knew they were never to see him alive again. The woods swallowed Victor Forrest. A low keening was to be heard. Aunt Phoebe had turned and was going more feebly, more slowly than ever towards her house.

Those that know whereof they speak say that when Lafe Coleman was found he was not a pleasant object to see. There was no bullet in him—nothing like that. It was the marks upon his neck and the horror of his blackened face.

And Victor Forrest died, as the other two had died, upon another tree.

There is a country road upon either side of which grow trees even to its very edges. Each tree has been chosen and transplanted here for a reason and the reason is that at some time each has borne upon its boughs a creaking victim. Hundreds of these trees, there are, thousands of them. They form a forest—"Creaking Forest" it is called. And over this road many pass, very, very many. And they go jauntily, joyously here—even at night. They do not go as Victor Forrest went,—they do not sense the things that Victor Forrest sensed. If their souls were not deaf, there would be many things for them to hear in "Creaking Forest." At night the trees become an ocean dark and sinister, for it is made up of all the evil in all the hearts of all the mobs that have done to death their creaking victims. It is an ocean arrested at the very edges of the road by a strange spell. But this spell may snap at any second and with that snapping this sea of evil will move, rush, hurl itself heavily and swiftly together from the two sides of the road, engulfing, grinding, crushing, blotting out all in its way.

LAI-LI

MAE V. COWDERY

Lai-li was dancing in the moonlight...Once more. Her brown body gleamed like gold in its path.

Fearfully he whispered her name......Once more.

"Lai-li......Lai-li......"

She did not answer...Ah! there was no need......She was coming nearer, nearer. Slowly she danced. There was not sound save for the pounding of his heart and the magic melody of the waves rolling slowly to shore......All was as on that night when first he saw her, Lai-li......"Moon Flower."

Many, many, years had passed since then. Time had dealt gently with her. She was even more beautiful.

He could feel her breath on his cheek, fragrant as the perfume imprisoned in the crimson petals of the flowers she wore in the ebon coils of her hair. Closer she came, her tiny feet making no sound as she beat her love song on the silver sands.

Would she know him? Would she forgive?........Had her heart forgotten the wound he had dealt in the reckless days of his youth? ......He surely had suffered.

Again he whispered her name.

"Lai-li......Lai-li......"

Her golden arms were twining around his neck. Her body yielded, as on that night—so long ago. Her lids drooped over eyes like midnight pools, hiding the fire within......Her lips were cool, like dew, on his feverish ones......As on that night......so long ago.

Once more they would dance the strange jungle dance she had taught him......once more they would dance......she had forgiven......

God! He had forgotten he was no longer young......Time had dealt roughly with him...It was his punishment. His limbs could no longer bend and whirl......His arms could no longer hold close their precious burden, as he sought to lift her and dart to the shadows......once more.

"Lai-li! Lai-li! Do not go! Stay! Stay! I am coming—I......am......coming."

The moon passed behind a cloud. They waves paused an instant on their home-ward flight. Air hung silent.

Again two figures danced a jungle dance in the moonlight......Cold and ivory blending, caressed by the moon's silver breath......Two figures slept once more in the soft embrace of the sand, watched over by the cool shadows......Two loved once more......

In the pale grey light of morning the waves still crept to the shore. The sun was lazily peeping over the eastern hills. All was as it had been the day before. In the cove a fishing sloop of olden days lay, her decks deserted. As the sky turned to its usual topaz blue, two figures appeared on deck. One scanned the shore with searching eyes. Quickly they descended into a small row boat and rapidly made their way to the lonely beach.

"Wonder where the Capt's gone? Can't see a thing on this dump of sand.....He sure must be a little off in the upper story to come to a place like this. He's a regular circus in all the sea ports with this ole sloop. I sure wouldn't have come on this trip if you hadn't been so blamed curious! Drat you......I'm just a soft hearted ole nut after all!"

"Well it ain't doing yaa a bit a good to grumble about it now. You oughta thought about that 'foe ya' come, perhaps we wus both a coupla nuts, but the Capt's been mighty good to us when we wus down and out. Any how he can't last much longer with that cough......Did you notice how he changed as we neared the blame island? He was blattin' to hisself about some Lilly, or somethin'......Bet he had one of them native sweeties.

"Well I'll be jiggered! Here's the ole boy fast asleep!"

"Yeh? Well he won't be waking in this place. Poor ole Capt. I'm glad he's happy! Lookit the smile on his face! There ain't a blooming wrinkle on it. I'm so glad he's happy......

"S'awright Pat. We're just a pair of soft hearted blokes, but I'm blamed glad we brought him here. Let's bury him here. Seems like that wus what he wanted......He knew he wusn't gonna last much longer......"

The two slowly made their way back to the sloop and as the sun finally beamed bright in the sky the sloop sailed around the bay and on into the open sea. The two on its deck failed to see......to hear......

Lai-li and the "Capt." Walking arm in arm (as of yore) and singing to them a farewell song......could not see their figures blend in the spray of the waves as their lips met.

"Lai-li......Lai-li......Lai-li"

THE CORNER

EUNICE HUNTON CARTER

My friend lives in the house on the corner. She lives high above the street in a doll's house of white enamel and soft blue with lovely old furniture and oriental rugs of faded brilliance on dark polished floors; in a miniature home with a real fireplace and polished grasses and flowers all about in crystal bowls. She lives high up there but below are the street and the avenue. And one Fall night as I waited for her in the loveliest room of all, I turned from watching the fire flicker and dart across the room and great chrysanthemums casting sleeping shadows on the wall. I turned from this and watched the street. It was alive with light and sound, the light and sound of the city, the black city. Motor cars whizzed by carrying throngs of pleasure seekers, alien many of them, in search of novelty and thrill, come to the black city for something new. And in the small morning hours they went back to their homes in Westchester and the Bronx, on Park Avenue and Riverside Drive, back to their haunt on Broadway and thereabouts, serene in the belief that in Harlem cabarets they had found something new, that in black and tan replicas of downtown cabarets, roofs and upper clubs, promoted by quacks of every race, they had seen life in the black city.

In reality as their cars swept past the corner, they were passing life by. They had missed a chance of seeing life when they didn't stop and watch the boy on the corner who for clapping companions in front of the drug store was doing a dance that was a bit of Buck and Wing, a bit of "Charleston" and many other things. They didn't hear the errand boy who came out of the drug store singing a song that had drifted out of the cabaret to come from him purified by the sheer joy and spontaneity of his singing.

Around the corner on the Avenue, a man mounted on a soap box was making a political speech in which he was putting race first and country after and the crowd around him was eager and interested—until a pair of detectives passed leading a troupe of gypsies toward the police station.

A group of school girls, bright felt hats perched jauntily on sleek bobbed heads, with short fur coats from which bright scarves fluttered in the night, passed by linked arm in arm, chattering as they went home from a late moving picture. To me, from my high perch, they looked like school girls the town over, but a passerby would have seen skins of olive, tan and copper beneath the bright felt hats.

A man without legs wheeled himself alone on a wooden platform and with an instrument or two gave the effect of a whole brass band as he attracted attention to the box for largess fastened onto his platform. A girl of the town dropped a coin or two as she went on her way but slim brown girl and boy passed him by unheedingly as with eyes locked, they walked on into the night.

Across the street the crowd around an automobile from which a swarthy man in morning clothes and a fez di playing gruesome pictures and dispensing patent medicines parted to let a girl, glitteringly shod and swathed in furs, enter a waiting taxicab.

Beneath the window a crowd of youths were in heated argument gesticulating fiercely. I leaned from the window and listened. For want of a better meeting place a group of college youth were discussing philosophy.

Inside the lovely room, the fire had burned low. The silver chimed clock on the mantle struck many times. I decided not to wait longer for my friend. I took my hat and coat and went down into the street and turned into the Avenue. I started to cross. A taxicab filled with alien pleasure-seekers crossed my path. As they passed the tower, they heard nothing but their own maudlin laughter, they saw nothing but their own vacuous faces. They passed on to the cabarets, illegitimate offspring of their own resorts, looking for life, Harlem life, and blindly, feverishly, rushing by it.

SUBVERSION

EDYTHE MAE GORDON

The deepening twilight wrapped the world in a dusky veil of mystery. Like a tired runner, the wind sighed among the bare branches overhead. Houses and stores, people and automobiles, streets and sidewalks, all sank into indistinguishable shadow.

John Marley was a music teacher—a teacher of piano, and an unsuccessful one. His face was deeply furrowed, and the coat which he pulled protectingly about him was threadbare. In his tired, muddy eyes there lay a puzzled expression. Where was he to get the money to pay the note that was due? An immense self-pity gripped his throat.

He again ran over in his mind his most likely friends. ... Suddenly his muddy eyes grew clearer. How had he forgotten Charlie Delany?

Delany was a bachelor, and, incidentally, a prosperous realtor.

"No luck this year," muttered John Marley. He stumbled with an uncertain gait up Broad street on his way to Delany's house.

"I've never asked him for anything," the music teacher thought. "And we've been good to him. ... No luck this year. No luck any year. The doctor said one lung's gone. Maybe I won't live long, anyway. I bet my wife will be glad. I'm a miserable failure. ... Then she'll have some money ... my insurance."

When he reached the intersection of Broad and Waverly streets he slipped and fell on the sidewalk. Automobiles whizzed by. A crowd gathered. John Marley looked foolish. He turned his head round to see who had noticed him fall. He shuffled to his feet. A few yards away in the street lay his hat. He picked it up and smoothed out the folds made by the automobile. As he buttoned up his coat, he shivered and continued on his way.

"What's happened to you, Marley?" Charlie Delany asked, opening the door wide. He slapped Marley gently on the shoulder as he propelled his friend into the warm living room. "Slipped on the icy sidewalk. Got all wet." John Marley looked ruefully at himself, then went over and stood in front of the sizzling radiator.

"Too bad! You can't go out in this condition ... a wet coat. Take mine. I'll get it later."

Charlie Delany's coat was of black broadcloth with collar, cuffs, and lining of soft beaver. Finally, several bills of large denomination having been pressed into Marley's hand, he prepared to go. He said:

"Don't forget Lena and I expect you to dinner tomorrow, as usual." Being assured that Charlie would be present, he shut the door with vigor and departed.

Charlie Delany was an old friend. Since he was not married he always ate Thanksgiving dinner with the Marleys. They would not think of having him eat dinner in a restaurant on Thanksgiving Day.

On his way home Marley gradually began to see things in a different light. Life seemed a bit more cheerful. His cough seemed less painful. Perhaps it was Charlie Delany's beaver-lined coat, with the beaver collar and cuffs, that made him feel different. One would feel different in a warm coat. Charlie Delany had given him a glass of gin—"to heat you up and keep you from catching more cold." It did more, for it enkindled in him the fire of renewed manhood.

Why didn't he get a good warm coat? Didn't clothes help determine what people thought of you? Didn't you have to be the master of your own fate? If he had had a warm coat three years ago perhaps he'd have two strong lungs today. People didn't want him teaching their children when he was continually coughing. And he could not blame them. From one of the easy-payment stores he could get a fairly good coat. Ten dollars down and a dollar a week. ...

He straightened his shoulders and almost strutted up Broad street. When he reached a brilliantly-lighted store, whose window displayed a variety of merchandise, he turned the knob smartly and sauntered importantly through the door. He felt happy, and he must buy something for Lena. He wanted to make her happy, too. From the variety of things in the store he finally decided upon a pretty but inexpensive scarf for Lena and a toy airplane for the boy.

He hoped the scarf would please his wife. Perhaps she would show him more affection. Perhaps she would not be quite so cold. He remembered how Lena had loved him before worries came, before the cough came, before slender times came. After all, who knew but that the doctor might be mistaken? He might live a long time. One could live quite a long while with one lung. He might even increase the number of his pupils, if he tried hard enough. He would then have more money ... Lena would then love him as she had long ago.

He thought: "Lena used to quarrel every time I invited Charlie Delany to dinner. She'd make mean remarks. Gradually she changed her attitude toward him. Why shouldn't she change her attitude toward me, and love me again if I am more prosperous?"

John Marley went to one or two other places, among them the barber shop. He got a haircut and had his face massaged. It was eight o'clock when at last he reached home.

He was thinking, as he mounted the steps:

"What will Lena say when she sees me wearing this beautiful coat? She'll brighten up and run up to me and kiss me, I'll bet." He paused in the dark hall. He put his hand into the coat pocket for the key but it was in his own old coat, and that was at Charlie Delany's. He rang the bell. In the dark hall Lena gave him a kiss and put her arms about his neck. She stood very close to him and stroked the beaver collar. She kissed him again and again and buried her head against the coat, now cooing softly:

"Marley isn't home, yet. The boy cried and called for you today."

Keen knife-thrust was Lena's voice. How weary he felt! How useless was life! How futile everything!

"Yes," answered John Marley, his voice striving treacherously to betray him. He kissed her tenderly. "Yes, he's home."

At dinner next day John Marley sat very quiet. At the table Lena tried hard to act as if everything was all right. One who noticed would have plainly seen that she was ill with fear. She wondered what her husband was thinking. She wished she had a chance to tell Charlie of last night.

While Charlie talked and laughed over his own stories, John sat staring at his son. He thought he saw Charlie's eyes and chin. Lena, Charlie, and the child ate. The husband hoped they did not notice him. He wondered what Lena thought, but could not look at her.

"You seem very quiet today, John." Charlie reached for the after-dinner mints. "Thinking about the accident of last night, I guess," he hazarded, sympathetically.

"Yes." John pushed back his chair, putting his hand to his mouth as if to hide the convulsive tremor of his lips.

"I'm thinking about my boy!" There was a pause, then he continued:

"I'm thinking of something else, too. I don't believe I'm going to live much longer. Life has given me all the joy it ever will."

As he spoke a vague incomprehensible solitude encompassed him.

"I want to thank you for your friendship, Charlie. When I'm gone be kind to Lena and the boy. I can think of no more appropriate person to ask such a favor of."

Charlie Delany mumbled incoherently and was vividly red in the face. He looked away. Lena's eyes were twice their usual size. She acted as if she was going to cry.

TWO GENTLEMEN OF BOSTON

FLORIDA RUFFIN RIDLEY

Usually homeward journey from school was a dignified process; it was decidedly fitting that thirteen-year-old ranking scholars of the eighth grade graduating class should have occasion for serious conversation. The closing half-hour of school, devoted to the consideration of "Gems from History and Literature," always left Arthur and Morton in a contemplative mood and ready for serious debates on the lives and deeds of Napoleon and King Arthur and Marmion and all the others.

From my shaded seat on the porch I could see them from the time they left the school yard all the way up the tree-bordered street, and as I watched the straight, manly little figures, I took delight in imagining the course of their absorbed conversation, and in observing the companionship which seemed to promise so much in the way of mutual benefit and pleasure.

They were so markedly different in outward characteristics! There was always something happening to separate Arthur's blouse and trousers, or to snap his garters, and in the midst of the most intense discussion even of so vital a question as to "which you'd rather be the greatest orator in the world or the greatest football player in the world"—it was always necessary for him to make some clothing adjustment; to Arthur, clothes at best, were only necessary accompaniments, and at worst, impediments to the pursuit of happiness; but these lapses from dignity and solemnity in the daily conversational intercourse of the two boys, were more than redeemed by Morton, who at thirteen years of age, reflected an indelible impress of three years contact with foreign salons —the reaction of an only child, accompanying parents of social and literary aspirations in their old-world journeyings. No intriguing considerations of "Horatius at the Bridge," could be great enough to upset the poise with which Morton would at once readjust a garter which dared to begin a false move.

Today, however, the approach of the boys was distinctly out of form—it was not that there attendants, to the number of eight or ten; very often their debates were extended to include followers, who gave more life and vigor to the scene and the occasions by supplementing their points with side whacks at shrubbery and high leaps at curbs. I was used to this variation from the usual, but today the formation was entirely out of the ordinary, one striking feature being that the comrades walked apart and silent, the followers compact and in earnest conversation. As the group drew near, I was startled by the sudden realization of what the scene meant. Without doubt Morton, the dilletante and Arthur, the dreamer, had disagreed, had gone so far in the disagreement as to fight, and had had a bloody fight at that! There was no sign of belligerency in their attitudes, they walked quietly and apart; characteristically, Morton had restored his clothes to some order—his Norfolk jacket was tightly buttoned to hide the dust and mud left on the blouse from its contact with the earth, but his scratched and bleeding knuckles couldn't be hidden in his efforts to cover a blackening eye with a very grimy handkerchief. Arthur was frankly dishevelled, and seemed utterly indifferent to the fact that he was without hat or tie; his face carried some slight intensification of its inclination toward griminess, which for racial reasons, was never as readily discernible as upon his friend Morton; his lack of bruises and general bearing indicated quite clearly that he had been the victor in the fray.

I was rather sorry that I had disclosed myself by an involuntary move toward the approaching group, for it at once became evident to me that Morton had intended to pass without stopping (what more natural) on seeing me however, he stopped and, with the courtesy that was so charming and so marked an attribute, he tried to drag his cap from his disfigured head. "It's all right, Mrs. Allen," he said, "*merely* a little difference of opinion," and replacing his cap, he swung down the road alone, leaving me to recover, before turning to those who were left, the poise which the approach and his speech had rather upset.

I turned to my son who was evidently suffering under the disadvantage of having a "smooth talker" get in his work first. "I'll fight anybody that attacks my good name," he volunteered, with great, emphasis, and then with the evident desires to level up intellectually in the eyes of the cortege, "he who steals my purse," he began, and stopped short, whether from some budding sense of good taste, or from the realization that a hint to his meaning was all that was necessary to his followers, it was not clear, but he began to edge toward the screen door in silence.

It was plain that he had decided to say no more—Morton had offered no explanation, made no accusations—attempted no defense should he, Arthur, take advantage of the absence of his companion to make out a case for himself? I read in a flash their code, and was convinced that any explanation of the affair would have to come from others was clearly out of it, how force the confidence of these gentlemen? How was it possible to chide a man for defending his good name? How call to order men who are adjusting "a mere difference of opinion" in their own way? The dignity of thirteen years must be sustained, its obligations respected, its ethics acknowledged. I accepted my evident limitations and confined myself to a meek suggestion to Arthur that it would be well to "bathe his hands in sulphur-naphthal solution." The round-eyed caravan dissolved, as Arthur passed through the screen door. I settled myself with more complacency than I felt to think over the situation. It was all so unlooked for! The companionship had been so smooth, so complementary, and then too boys now-a-days were not in the habit of disfiguring each other as in the old days—what could have ruffed Arthur's good temper and thrown Morton out of his natural poise sufficiently to bring about a bloody row?

Only the day before, Morton had graciously accepted an invitation to stay to lunch, being largely influenced, I have no doubt, by the sight of the hot biscuits which were being taken from the oven as he came through the kitchen; he had conditioned his acceptance however, upon the loan of a clean collar. We had sat at the table in the peace and contentment that accompany a satisfactory meal, eaten in congenial company. We had dallied over the meal even longer than it took the boys to demolish two large pans of biscuits with accompaniments; the day was warm and Morton was waiting for a telephone call. He began talking of France, his parents were going over again in a few weeks. "You ought to go to Paris, Art," he said, "why couldn't you send him over to join us, Mrs. Allen?" He tossed this remark casually, as he gracefully broke open another biscuit. "I'd rather go to Canada and raise silver foxes," Arthur had turned to say. "Well if you came to Paris you would see where Napoleon lived—will you excuse me Mrs. Allen if I see what time it is, you know I have my violin lesson at two o'clock."

After so large and cordial an invitation, and so intimate an afternoon, it gave me some surprise to find that the friends at their very next meeting had engaged in battle.

The growth of their intimacy had been of great interest to me. In the big American public schools, democracy is most truly demonstrated in the freedom with which children make and develop friendships, even the guiding hands of parents cannot always be effective here. Arthur and Morton were neighbors, but the fact of their difference in race kept the families apart as far as social contact is concerned; Arthur being the only one of his kind in the neighborhood, the children generally had played in and out of each other's houses. Not being dependent on close social contact, and entirely unconcerned about it, the limiting of social recognitions to courteous out door exchanges between us parents was entirely acceptable to me.

I had at first hesitated at encouraging the close companionship between Arthur and Morton which loomed inevitable. American standards of simplicity had been too strongly bred in me to accept whole-heartedly the polish with which Morton literally shone; still Arthur with his inherited indifference to externals, could stand quite a little working upon, and I not only realize the benefits that Morton would bring Arthur, but also those that Morton would receive; in fact, I felt sure Morton had the advantage. Morton was never, as Arthur, so absorbed in a book that he overlooked offering a chair when necessary, but, although I worried and grieved over my young barbarian who would bring to the table along with his immaculate young guest a pair of hands that never should have left the cellar, yet I could not but warm to the fact that he had forgotten himself in seeing that his pets received their daily attention, and on time.

In the days that followed the battle, I kept "a weather eye" open for any hint or suggestion that would enlighten me as to its cause. There was some estrangement, Morton's missionary zeal had received a set-back, the two boys did not walk together on the homeward journey, neither were there any interchange of visits—it was impossible for them to keep entirely apart, their interests were too close—but there was a barrier and as I watched them in the week that followed, I became convinced that the barrier had been raised principally from the outside.

The time was drawing near for Morton's family to start upon the European trip and I was still in the dark. My enlightenment came suddenly, however.

I was at my kitchen window making out a batch of cookies that were great favorites with the young literat; two classmates of the duelling pair were lying upon the grass beneath the window and their voices came up to me. "Art and Mort had a fight last week, when you were absent." "Gee, I never saw Mort get into a fight." "Naw, he didn't want to this time, but Art made him!" "Who licked?" "O, Art." "Did he make his nose bleed?" "Yes, and blacked his eye!" "Gee, wish I'd been there," and, after a pause, "what'd they fight about?" "Well," with deliberation, "Mort attacked Art's good name, I'd fight for my good name, wouldn't you—Mort tried to talk out of it but all the fellas were on Art's side!"

"Sure, I'd fight for my good name—did he call him a liar?"

"Worse than that, he went to the guild and he had to report his good deed, and he said he had been 'elevating a little colored boy!'"

"'Elevating a little colored boy!' Gee, wish I'd been there—is that your dog—come on" and two pair of legs went scurrying across the lawn.

A little later, Morton came in with Arthur. "We're leaving tonight Mrs. Allen and I came to bid you good-bye and to wish you a very pleasant summer," and the little hand was extended with its usual grace. Our young Chesterfield sailed for Europe three days later, leaving more questions in my mind than before. What had been his reaction from the fight? In his relations with Arthur, how much had he been influenced by adults? What were the parents reactions? Were they possibly those of the rebuffed missionaries who only feel pity that the heathen do not know what is good for them? As for my little son—I never discussed the matter with him, I felt he had shown himself wiser than I. With instinctive wisdom, he had sensed a situation to which I was blind, and had met that situation adequately. I had not recognized the "patronizing pose," neither would I have had the directness and courage to reduce it to its lowest terms and deal it the "knock out" blow.

WOMEN OF THE HARLEM RENAISSANCE
ANTHOLOGY SERIES TITLES

SHORT-TAKE ANTHOLOGIES

ON BEING COLORED ME: Reflections on Race and Gender by Women of the Harlem Renaissance

CROSSING THE COLOR LINE: Short Fiction on Passing by Women of the Harlem Renaissance

HARLEM ON HER MIND: Prose, Poems & Plays by Women of the Harlem Renaissance

PRIZE POEMS BY WOMEN OF THE HARLEM RENAISSANCE

POEMS BY BOSTON'S WOMEN OF THE HARLEM RENAISSANCE

RONDEAU: The Collected Poems of Jessie Redmon Fauset

HOW BRIGHT THE FLAME: The Collected Poems of Mae V. Cowdery, 1927-1935

EXPANDED ANTHOLOGIES

FAITHFULLY YOURS, JESSIE REDMON FAUSET: Stories, Poems & Personal Essays

ESSENTIAL SHORT STORIES BY WOMEN OF THE HARLEM RENAISSANCE: Volumes 1 & 2

THE SATURDAY EVENING QUILL: Stories, Poems & Plays by Boston's Women of the Harlem Renaissance

---

VOICES RESTORED: The Performance Edition
(A companion anthology of poems performed at a spoken word event)